Crystalle Valentino writes erotic fiction. She is the author of *After Hours*, *Personal Services* and *A Private View*, all coming soon from *Black Lace*.

Personal
Services

CRYSTALLE VALENTINO

BLACK
LACE

1 3 5 7 9 10 8 6 4 2

First published in 2000 as *Coming Up Roses* by Black Lace,
an imprint of Virgin Books
This edition published in 2013 by Black Lace, an imprint of Ebury Publishing
A Random House Group Company

The Random House Group Limited Reg. No. 954009

Addresses for companies within the Random House Group can be found at:
www.randomhouse.co.uk

A CIP catalogue record for this book is
available from the British Library

The Random House Group Limited supports the Forest Stewardship
Council® (FSC®), the leading international forest-certification
organisation. Our books carrying the FSC label are printed on
FSC®-certified paper. FSC is the only forest-certification scheme
supported by the leading environmental organisations, including
Greenpeace. Our paper procurement policy can be found at:
www.randomhouse.co.uk/environment

Printed and bound by CPI Group (UK) Ltd, Croydon, CR0 4YY

ISBN 9780352347589

To buy books by your favourite authors and register for offers visit:
www.blacklace.co.uk

Chapter One

Rosie Cooper's bad day started like this: her dilapidated van broke down, again, so she transferred her little hand mower, her strimmer, all her vital bits and pieces, into her car instead. She tried to be upbeat about it, though, picking a sunflower from the pocket handkerchief that passed for her front garden and inhaling the fresh, fruity fragrance as she left her ground-floor Richmond flat.

She got into her prized and beloved brand new Beetle, with its peach metallic finish and the dinky little flower holder on the dash, and noticed that a small circular dent had appeared overnight on its formerly pristine bonnet. She also found that the sunflower she had brought with her from her pathetic little city garden had too thick a stem to fit into the holder, and the petals started dropping, and all at once her mobile was ringing, and it was a cancellation. *Another* one.

'What do you mean, it's a cancellation?' Rosie asked angrily, stuffing bright yellow petals into the ashtray. More dropped off the sunflower head. Did sunflower pollen stain? she wondered, gazing worriedly down between her tatty jeaned legs at her dark-peach carpet.

'Hey, girlfriend, don't shoot the messenger,' said Lulu on the other end of the phone. 'The woman said cancel, so here I am calling you, cancelling one lawn-mow and edge-cut and nerine-bulb planting, all scheduled for this a.m., and she did apologise, short notice and all, but there you go, that's life.'

Rosie unthinkingly put a long curly strand of her untidy bright ginger hair between her teeth and started gnawing on it. Since the age of two, in moments of extreme angst, she had gnawed her hair. Why change the habits of a lifetime? She could speak and gnaw at the same time, no problem.

'Look, was she saying cancelled just for this once, or for all time? I mean, I'm calling on her again next week, right?'

'Wrong,' Lulu said succinctly. 'She don't want your sorry ass on the premises again, ever, amen. She didn't say that in so many words, but I think I know a kiss-off when I hear one.'

Rosie spat out the hank of hair and viciously threw a sunflower petal at the steering-wheel. 'Lulu, that's the sixth one in three weeks. We're losing clients at a rate of two a week.'

'Hey, have Mensa heard about you? Quick as a flash, that mental arithmetic. Don't know how you do it, girl.'

'Fuck off, Lulu,' said Rosie. 'What am I going to do about this? It can't go on, this rate of loss.'

'Think you'll find it can,' Lulu said placidly. Rosie

could hear her rustling sweet wrappers as she spoke. 'Not only can it go on, but it now looks as if it *will* go on, probably until you go belly-up.'

'You're such a comfort,' Rosie said irritably.

Lulu never seemed to get hyped over anything, and at times it just about drove Rosie crazy. Lulu was black, six feet tall, with a megawatt smile and a voice like the thickest maple syrup. She had been answering the phone for Rosie's up-and-coming London-based horticultural business for six months now, and it felt like for ever. Lulu was terrific at soothing irate clients, charming contacts and cooling tempers – maybe because she didn't seem to have a temper herself. Whereas Rosie was everyone's idea of the archetypal redhead. A bit combustible, if not downright fiery. Red hair, white skin, gooseberry-green eyes. Medium height only, but strong with it and nicely proportioned. And with more than her fair share of pheromones. Oh, and a few freckles, like a saddle sitting over the bridge of her nose, which incidentally she hated and scowled at in the mirror every morning.

'At which point,' Lulu went on smoothly, 'I will have to get another job, which tees me off no small amount I can tell you. I *like* this job. It suits my schedule.'

'So suggest something to me. Something to save your job and my business.' Rosie's voice was light but there was a sharp edge of deadly seriousness behind it. This *was* serious. She didn't fancy being bankrupt in the least. The loan company would repossess her darling little car. She'd have to work for someone else.

Well, she *could* do that. If she absolutely had to. But

the thought made her innards shrivel. After two years at Sharsholt College she'd applied for a job with the Hampshire parks department, and within weeks she'd had enough of that. Supercilious men had bossed her around and ordered her to use chemicals she considered unsafe for people and ruinous to the delicately balanced wildlife. She'd been very pleased to leave and, although they had given her a good enough reference, they had been equally pleased to see her go.

At a loss to know what to do next she had, on a whim, moved from her quiet country life on the family-run farm to London. The flat in Richmond had come up and she'd taken it, pleased because it was within easy walking distance of the Botanical Gardens at Kew, which constituted three hundred acres of easily accessible green space, and the river. She'd briefly tried office work and hated it, suffering it like a wild animal confined indoors. So, with no luck at job-hunting with other gardening firms in the city, she had decided to set up on her own, and for a while she had seemed to be doing pretty well at it too.

Until now.

Had she gone to horticultural college, got her quali-fications, slogged over books and soil samples, double-digging, endless tests and numerous hurdles, just to lose it all now that it was only just beginning for her?

'No can do.' Lulu finally answered her question through a mouthful of chocolate.

Perhaps that was how Lulu kept so calm, thought Rosie. Endless supplies of chocolate for maximum oral gratification. But that would mean always having to wear her 'fat day' jeans instead of the ones she had on at the moment, her sexy skin-hugging kick-ass 'thin day' ones, or schlepp to the gym which she knew she would hate. Gardening kept her fit enough, her metabolism ticking over fast enough, not to have to worry about what she did or did not eat. Ingesting vast quantities of chocolate wasn't going to help her keep her balance on the tightrope.

She sat and thought a moment, chewing on her hair again, her green eyes distant.

'You still there?' Lulu asked anxiously. 'You ain't got no hose stuck in that car window, have you?'

'Nope,' said Rosie, straightening up and snapping on her seat-belt, not bothering about the debris from the shattered sunflower any more. Any more hanging around here, she thought, and her business would be in bits just like that flower, and she wasn't standing still for that, no way. 'Lulu, if anyone else phones to cancel, assure them they'll be welcomed back at any time and with a discount thrown in.'

'If you say so,' chomped Lulu.

'I do say so. Now let me check this morning's cancellation with you. Mrs Squires, right? And the address, read that to me again.'

Lulu did, but with an air about her of humouring her boss. After all, when the rot set in with a business, in her experience it was nearly impossible to cut out the bad wood before the whole fucking tree fell down. Usually on your head.

*

Mrs Squires lived in a select square in Chelsea. Just like everywhere else in Chelsea, the roads all around were crammed with cars, so Rosie had to cruise around the area twice, grumbling profusely, before she found a parking slot. It was some distance from the house, but she was fit enough and certainly charged up with enough adrenalin to stomp all the way there in her unfashionable but workmanlike trainers, jeans, T-shirt and lumberjack shirt.

As she walked, she ignored the roar and hoot of the nose-to-tail traffic, the young, beautiful and rich chattering loudly into tiny mobiles, the wind-driven litter, and she concentrated on admiring the greenery. She always did this. It was spring – not cold any more but not yet hot – and the lime trees were in bud, throwing out dusty catkins, unfurling leaves, sap rushing up from their roots, shooting through their trunks, and zapping through their branches. A natural miracle was happening and most of humankind was unaware of it.

When she reached the row of elegant terraced houses where the wealthy, fortyish Mrs Squires lived alone with two yapping, tedious Pekinese, Rosie slowed down. There was a large communal garden in the centre of the square, but that was not her concern; she tended the little garden behind Mrs Squires's house, often having to carry her tools and bags of peat and whatever else the garden required through the house to reach it, when Mrs Squires forgot to leave the back gate unlocked.

She was always very careful to lay down dust-sheets before she transported anything through the mini-palace that Mrs Squires called home. The place was stuffed full of valuable, fragile antiques and collectables. She was always *extremely* careful not to turn around too fast and knock anything over. Mrs Squires had litigation written all over her; she'd sue at the drop of a hat, and enjoy it. Rosie suspected that Mrs Squires's life was in fact so headachingly dull that even a courtroom scrap would have its charms.

And now look at it, Rosie thought angrily. After all that care and attention, the love she'd lavished on that barren little plot, the glorious way it was shaping up now she'd worked so long and so hard on it – all that had been snatched away from her. Someone else would reap the benefits of her hard landscaping, her painstaking choice of architectural 'framework' plants; someone else would fill in the gaps in the borders and take the credit for the overall look of the thing, which would be wonderful, because of the work *she* had done.

It wasn't fair.

But then, when was life ever fair for a self-employed and fairly impoverished gardener?

Rosie went around the back of the row of terraces, where there were garages and fire escapes and high walls shielding the privacy of the back gardens from statuary- and plant-thieves, or the passing and just plain nosy. There was another line of cars here, natch. She could hear the ill-tempered little Pekes yapping away, the sound muffled. They were indoors. Rosie could see the upper-floor windows with their curtains pulled closed. She listened carefully for sounds; nothing except a distant car alarm shrieking unheeded, a passing police car, the laughter of children somewhere nearby. Closer, she thought she could hear whispering, maybe a faint creaking.

But maybe not.

And anyway, what was she *doing* here? What was the point of coming over here in a temper? The woman had every right to cancel if she wanted to. What am I going to do now? wondered Rosie with a flash of humour. Bang on her back door and demand an explanation? Ridiculous. She'd make a fool of herself, and Mrs Squires might even call the cops, and that would certainly put a crimp in the rest of the day.

She was *sure* she could hear whispering over the frantic barking of the two Pekes. Maybe Mommy had gone to the shops and left Bubble and Squeak to fend for themselves for an hour or so. Rosie liked dogs as a rule, but Bubble and Squeak possessed all the charm of a pair of rabid sewer rats as far as she was concerned, and she would not be sorry to see the back of them. Very often she had been nipped about the ankles by one or the other of them, and Mrs Squires had always laughed and said the little darlings were only playing. Rosie now wished that she had booted the miniature canine hooligans while she had the chance.

But this was plain silly. She might as well just give it up and go home. Well, maybe she would, but a quick look over the wall wouldn't hurt, would it? Rosie stuck her trainer-clad foot into a gap in the pointing on the wall, and heaved herself up, scrabbling at the curved top with her hands. She got a grip, and looked over. Well, she could *look*, couldn't she? After all, she was the one who'd done all the work.

Rosie caught her breath.

She was looking at the garden all right, but she found that she was also, quite unexpectedly, looking at a naked back. It was a male back, very broad and lightly tanned and quite nicely muscled. *Solid.* And, shockingly, this unknown man was kneeling very solidly between Mrs Squires's naked thighs. Mrs Squires – *Jesus!* – was sitting on the swing, the very same swing that Rosie herself had strung up some months ago in the branches of the ravishing red copper beech and Mrs Squires – the elegant, composed, overbred Mrs Squires – had her wrists tied to the ropes of the swing, for God's sake! She was trussed there like a Christmas turkey. Mrs Squires was stark naked and, Rosie noted incredulously, she was in amazingly good shape for her age.

I was going to plant the nerines by that swing, Rosie thought in a state of shock, and some red-hot pokers, so that in autumn the whole thing would be ablaze with colour: the purple of the beech, the bold pink thrust of the nerines, the shrieking orange of the pokers. It would have looked amazing. And now look, talking of pokers, talking of poking . . .

She really shouldn't watch.

She *knew* she shouldn't watch.

Still, she went on watching, almost mesmerised.

Could those humungous tits be real? Other women's tits were a constant source of amazement to her. They looked all skinny and contained when they were clothed, but when they were whipped out of their fancy bras – and yes, Rosie was pretty sure that was a frighteningly expensive designer bra she could see abandoned on the lawn, tangled up with a checked work shirt and a pair of hastily discarded tights – and wham! Huge tit alert.

And wow, that was one very impressive back, she thought, clutching on harder to the wall as her fingers started to go numb with the effort. Maybe he worked out? Rosie stared hard at what she could see of the man. He was still facing away from her, whispering in Mrs Squires's ear, and he was wearing very worn stone-washed denim jeans that looked absolutely great clinging to his well-muscled butt. He had a close-cropped head of thick corn-blond hair into which all the timid spring sunshine seemed to be concentrated, like a star about to go supernova.

He also had a muscular neck, shoulders that looked as if they were used to hard work, shovel-like hands that would make a manicurist pass out. This was no office worker, and this was no fashion slave either. Going by gut instinct alone, Rosie reckoned that this bloke had never seen the inside of a gym and that, if he *did*, he would probably laugh out loud.

He was unbuckling his belt!

She found it hard to tear her eyes away. She was aware of a pulse beating away between her legs, of a spreading delectable dampness there. Mrs Squires was in a similar condition by the look of it. Actually Rosie thought that Mrs Squires had gone beyond dampness and was into soaking wet by now. Her pale but well-developed thighs were clamped around the man's waist and her eyes were directed downward as he worked his buckle loose.

God, I bet he's huge, thought Rosie, feeling a shockingly hard jolt in the region of her clit. He was talking to the enraptured Mrs Squires, whispering, making her blush and giggle. Mrs Squires was *giggling*. Oh wow. And now he was unzipping himself; Rosie could hear the zipper coming down. Mrs Squires's eyes opened wider and she said something. The man laughed, low and seductive. And then he pushed the jeans down, bunching them around his thighs.

Oh, nice ass. *Exceedingly* nice ass.

All the variations in men's buttocks were just as intriguing as those in women's breasts. Some were thin, some were flabby – oh yuk – but the best, the absolute best, were firm like these, full of muscle and implied strength, enough strength to drive a good-sized cock just as deep into a woman as she wanted. And Mrs Squires wanted it all right.

Even from where she watched, being careful to keep her head just below the level of the wall and only occasionally taking tiny surreptitious peeks, Rosie could see how desperately aroused the woman was – totally oblivious to the hysterical barking of her 'babies'. Her chestnut-brown nipples were taut with excitement, rising crisply from the fat white pads of her quivering breasts, her mouth was half-open, drawing in panting breaths as the man kneeling between her legs pulled her thighs open wider. Rosie got a glimpse of a damp pink slit lavishly fringed with ash-coloured curls as the man pulled Mrs Squires wide open to take his cock inside her.

Mrs Squires was clutching at the ropes of the swing with her fingers, not unduly hampered by her bound wrists, so that the seat swung up underneath her as the man pulled her in close. Avid with curiosity, Rosie leaned as far to the left as she could, but she still couldn't get a look at his cock. She could see silky blond fur dusting the cleft of his behind, darkening at his apex where she could see the merest suggestion of his balls, which were obviously up so high with arousal that she was being cheated of a better view.

Action! His head was dipped, his hair glistened in a shaft of spring sunshine, and his shoulders bunched powerfully as his hands worked at his groin. Oh God, he's putting it in! thought Rosie, and again there was that deep, deep tugging ache at her clit. Rosie felt her own nipples contract and harden, and her wet pussy opened like a flower – opened for nothing, because it was Mrs Squires who was getting the benefit of his fucking, not her. For a moment she almost felt as if his cock's head was pushing up between her own thighs, invading her own cunt, and she found herself pressing her thighs together like an overexcited wanking teenager as Mrs Squires let out a howl of pleasure.

It was pressing her thighs together that unbalanced

her. She flung out a hand as she started to slip, but she couldn't grasp the wall. She only succeeded in snapping off a fingernail. She cried out involuntarily with the sudden pain and then cried out again when her ass hit the pavement with a great deal of force.

Damn! They must have heard her!

Rosie scrambled to her feet and, hobbling painfully and sucking her bleeding finger, she hurried off along the back of the mews. She shouldn't have watched. It was an intrusion for one thing, and for another she was now so horny that her pants were soaked. When she reached the end of the mews she turned and looked back, expecting retribution; but there was no one there.

Of course there wasn't.

Only the line of cars and vans, one of which she now noticed was a mid-sized red flatbed truck with gardening equipment stashed in the back. On the side of the van *Countryman Gardens* was written in gold Gothic letters, and beneath that were two telephone numbers, landline and mobile, plus a website and e-mail address. Without paper or pencil, Rosie memorised the web address and telephone numbers as best she could, and shambled off, aching, back to her car.

Chapter Two

'You limping?' Lulu asked with mild concern, looking up from her latest sex toys catalogue as Rosie arrived back at base.

'Base' was a corner of Rosie's Richmond flat, a corner stuffed with desk, files and computer gear, plus a big Harrods bag of assorted chocolate delights in case Lulu got peckish during the morning, which she frequently did. Lulu only ever worked in the mornings; Rosie had no idea what Lulu did with her afternoons, and she had never dared ask, but they seemed immutable and immovable, almost sacrosanct. It was understood between them that Lulu only *ever* worked mornings. So in the afternoons Rosie picked up what calls she could on the mobile if she had to be away from base. And she didn't question Lulu about the afternoons, because Lulu was spectacularly good on the telephone during those hours that she consented to be on duty, so why upset the status quo?

'I'm not limping,' Rosie said irritably, dumping a bag

of bulbs on the desk. Puffs of dirt and shreds of bulb skin billowed out of the netting. She looked tetchily at the sex catalogue Lulu clutched in her well-manicured hand. Here she was, trying to retrieve her business, her car, her entire way of life, and Lulu was slumped here enjoying perversions.

'And what the hell is that?' asked Rosie, her gaze suddenly riveted to a small blue bomb-shaped object in the catalogue.

'You have led *such* a sheltered life,' mourned Lulu. 'It's a love bullet, dumb ass. Used for all-over massage.'

Rosie snatched the catalogue. She turned it sideways, then upside-down. 'And what about that?' She pointed with her bloodied finger.

Lulu looked at her friend and employer in disbelief. 'That's a vibrator, of course. Whatchoo think it is, a scary-looking ice lolly?'

Rosie pulled a face, but it was true that she was amazingly inexperienced in the wilder aspects of love-making, whereas Lulu seemed to be worryingly expert. Rosie wouldn't admit it to a soul, but she'd never tried a vibrator, not even one that didn't look as downright terrifying as the one in the catalogue.

'You *are* limping,' said Lulu, snatching the catalogue back. She pushed the bulbs fastidiously aside and unwrapped a fresh bar of chocolate.

'Give me some of that,' Rosie ordered.

'Oh, this is bad,' said Lulu, shaking her head so that the multicoloured beads woven into her hair extensions jangled and swung. Lulu snapped off a chunk of chocolate and Rosie grabbed it. She winced and stuffed it into her mouth. 'You've hurt your hand too. And you're comfort-eating. I know the signs, girlfriend. This is *bad*.'

'We've got a small problem,' admitted Rosie through a mouthful of chocolate.

God, was there anything in the world better than chocolate when you felt freaked? Only sex, she decided. And she'd had precious little of that lately, because she'd been so busy with her thriving business. But now all that was in danger. Her precious little car was in danger. Her flat could go. Hell, her very *ass* was in danger.

'How small a problem?' Lulu's spectacular almond-shaped eyes narrowed suspiciously.

'Well, smallish.' Rosie filched more chocolate. Lulu watched her in horror.

'Steady. I'd share my man with you and you know it, but ask me for my chocolate stash and I've got to say no.' Lulu carefully tucked the remains of the chocolate bar back into the Harrods carrier. Then she straightened up in her chair and ran her hands down over her red T-shirted and exuberantly large breasts, steadying herself to receive Rosie's news. 'So give. What's this smallish problem we got, which looks like a pretty damned big problem from where I'm sitting, by the way.'

'Competition, that's the problem,' said Rosie, hiking one buttock on to Lulu's already overcrowded desk.

Rosie grabbed a spare piece of paper and a pen. She jotted down Countryman's telephone numbers and

web address before she forgot them. She marvelled at
the unkempt state of the desk – how could Lulu find a
thing?

But Lulu seemed to manage very well. Lulu seemed
to function best in an atmosphere of chaos, and was
strictly an indoor girl. With Rosie, it was a measure
of orderliness, and outdoors. She always felt faintly
overheated when she was indoors, and was prone –
much to Lulu's annoyance – to throwing open windows,
even in the depths of winter.

Lulu snorted. 'Competition's a fact of life,' she said
stoutly. 'What you gotta do is offer a better service, or a
cheaper service, or some damned thing like that.'

'Yeah?' Rosie glared at her. 'And what if your
competitor's offering something you can't offer?'

'Like what?'

'Sex.'

After a thoughtful moment Lulu gave a dismissive
gesture. 'Ha! You can do sex, Rosie. It's like riding a bike
– you never forget how to do that funky thing. Just get
in there and grind away.'

Rosie gave her a calculating glance. 'Look, can you
do something for me?'

'Is this about the sex?'

'This is about competition.'

'Oh.' Lulu looked briefly disappointed. 'Well, try
me.'

Rosie nodded at the computer screen, which was
currently given over to a slow-mo flower-opening
screen saver. 'Call up our database. Then match the

clients that have cancelled our services with their details on the database.'

'That's simple,' said Lulu, frowning. 'I can do it right now.'

'Go on, then.'

Rosie stalked morosely around the room while Lulu's fingers flew over the keyboard. She opened the window wide. Lulu shot her a glare. Within minutes Lulu called her back, showing her two printouts – the cancellations, and the more detailed descriptions of those now ex-clients from the database. Rosie said nothing, just took the sheets and examined them.

'Well?' prompted Lulu after a few tense minutes.

'It's most of our female customers,' Rosie said, tossing the sheets on to the desk. 'This Countryman bloke's targeting the divorcees, the singles, the widows – all women and all under fifty. And he's giving them what I can't give them. Yes he's doing their gardening, but I also think he's offering them sexual services. The bastard.'

'What makes you think that?' asked Lulu, fascinated.

'I found him this morning with his cock up Mrs Squires.'

'Really?' Lulu looked more interested than scan-dalised, to Rosie's annoyance. She still felt uncomfortably wet between her legs from seeing the wretched man with his cock up Mrs Squires, and that made her feel even *more* irritated.

'Yes, really. He had her tied to the swing that *I* put up, and he was giving it to her just like she wanted.'

Lulu's brow clouded. She pouted, thinking it over, then she grinned. 'Well, you could do that too. If Mrs Squires swings both ways.'

Rosie gave her a look of total disbelief. Then she shook her head. 'Look, thanks for your input, Lulu, but I don't want to boff Mrs Squires, I just want to dig her garden.'

'Oh yeah? While meanwhile that man there is providing a Profit Enhanced Product. Not only the garden, but also the fuck. He probably gives out loyalty cards.'

Rosie had the distinct impression that Lulu was finding this situation funny.

'Look,' she said tetchily, 'can you do something else? Can you get into *his* computer, get at *his* database? It's important.'

Lulu shook her head. 'No, that's not my line of country,' she said regretfully. 'You need a real pro for that, a hacker. It's beyond me.'

'So where do I find a hacker?'

Lulu grinned one of her huge piano-keyboard grins. 'Hey, no sweat.' She winked. 'Sure, *I* can't do it. But I sure as hell know a man who can.'

The 'man who could' opened the front door of his Shepherd's Bush terraced house three hours later and found Rosie Cooper standing on his doorstep. He saw a tangle-maned redhead wearing no make-up and smelling sweetly of essence of rose, clothed in black pedal pushers, block-heeled black gator-effect mules, a white T-shirt and a pretty sexy black leather biker jacket.

'Hi, I'm Davey Taylor,' he said, and stuck out his hand.

'Rosie Cooper. Lulu phoned you about what I wanted?' Rosie took his hand and shook it briefly. Actually she was rather impressed. She had expected a geek, a sad, bifocaled loser, but this guy wasn't even wearing specs. He was tall, with a fuzz of dark curls, a healthy tan and snappy brown eyes. He was slightly skinnier than Rosie's ideal, but he had a good pair of shoulders and well-muscled arms. He wore a baggy khaki T-shirt, combat trousers and high-top trainers. And he smelled clean.

'Yeah, she told me the details. Come in.'

Rosie went past him into a plain cream-painted hall. He opened a door, and there was a cream-painted lounge. There was nothing on the walls, and the polished wooden floors were bare too. There was a large-screen television, a huge burgundy-coloured leather sofa, and in the far corner there was a desk sagging under enough computer equipment to launch a shuttle. Above the desk was the room's only window, draped with white muslin. Through the muslin Rosie got a misty view of a garden ravaged by weeds.

'She gave you his name, his telephone numbers, his website address?' Rosie asked anxiously. 'She told you what I want? *Exactly* what I want?'

'She told me.' Davey went over to the desk. 'Take a seat.'

Rosie sat on the edge of the gargantuan sofa. 'Can you do it?'

Davey shot her an affronted look. 'Sure I can do it,' he said. 'But it'll cost.'

Rosie nodded, relieved. 'Of course I'm more than happy to pay for the work you do.' She thought about her dwindling resources. There was the van to be fixed. There was that irritating dent on the Beetle's hood to be knocked out. 'Um, how much is it likely to be?'

Davey was bashing away at the keyboard; lines of incomprehensible figures were flickering on the screen as he scrolled up.

'Oh, pretty reasonable I'd say.' Davey turned in his seat and flashed her a fetching even-toothed grin. 'I want a fuck, that's all.'

'Excuse me?' Rosie was sure she must have misheard him.

'A fuck,' Davey repeated patiently. 'Well, not just a fuck, maybe. A strip first. I've always wanted to hump a redhead. It's been an ambition of mine since college. Can't resist a red pelt.'

Rosie stared at him in complete outrage. She sprang to her feet. 'For God's sake!' She burst out. 'I said I was willing to pay you.'

'I'd prefer payment in kind. Call it bartering, if you like.'

'I *don't* like.'

'Then you don't want me to go ahead and hack into Countryman's files?'

Rosie bit her lip and glared at him. He had her over

a barrel here. But she thought about it, and what she thought was, Why the hell not? She'd be the first to admit that seeing Countryman and Mrs Squires at it in the garden had turned her on a lot. Even a long shower and a very satisfactory wank hadn't quite cooled her down, not yet. And Davey was handsome enough, and yes, she felt horny enough to go along with this.

'All right,' she said, walking over to where he sat at the desk. 'Go ahead and access the files. I'll do it.'

'Great.' Davey grinned happily, his fingers hopping about on the keyboard, his face rapt as he stared at the screen once more. 'Take the trousers off, but keep the rest on, including the shoes, OK?'

It seemed a trifle offhand, but she reminded herself that she had agreed to this. A strip first, he'd said, and she had agreed to do it. But she was a gardener, not an exotic dancer, and she had no idea how to strip in a flirtatious or seductive manner. Feeling herself blush at the suddenness with which she found herself plunged into an unknown role, she kicked off her mules, then, after a moment's deliberation, she hooked her thumbs into the elasticated waistband of the pedal pushers and hoiked them down.

Rosie was suddenly aware of Davey's eyes on her as she kicked off the black trousers and stepped back into the high-heeled mules. She stood there gazing through the muslin drape at the frazzled garden beyond, wondering what the hell she should do now.

Davey cleared his throat and said, 'Um. You're not wearing any pants.'

Rosie glanced down at him, saw where his gaze was directed, and looked quickly away with a shrug. 'Visible panty line,' she explained.

God, she felt ridiculous. She was standing here with a total stranger, wearing a T-shirt, a waist-length leather bomber, and below that she was naked right down to her feet; then there were the mules. Trying to get into the spirit of the thing, she put one foot slightly in front of the other for a more seductive pose, pure 50s starlet. She still felt foolish. Particularly about the fact that her buck-naked red-furred pussy was on a level with and about a foot from Davey's eagerly staring eyes. She considered crossing her hands in front of her thick brilliant red bush, but rebelled against anything so defensive.

Davey cleared his throat again. 'Walk around a bit,' he ordered.

Rosie hesitated, then turned and walked slowly about the room. There was nothing of any interest in here to look at, and the only thought that seemed to be circulating in her fevered brain was that he was looking at the wobble and roll of her naked white ass beneath the short black leather jacket, and at her long bare legs.

At this thought her clit woke up and reminded her that this was in fact an extremely sexy situation for a woman to be in. So why not enjoy it? Davey obviously was, she saw, as she glanced back at him with a seductive smile. Under the combat trousers, something interesting twitched and stirred.

'Shouldn't you be concentrating on getting into Countryman's files?' she asked teasingly.

'I'm doing it, I'm doing it.'

'Yeah, but you're more interested in getting into me, right?' Rosie grinned. She gestured down at her T-shirt. 'You want me to take this off? You want to see my tits, Davey?'

Davey gulped. 'Yeah, why not?' Then he turned back to the screen and his fingers moved over the computer keyboard even more rapidly than before.

'I suppose you get on to the porn sites with that thing?' asked Rosie, not really interested but just making conversation.

She threw the bomber jacket on to the couch prior to giving her stiff-nippled tits an airing. And oh, she felt hot down there now. Incredibly moist. Into her mind's eye sprang an image of Countryman's busily pumping backside between the milky thighs of lucky Mrs Squires. The wetness increased and the racing of her pulse was accompanied by a shiver of awakening pleasure.

Davey threw her a grin. Nice teeth too, she noted.

'I can do anything on this thing,' he bragged. 'I can call up a cyberdildonic sex toy, did you know that?'

Rosie shook her head. 'A cyber *what*?'

'Yeah, I can. So's I can have Net sex with a webcam girl. Practise my auto-cunnilingus.'

Rosie looked at him with more interest. 'You like giving cunnilingus?'

'Oh, sure.' Davey was looking at her naked snatch again, and Rosie knew he was imagining what she would taste like. His eyes rose hotly to where her nipples were pushing against the T-shirt. 'Come on, do the deal! Let's have a look at 'em.'

Rosie happily concurred, although she still felt mildly foolish, despite her arousal. She admired lap dancers and hookers, she really did. You had to really concentrate on your stance, your overall technique, when you were stripping for a man.

She decided to tease him just a bit further.

'Do you think they'll be nice?' As she said this she cupped each breast in her hands and lifted them under the concealment of the shirt. Her nipples protruded outrageously, and suddenly she wanted his mouth there, right there, on her hard little nubs, his tongue cooling their heat with long, slow, leisurely laps.

'They look pretty full,' Davey remarked, and Rosie hid a secret smile as his hand dropped into his lap and gave his restrained and straining cock a hungry squeeze.

'They were last time I looked. Is that sore? It looks pretty full too.'

Davey laughed, and there was the higher pitch of excitement in its tone. 'Oh, it is,' he agreed, his voice growing husky with need.

'Well, let me see it then,' Rosie said boldly. 'What do you call it, Davey? Your old man? Your dick? Your penis? I think you look like a dick or cock man to me.'

'Yeah, you're right.' He grinned, obviously pleased by her perspicacity, and clamped a friendly hand around the outline of his rearing organ. '*I* call it my dick. And it's a little uncomfortable right now because I think it's just fallen in love with that gorgeous red-haired cunt of yours.' His eyes were fairly glittering with lust. 'Come on, Rosie, let me have another look at that flaming bush.'

Rosie turned obligingly, hands on naked hips, one leg cocked seductively in front of the other. She was getting the hang of this stripping business now. She wasn't up to bump-and-grind yet, but the posing she could do. She posed there like an old-time Windmill girl, her bush glowing warmly in the subdued light of the room.

'Oh, wow,' moaned Davey, his mouth open. 'Now the tits. Lay those tits on me, Rosie, right now.'

Rosie grasped the hem of the T-shirt and pulled it off over her head, making her breasts bounce heavily as she moved. She looked down at them quite proudly; happily they were more grapefruits than bananas, being firm and round and full and pert and very white. Her nipples were astonishingly dark for a redhead's – the colour of strong chocolate, almost shockingly intense against the whiteness of the soft surrounding flesh.

'You like?' she asked saucily, totally nude now but for the black high-heeled mules. She stood with hands on hips, displaying the goods. 'Hope I'm not distracting you too much from Countryman's database, Davey.'

Davey's breathing was getting just a little hoarse. 'You're going to let me have a fuck, right?'

Rosie looked at him blandly. Did he really imagine that she wasn't gagging for it too now?

'A fuck was the deal. Also the strip, which as you see –' she held out her hands and gave a little shimmy, which sent her tits bobbing merrily, '– has been done. I keep my promises, Davey. One hundred per cent.'

Davey looked distractedly back at the ever-shifting information on the screen. 'Passwords,' he said almost to himself. Then to her he added, 'Any ideas about passwords?'

Rosie frowned. 'No. Well. I don't know.'

'Trying all the obvious ones.' His hands flew over the keyboard. 'Countryman, country, man, gardens . .' He shook his head.

'Try poached,' suggested Rosie.

Davey looked at her.

'As in stolen,' Rosie explained. 'Also filched, nicked, purloined.'

Davey tried. He shook his head. Tried a few more of his own. No go.

Rosie had an idea. 'Try *Coming Up Roses*.'

'But that's *your* company name. He wouldn't use that. Too obvious.'

'Rose?'

He tried. 'Nope.'

'Roses?'

He tried. Then he laughed. 'We're in.'

'Great.' Rosie snatched up the leather jacket and hurried over to where he sat grinning at the screen. She shrugged the bomber jacket on and forced her feverish thoughts into order. 'Get me a printout of his database, and anything else you can get your hands on, OK?' she ordered.

Davey nodded and started to download the

information. The printer whirred. While it did so, Davey oh-so-casually raised his hand and lazily caressed the pliable globes of her naked butt. Still staring at the screen, he raised his other hand and slipped his index finger in under her flaming bush to open up the lips of her sex for him. He then leaned his head over and inserted his tongue into the gap he had created, tickling her hot little clit with its tip.

Rosie moaned with pleasure and pushed her fingers into the dark fuzz of his hair, pulling his head in closer while opening her legs a little wider. The printer whirred busily while Davey got even busier with his tongue. Yes, he really did like to give tongue, thought Rosie blissfully. He was delving deeper, lapping her liquid warmth, searching for hollows, crevices, and then when he found the one he sought he was suddenly pushing, pushing up, fitting his tongue deep into her so that his slightly bristly chin scratched hard against her erect clit.

Rosie let out a groan and threw her head back in ecstasy, relishing this unexpected bonus.

But suddenly Davey pulled back. 'Gotta get out of there quick now,' he explained, indicating the screen. He tapped keys and the screen went blank. There was a neat stack of paper in the printer's tray – evidence of a job well done.

'Now for the payment, yeah?' Davey grinned, and his hands went to his fly, unzipping briskly.

To Rosie's surprise he was wearing underpants. He hadn't looked the sort to bother. But he was equally brisk with the bulging Calvin Kleins, yanking them out and then down and on to his thighs along with the trousers, leaving his prodigious and naked erection standing there like a white mast.

Rosie was torn between ogling Davey's cock and trying to pull the jacket closed over her hard-nippled breasts in a sudden attack of shyness.

'Now that wasn't part of the deal,' Davey protested mildly, looking up at her face with a reproving expression. 'I like the leathers on you, but keep it open. So that your nipples are naked.'

Rosie obliged, pushing the butter-soft leather back to expose her breasts completely.

'Oh, that's better,' said Davey admiringly.

She stuck the goods out further, and heard Davey's intake of breath with renewed confidence. The scent of the leather mingled with the aroused-male scent of his sex, tantalising all her senses. Oh, this was good. It felt distinctly naughty, and that aroused her even more.

Davey pushed his castored chair back and around, and Rosie was upon him like a female vampire ready to suck. She swung one leg over his lap and sat down facing him, smiling into his eyes. A musky perfume rose from between her wide-stretched thighs.

Lazily she hitched forward and rubbed her furry mound against his twitching cock. The pressure on her clit made her pant a little, but it felt good. She thought of Countryman tying Mrs Squires to the swing, and into her mind sprang an image of herself, tied to that same swing, with Countryman nudging his cock, his very big and very hard cock, between her thighs and up, up, up into her.

With a moan, Rosie rubbed harder against Davey's fat penis. He seemed to like that, and dipped his head down and took one of her nipples into his mouth while rubbing the other with the palm of his hand.

Rosie hitched herself up higher, stretching between her own wide-spread legs to run her hands up and down his dark-furred thighs. She let her fingers brush with tortuous and exquisite slowness against the fork of his thighs, where his skin felt so hot and where his hair was thickest. Gently she took his balls into her hands, cradling them and caressing them, then slid her fingers higher until the root of his dick was silky and hard underneath them.

'Nice dick, Davey,' she cooed, outlining the curve of his ear with a long, lascivious lick.

She scooped his cock up between her fingers, relishing its fine texture and its rigidity, swirling her fingers right up to its pinkened and moist tip. The little eye there was standing open and spurting just a tiny bead of pre-come. Rosie steered the engorged prick down from his belly, down and under her bush, and wiped that little bead away with the tip of her clitoris. Then she held his cock right there, and rubbed her hot little clit along the hollow at the tip of his glans.

It felt good.

She did it again. And again. And again, building up a rhythm until she was comprehensively fucking him while bringing herself off at the speed of light. She crouched over him, nudging him over and over with her clit, her head back, her eyes closed, the feelings so intense, so incredibly good, and then Davey pushed a finger up into her and clutched hard with his free hand at the globe of her arse; the combination of pleasures suddenly exploded in shimmering waves and she screamed, coming like crazy.

Davey quickly replaced his finger with his cock, jamming it up inside Rosie's aching pussy with extreme desperation. Rosie was aware that he was going to come at any second, she was driving him wild, clamping her muscles tight around his cock, bouncing up and down upon his slippery pole, urging him on with breathless little cries. He pushed one hand into her bush, tangling his fingers in the damp red curls, exerting pressure on her mound.

Rosie moaned and came again, more slowly this time, her face twisting almost with anguish as the pleasure shot through her.

'Oh, Davey,' she groaned, and he was suddenly pushing up against her bucking hips, almost unseating her with the violence of his movements. He came, shouting aloud, his penis rock-hard inside her and then pulsing, shooting his seed, pulsing again, filling her so full that she cried out in surprise and delight.

And finally, gently, their movements slowed and at last they were still, panting against each other, both grinning, their faces close together, their glances suddenly shy.

'Wow, you are so good at this,' gasped Davey

admiringly. 'What did Lulu say you were – a gardener? I'm telling you, you'd make a fortune as a whore.'

It was a comment that Rosie would remember more than once over the coming days.

Chapter Three

By the time Rosie had finished up at Davey's, it was past one o'clock and she had no time to stop for lunch back in Richmond. Instead she returned to base – empty now of Lulu's larger-than-life presence – dumped the printouts in the filing cabinet, locked it, and took a short shower to wash the heady smell of sex off her skin.

She then put on clean jeans, trainers and a T-shirt. She loaded her gardening gear into the Beetle again, took time out to phone the garage to collect the van, and set off for Knightsbridge. She stopped at the deli for a bagel, eating as she drove.

She hadn't thought to look out for Countryman.

She thought of it now, though, as she battled her way across town, glancing occasionally in her rear view mirror, looking out for a red flatbed truck. But it never appeared.

Of course not.

He wouldn't be stalking her. Not a nice ordinary working girl like her. But then, he *had* used her name for his computer password. The thought sent a thrill of unease through her. Unease, yes, and something else. Lust, perhaps? He'd certainly been something, she had to admit that much. It was impossible for any red-blooded woman not to admire a body like that: so male, so well-honed, so obviously bursting with health and strength. And his hair. Thick and wheaty. Gorgeous. Such a succulent thought, weaving your fingers through its silky thickness, drawing him closer for a long full-on snog.

Rosie fidgeted uncomfortably as arousal stabbed at her all over again. What was the matter with her all of a sudden? After months of bearable if not entirely happy abstinence, she suddenly seemed to be constantly panting for it like a bitch on heat.

Irritated with herself, she swung right across the traffic, causing a chorus of honks and shouts. If anyone was following her, that should lose them. And on top of all her other problems, it certainly wouldn't pay to start rolling up late. She was relieved when at last she found a parking space not too far away from the garden she tended for Simon Willis, an architect whose practice was based in Docklands.

Simon's was a large Georgian property, detached and set in a garden that surprised her by its size. At the front was a kiwi-fruit tree, and at the back there were many established shrubs and an ancient and very beautiful walnut tree. Rosie loved working there, particularly in the walled and totally private back garden where she now went, passing through a side gate and closing it carefully behind her. She brought the tools and the small mower and the strimmer with her. No sense in ringing the doorbell – Simon seemed to work even longer hours in his office than she did grubbing around in the dirt.

Simon wanted one of the long borders completely emptied and refilled with more colourful perennials. They had discussed his plans for the border at some length a few weeks back, and Rosie was now halfway through clearing the ground. Working out a game plan, she first mowed the big lawn and then strimmed the edges; then, sweating, a bit out of breath and surrounded by the heady scent of freshly mown grass, she took up her spade and continued with clearing the border.

The sun was beaming down; it was more like July than April. Rosie paused, running the back of a muddy hand over her sweating brow, and wished she'd at least brought some mineral water with her. She carried on digging. Simon wanted dark ruby-red dahlias, scarlet crocosmias and delectable orange canna lilies in this border, and she could already picture the fiery colours, vivid in the sun. It was to be a 'hot' border.

Wow, it sure was a hot day.

A thought occurred to her, and she looked about. Well, why not? Simon was at work, and the garden was completely enclosed. And it would feel sort of naughty, which was also sort of exciting. Mind made up, she gripped the hem of the T-shirt and pulled it over her head, tossing it on to the mower's grass-box.

Oh, now that felt good. She could understand the

buzz that naturists got. Her nipples were immediately hard, stimulated by her own low-level state of arousal and also by the soft, warm breeze. Naked to the waist, she took up the spade and carried on digging, her breasts swinging freely with her movements. Absorbed, she turned the soil and cleared out weeds, put aside shrubs to use elsewhere, and soon forgot that she was topless. She was reminded of it only when she turned at an unexpected sound and saw Simon coming out of the French doors on to the terrace. Rosie dropped the spade in shock and looked down at herself in horror, blushing furiously.

'Oh! I didn't, I mean, I thought you were at work. I'm so sorry,' she blurted out, covering her breasts as best she could with her soil-dirtied hands. It seemed to call attention to them even more, she thought in panic. He was going to be offended, she just knew it. And she'd lose another client, *another* one. She couldn't afford for that to happen.

'Sorry for what?' asked Simon perfectly calmly.

Rosie looked at him dubiously. Simon was roughly the same height she was, compactly made and dressed in what she knew to be his normal workaday uniform: a plain button-down shirt and heavy cords. He had straight dark hair, and wore tortoiseshell effect glasses that gave him a bookish air. They also accentuated his dark green eyes, which were now looking up and down her body with every appearance of interest.

'If you're sorry for working without your top on in my garden, forget it,' he said, not waiting for her reply.

'I thought you'd be at work,' Rosie said anxiously.

'I'm working from home on Tuesdays now.'

'You didn't tell me that!'

'Didn't think I had to.' Simon smiled, very cool and calm. 'Actually I'm bloody glad I didn't, or I'd have missed all this. I've been watching you for about a quarter of an hour, and I have to tell you, Rosie, you've got a truly beautiful set of tits. I was just praying for you to take your jeans off too. I've heard of the Naked Chef, but the Naked Gardener? That'd be really worth seeing.'

'Oh.' Rosie stared, completely wrong-footed. Far from being offended, he seemed positively pleased by her state of undress. *Really* pleased. The front of his cords was tented up by a good-sized erection.

'Fifty quid extra in it if you take them off and carry on gardening,' said Simon blandly.

Fifty quid! On top of what he paid her anyway for the gardening, that was a very tempting offer. She looked down at her body. She was standing here cringing like a propositioned maiden instead of a full-grown new-millennium woman, her grubby hands each clutching a handful of tit. She felt ridiculous. And, in view of all that Countryman had inflicted on her cash flow, she could really use another fifty quid.

'Well,' she said doubtfully. 'I don't see why not.'

'Neither do I,' agreed Simon, stuffing his hands in his pockets in anticipation of yet more delights being revealed.

Well, he obviously expected her to do it. And she

needed that fifty pounds. It wouldn't even cover the cost of repairs to the van, she suspected, but it would certainly help. And, hell, she rather wanted to do it too. Simon was a very attractive man, and this was pretty exciting. She almost smiled as she thought of shagging Davey earlier in the day. It seemed to be all feast or famine, this sex game. None for months at a stretch, then two in one day!

Rosie let her hands drop. She was aware that already her aureoles were dimpling, and the centres of her nipples were stiff. Feeling Simon's attention on her, she fiddled the button loose on the waistband of her jeans, then unzipped them. Kicking off her trainers, and thinking how dewy and softly sensual the newly cropped grass felt beneath her feet, she slid the jeans down and kicked them off, then looked back up at Simon on the terrace.

But it wasn't just Simon on the terrace.

There was another man there too, a much younger man. Three in a day, she quickly amended. He looked – what? – seventeen or eighteen? He had the same straight brown hair as Simon, but it was worn long and loose on his shoulders. The dark green eyes were the same as Simon's, too, although this younger man was taller, and had the badly-put-together look of someone who was rather coltish. Still some way off from the assuredness that only comes with age.

'Sorry, Rosie – this is my son, James,' said Simon, as if this were a garden party and he had been remiss over the introductions. 'Jay, this is Rosie. She does the garden for me. Rosie, I do apologise. I forgot to mention that Jay was here too.'

'It's OK,' said Rosie, feeling an absurd desire to laugh.

She was standing here in the buff with two fully clothed men staring at her. It wasn't an everyday occurrence – hell, it wasn't even an every *year* occurrence for her – and yet Simon was being relentlessly civilised about the whole thing. Making introductions. Rosie, this is my son. Jay, do you know Rosie? Ha!

'What's funny?' asked Simon, stepping down on to the lawn.

Rosie shrugged, and her breasts jiggled lightly. She felt the gazes of both men zoom nipplewards like Exocets locking on to a target.

'Nothing. It's just that I don't usually do this sort of thing,' she said awkwardly. 'And has Jay been watching me for a quarter of an hour too?'

'Nope,' Jay replied for his father. 'I just got up and came out here when I heard voices.' Jay gave a grin. 'I must say it's a very nice thing to wake up to in the morning, a naked redhead in the garden.'

Simon came closer, and Rosie found herself backed up against the trunk of the walnut tree. He smelled of soap-scrubbed skin, sandalwood and ginger. Medallions of sunlight dappled the lawn all around them under the tree's spreading shade. One highlighted Simon's hair, shading it with chestnut. Another burnished Jay's as he came closer too, and it was the same colour exactly. Father and son, she thought. Had any female gardener ever done anything like this with a father and a son? Never!

As she leaned back against the tree Simon reached out. He rubbed the back of his hand, lightly covered in pale-brown hair, against one turgid nipple.

'I thought I was going to carry on gardening?' Rosie teased, enjoying his touch enormously.

'No, this is more fun,' said Simon, and to her surprise – he had always seemed so remote, so patrician almost – he unbuckled his belt and unzipped the heavy cords in a very businesslike fashion.

Rosie looked at Jay, who winked at her encouragingly. Her eyes drifted downward. Oh, a big one under there. *Very* big. Her eyes moved back to Simon. His unzipping had revealed boxer shorts, navy silk by the look of it, and poking out of the slit in them was a long brown cock. Not quite as long as Jay's, but she guessed it was thicker. She reached out and stroked it enthusiastically.

Encouraged, Simon moved in closer and kissed her. Nice, clean toothpaste-scented breath. Nice dry lips. His hands were kneading her breasts as if they were dough. Another hand slipped down and fondled her bush. Her eyes flickered open in surprise. Either he had three hands or Jay was getting in on the act.

Jay was getting in on the act.

'Hey, I'm first,' Simon protested mildly, batting Jay's questing hand away.

Jay chuckled and moved back. The old lion still had supremacy. Rosie wondered how much longer that would last. Would Jay be batting Simon out of the way within a year or two, insisting he should be first? Probably.

But for now it was Simon's show. It was Simon who put his hand where Jay's had been, who tweaked at her pubic hair and slid a finger into her slit, where she was extremely wet. He moaned in satisfaction at this, and bent a little, lifting her up with a hand under each of her thighs so that her back rested against the trunk and her wide-spread legs came up on either side of his waist.

Rosie was vaguely embarrassed by Jay standing there watching as she got fucked by his father. Did he watch his father mounting his mother, she wondered?

The thought made her hotter than ever.

Rosie wrapped her arms around Simon's neck, and he pushed himself towards her well-lubricated slit. From there, Simon took off, bending his knees and pushing up energetically as his cock connected with her entrance. He slid his whole length into Rosie with a grunt of pleasure, and started to pump immediately.

And Jay, too, was showing some finesse. He slid his hand between her body and his father's, and stroked her hard little clit with what seemed to be a practised touch, fondling and tickling her while his father thrust indiscriminately. It felt so incredibly good to be doing this out in the open air. Simon was deep inside her, his passage oiled by her juices, and Jay's hand was pulling at her nub in a steady, ecstatic rhythm.

Rosie gasped as her orgasm started to flood her with sweet, searing heat. Deliriously she pushed down as hard as she could on to the father's penis and the son's caressing hand, seeking and finding that moment of complete release. She cried out hoarsely, arching her back against the trunk of the ancient tree, and was immediately followed by Simon, who squeezed her breasts quite cruelly as he came, pumping even more vigorously at her in the passion of his climax.

Eyes closed, breath coming in tiny shallow pants, Rosie slowly returned to earth to feel Simon slipping softly out of her. God, why were men always in such a hurry to do that? She preferred a man to linger, perhaps bring her off for a second or even a third time while she was on the plateau of arousal. But no. One quick hump and most of them were off and away. Thanks for the fuck, and goodbye.

She was surprised to feel herself being lifted up again – not against the tree this time, though. She opened her eyes, glancing around in curiosity. Simon was behind her. She could feel his naked and deflating cock warm and sticky against her buttocks. His arms slipped around her waist and his lips nuzzled against her neck, which felt very good. Jay, unzipping his trousers, came in closer, and while Simon lifted her up from behind, Jay grasped her thighs and parted them.

They *had* done this before, she was sure of it. They seemed to move so seamlessly together. Jay, who was wearing no underpants, flourished a longer, thinner cock than his father's up between her thighs as his hands hoisted her a little higher. With a quick movement he pushed into her, and Rosie let out a purr of pleasure. Maybe this was the answer to the man problem, she thought – two men at once. So when she was revved up and ready to continue, the second man could take over.

Oh, and Simon was getting involved too, pressing his hands very firmly against her mound so that her clit fairly hummed with excitement. She was going to come again. She tensed, her head thrown back on to Simon's supporting shoulder, as the pleasure surged through her again, weaker this time, but sweet and powerful nevertheless.

And still Jay fucked her, moving with long easy strokes, only his heavy breathing and the delicate flush of blood in his face betraying the depth of his arousal. Maybe he was trying to show that he could go on for longer than his father, maybe there was a touch of machismo at work here, a little male competition. Still, she was very much the one to benefit from it. She came again, crying out wildly, as Simon's hands attended to her clit and to her nipples too, roaming over her freely – a crazy counterpoint to Jay's ecstatic pumping.

And then it was over. Jay came in a wild staccato burst, flooding her with delight and, like Simon, he soon pulled out of her. Although Rosie could feel that Simon had grown hard again while he held her, she sensed that playtime was over. As she stood there, naked, breathless, and sated, she watched with amusement as both men tucked their cocks back into their trousers.

'Just carry on with the garden, OK, Rosie?' Simon said, giving her a last lingering kiss before both he and Jay went back up on to the terrace and disappeared into the house.

Suspecting that they were still watching her from in there, Rosie happily worked on in the buff, digging and moving plants about, smiling secretly to herself at intervals when she thought of their eyes out on stalks as they watched her. She was willing to bet they were each clutching a new stiffy, and she half-hoped they would come back out and start all over again.

But they didn't. When her two hours were up, Rosie regretfully pulled her T-shirt back on and yanked on her jeans and trainers. She took her equipment back out and put it in the car, and then rang the front doorbell. Simon came to answer it in seconds, obviously expecting her ring. No erection was in evidence now, but his eyes sparkled intimately at hers when he handed over her inflated wages.

'Thanks,' said Rosie, pleased with the bonus.

'The pleasure was all mine.' Simon smiled, leaned forward and kissed her briefly, his tongue tickling her lower lip. His hand slid to her waist, and then quickly up under the T-shirt to cup and caress her naked breast. 'See you next time,' he murmured against her mouth.

'Can't wait,' said Rosie, giving his fast-growing erection a friendly squeeze through the thick cloth of the cords.

Simon reluctantly removed his stroking hand, then drew back and closed the door. Sighing happily, Rosie went down the path under the big kiwi-fruit tree, and out of the front gate.

'Hi,' said someone close beside her.

Rosie shot up in the air as if someone had let a gun off

by her ear. She spun round to find a man leaning against Simon's front wall, arms folded over his broad chest. He was wearing jeans, lumberjack boots, and a red-checked shirt. He had thick, wheat-blond hair, joltingly intense turquoise eyes that were looking her over with interest, and an outdoorsy-type tan. He looked a bit like Kevin Costner, thought Rosie, almost salivating at the sight of him. She got a delicious waft of fresh male sweat, leather and oak moss. He was nearly a foot taller than her, and he was just stunning. Oh, holy wow, thought Rosie. And then she saw the red flatbed truck, and with a sudden chill her dazzled brain clicked into gear.

It was Countryman.

Chapter Four

'Oh – hi,' Rosie said automatically. He had a very direct, piercing stare, which made her look nervously down and away. She was uncomfortably aware of how dishevelled she was, sweaty from working and also exuding the musky aroma of sex.

'You're Rosie,' he said.

His voice was very nice, she thought. Low and almost soothing. And then she thought, hey, wait a minute. This was the guy who was poaching her business. This was the guy on whom she had only today sworn revenge. This was the guy into whose computer files she had just hacked. She swallowed nervously, feeling a guilty flush suffuse her face. But of course he didn't, couldn't, know what she'd been up to. That fact reassured her just a little – only a little, because up close he was very tall, intimidatingly cool, and his hands really were as big as shovels. And if he knew what she'd been up to, he could throttle her as casually as wringing out a wet cloth.

'You seem nervous,' he said.

To Rosie's consternation he pushed himself lazily away from the wall, letting his hands fall to his sides as he came closer. Before she even realised she meant to do it, Rosie backed up a couple of paces. But he just kept coming. Rosie stepped back again, teetered on the edge of the pavement, and stumbled back against the side of her Beetle. She was now flattened against the driver's door and he was still coming.

'I think I ought to warn you,' she said in a shrieky little voice that sounded nothing like her own, 'that I know karate.'

'Really?' He came closer still. 'Then we have more than the garden business in common. I'm a black belt.'

Rosie let out a nervous neighing laugh. 'You're kidding,' she said breathlessly.

He came closer still. When he stopped moving he was no more than a foot away from her, looming over her in what could only be described as a subtly threatening fashion. He folded his arms over his chest again. Those vivid eyes – yes, they were turquoise, a bright turquoise blue, she thought dazedly – stared into hers.

'Want to find out?' he said softly.

'Not particularly, no,' said Rosie. Damn, now she sounded like the Queen.

'Only someone hacked into my computer files this morning, and I wondered if it might be you.'

Rosie returned his stare as levelly as she could. Her heart was whacking away so hard in her chest that she wondered whether or not she was about to have a seizure. 'I don't know anything about computers,' she said truthfully.

'Only gardening and karate,' he said, and there was the faintest smile playing about his lips, the bastard. He was really getting off on this.

'That's right,' she said flippantly. 'And I think I ought to warn you I've got a rape alarm in my jeans pocket.'

His eyes widened a bit at that. 'Lady,' he said succinctly, 'I'm not interested in forcing you, you know.'

Pity, thought Rosie, she was immediately appalled at the thought. This man was her enemy, she reminded herself. He was poaching her clients, ruining her business, and now he had the absolute *gall* to stand there eyeing up her thinly covered tits as if they didn't quite come up to expectations! Suddenly she wished she was wearing a bra. A real, heavy-duty, passion-killing beast of a bra. Because her nipples were getting hard. She could feel them puckering and tingling, and it was because he was staring at them like that. They were poking up lustily beneath the thin fabric of the T-shirt.

'It's rude to stare,' she pointed out, sounding irritatingly like the Queen again.

'Really?' His eyes lifted from her breasts and his gaze met hers. 'Only you seem to be enjoying it.'

'I'm not,' Rosie said furiously.

'Well it's hardly a cold day, is it,' he said with infuriating logic.

'I don't think the state of my nipples has anything to do with you,' said Rosie with frosty dignity.

'Hey, lady, I'm agreeing with you on that.' His eyes

looked flinty now, greyer, angrier. 'Just back off from my clients, OK?'

'*Me* back off from *your* clients?' Rosie let out a breath of wonder at his audacity. Angrily she burst out: 'Why don't you back off from mine, *asshole?*'

'What?' he said tightly, and now they were glaring at each other nose to nose. 'What did you call me?'

'You heard! Just leave my clients alone.' Rosie was good and mad now, all nervousness and caution thrown to the wind.

'Or?' His voice was suddenly silky with threat.

'What?'

'Or what, exactly?'

'Or . . . or you'll be sorry, OK?'

There was a long silence. Then he said, 'Miss Cooper, I'll take on any clients I choose, and I don't want to hear that you've been poaching any of mine, is that clear?' Those turquoise eyes were hard, boring like drills into her brain as they stared into hers. His eyes dropped to her chest. Her nipples were still hard. Shamefully, irritatingly hard. 'Yes, you may have a superb set of tits, but frankly you're starting to get on my nerves.'

'Ha!' Rosie was almost beyond reason now – so furious that all she could do was lash out at her tormentor. 'What do *you* know about my tits? You're too busy playing Mellors and Lady Constance with *my* female clients.'

He moved fast for such a big man. That was all she could remember afterwards, because her mind just shut down, refusing to recall the extremity of her embarrassment at what he did next. All she remembered was the speed with which he pulled up the hem of her T-shirt, holding it up above her breasts at shoulder level so that she was pinned against the car by his hands and her breasts were exposed, naked, pale and vulnerable. There was no one in the street. This was London, she thought frantically, and yet there was no one in the street, no passing heroic male pedestrian to leap to her defence, no patrolling policeman to break it up, not even an old lady with a stick to hit the bastard.

I am not going to dignify his actions by struggling, thought Rosie mulishly. She stayed still, breathing hard, while he stared down at her nude and heaving breasts, so pale and full, with their hotly aroused cinnamon-coloured peaks bare to the fresh spring air.

'Oh wow,' he said quietly, and there was something in his voice, something genuinely admiring, that kept her still.

'You enjoy intimidating women?' Rosie asked in a strangled voice. She was wet all over again, soaking wet, wetter than she had been with Simon and Jay. It maddened her how aroused she was, how soft, how malleable, how totally liquid she felt while this stranger held her still and looked her over.

Her nipples felt so stiff, so painful, and so needy. She wanted his hands on them, his lips. She wanted his tongue to lap them, to pull them into his mouth. She wanted him to suck them. She knew it, and hated herself for it.

'No, this is a first,' he said after a long moment.

'Seen enough?' Rosie asked roughly, thinking that if he stood there looking at her breasts for one more minute she was going to buckle at the knees, beg him to take her somewhere and fuck her quickly. She could already imagine it, unfolding in her mind like scenes from a blue movie. She wanted it.

'Not nearly enough,' he answered, his voice suddenly low and husky. He came in closer still, and she let out a groan as the rough fabric of his shirt abraded her nipples. 'But if I see any more right now, I'm going to come in my pants like a schoolboy.'

His hands, which had been securing the lifted T-shirt against her shoulders, moved a little lower, so that his thumbs slid in under the heavy curve of each breast. Now his hands were framing her breasts, his thumbs lifting their weight a little so that her perky nipples were forced to jut even higher. It was torment, it was sheer hell, because his fingers were clasping her beneath her arms, right beside the burgeoning globes of her tits, resting ever so slightly upon the silky, ultra-sensitive point where her curves began, but not intruding upon them. And oh, she wanted that intrusion. She felt flushed and weak and entirely willing, and he had barely touched her yet. Her pussy was open and aching. Her nipples felt ready to explode with sensation. He pressed closer, closer – and now she could feel his erection.

'Oh God,' she moaned, unable to help herself.

But then he pushed her T-shirt back down, smoothing it decorously at her waist. From the corner of her eye she saw why. Someone was coming down the street, coming closer. She was saved! Funny how it didn't feel that way, though. Half of her felt sorry at the interruption. Half of her was relieved. She stayed there, her weight supported by the car. She wasn't entirely sure she could stand up by herself at this moment.

The man passed by, glancing curiously at them as he did so. Countryman glanced back, and the man looked away. A fat lot of use he'd have been anyway, thought Rosie. He was a foot smaller than Countryman, and weedy by comparison. Countryman! She thought angrily. What a stupid bloody name for a company. She didn't even know his real name.

'What's your name?' she asked suddenly.

'Why?'

'Look, you know mine. Why shouldn't I know yours?'

Rosie glared at him, the hot flush of her arousal beginning to recede. God, he was good-looking. In other circumstances, she'd love to play around with him. But he was a rival, and so she had no intention of letting her personal life get tangled up with business. It was a rule she always stuck to – never mix business with pleasure. And she wasn't going to break that rule. Not for anything.

He shrugged. He still looked angry enough to chew up her ass and spit out the bits, but he was also quite clearly getting a grip on his temper.

'Ben Hunter,' he said brusquely.

'Right.' Weakly Rosie pushed herself away from the car, fumbling for her keys. 'Well, I wish I could say it's been fun, but it hasn't. Gotta fly.'

He looked at her broodingly.

'If just one of my clients goes missing, you'll regret it,' he reiterated.

'Hey – I'm shaking in my boots,' Rosie snapped back, realising that she was. She still felt very shaky indeed. She felt a sudden urge to see a friendly face and be plied with hot coffee and lots of sympathy.

'Well, I did warn you,' he said, and stepped back so that she could get the door open.

Rosie stuck the key in the lock. A hand twice the size of hers closed over her fist. Very very gently. Not squeezing in the least. But the implication was there. He could squeeze if he wanted. He could very probably break her hand into little pieces, and let's face it, she wouldn't be doing much deep-digging then, would she?

'Remember what I told you,' he said close by her ear.

'It's burned on my brain,' Rosie said with sarcasm, trying not to shiver as his breath brushed over her neck. 'Can you let go of my hand please?'

He let go. Feeling as if her legs were about to give way, Rosie piled into the Beetle and pointedly locked the door behind her. Not looking at him again, she pulled out into the road and sped off. God, she badly needed some TLC right now. On an impulse, she took a right instead of a left at the end of the road, and headed for Lulu's. She'd never been there before, but she knew that Lulu would give her a warm welcome.

'What the hell are you doing here?' Lulu asked her in obvious dismay when she opened the door to her big pre-war semi in Neasden and found Rosie on the doorstep.

Rosie stood for a moment, aghast. So much for the warm welcome. So much for the open arms of friendship. Lulu looked like she'd found a turd on the doorstep instead of the woman who was supposed to be her best friend, her employer and her long-time buddy.

Music and laughter issued from somewhere up the hall. Must be the television running or something. Rosie had always thought that Lulu was single and fancy-free, childless, husbandless, and not regretting it for an instant. She knew that Lulu had inherited this house after her Nigerian parents had died. She had *thought* that Lulu lived a sedate and orderly sort of life. Maybe went to the gym and to church or helped out in a local charity shop when she had some free time. But it sounded like there was a party going on in there. Well, maybe a family birthday or something.

'I just wanted a chat, that's all,' Rosie said lamely.

'A *chat*?' Lulu looked incredulous. 'Girl, wouldn't it have waited until tomorrow morning, this chat? What happened, the town burn down? The nursery run out of peat substitute? What?'

'Well, I. No. I'm sorry.'

A door opened down the hall. There was a sudden blare of music and laughter and a blonde girl of about twenty stepped out and closed the door behind her. She was wearing only slightly less than nothing at all. A red balconette bra hitched her fulsome breasts up to impossible levels, and a matching G-string only just covered the tuft of red-blonde hair between her unclad legs.

Rosie gawped.

The girl flashed a smile and more besides at the two women at the door, and then scampered off up the stairs. Rosie watched her white buttocks, divided by a sliver of silk, jiggle all the way up to the next floor. Rosie's eyes drifted slowly back and met Lulu's. Lulu was by now busy looking at the doormat.

'Um, my niece,' said Lulu. 'Priscilla.'

Rosie absorbed this gem, wondering what new shocks this day was going to throw at her before she fell into bed again in a state of mental and physical exhaustion.

'Lulu, she's the wrong colour to be your niece.'

'Well –' Lulu looked up desperately '– not *my* niece as such. Not my real niece anyway. My ex-partner's niece. She sort of adopted me as Aunty Lulu, know what I mean? And she stays here sometimes.'

'Interesting line in underwear,' said Rosie stonily. As far as she knew, Lulu didn't have a partner, ex or otherwise.

'Oh, she sells stuff for a lingerie company. Tries the stuff out sometimes for a laugh, you know what these girls are.'

'I know what these girls are, Lulu, yes. I heard a man laughing in that room, too.'

'Oh, her boyfriend.'

'Her boyfriend.'

'You got it.'

A tall red-haired man opened the gate and came up

the path, hesitating beside Rosie. He looked awkwardly at Lulu and smiled distantly at Rosie.

'Am I early? I'm here to see Anna.'

Lulu paused for a moment. Rosie watched her expectantly, one brow hitched up. Mixed emotions chased around over Lulu's countenance for a few seconds, then she said, 'No, that's fine. Go right in. Second door on the left right down the hall there.'

The red-haired man entered. He vanished down the hall. Lulu and Rosie stood on the step and looked at each other.

'It's not what you think it is,' said Lulu presently.

'It's not?'

'No way!'

'It's not?'

Lulu sagged. 'OK, I'm running a few girls in the afternoons. This is my own private property, I'm supplying a community service here; is there a law against that?'

'I think you'll find there is,' Rosie told her.

'*Shit!*' burst out Lulu. 'I hoped you wouldn't ever find out.'

A brunette woman of about thirty clonked down the stairs in impossibly high-heeled fluffy mules. She was wearing slightly less than Priscilla had been. Only the G-string. Her naked hips swung and her heavy dark-nippled breasts bounced exuberantly with every step. She gave Rosie an unselfconscious smile, then spun away, buttocks twitching enticingly, and went into the room the red-haired man had just entered.

'Lulu, be straight with me,' said Rosie after a judicious pause. 'You're running a brothel here, right?'

'Only in the afternoons,' protested Lulu, as if that made the whole thing much better. 'Hell, you'd better come in.'

They sat in Lulu's sun-drenched kitchen and drank real home-ground coffee. It was a nice kitchen – homely, not flash. A ginger cat sat just outside the open back door and cleaned itself industriously. There was a little garden out there, nicely kept. It was a pleasant suburban scene, perfectly normal apart from the fact that Rosie could distinctly hear the banging and moaning sounds of someone making very vigorous love in the next room.

'The walls are a bit thin,' Lulu said apologetically, stirring three sugars into her coffee. If Lulu could blush, then she was blushing.

'I never even suspected,' said Rosie, shaking her head. It was turning out to be quite a day.

'And why should you?' snorted Lulu, adding cream. 'My private life is my private life, after all.'

'Of course it is.'

'The minute I'm out of your office, my life's my own.'

'Absolutely.'

'Private.'

'Right.'

'Sacro – what the hell is that word?'

'Sacrosanct.'

'That's the one. Sacrosanct.' Lulu stirred her coffee.

A scream sounded in the next room, then there was silence.

'She OK in there?' asked Rosie, a bit perturbed.

Lulu gave her a look.

'What?' Rosie asked indignantly.

'Girl, you have led *such* a sheltered life.'

'Well, it looks like it's changing.'

'In what way changing exactly? In an interesting sort of way, would that be?'

'Well, I –' Rosie hesitated, feeling herself colour up with embarrassment.

'You're blushing,' said Lulu with a broad grin. 'Come on, give. You know my guilty secret now, so come on, 'fess up.'

'I, well, I had sex.' Rosie gulped down a mouthful of coffee, keeping her eyes on the tabletop.

'Must be a first,' Lulu scoffed. 'What, are you telling me that you had your cherry broke for the first time today? That you were, before this point in time, a *virgin?*'

Rosie snatched a hank of her hair and started chewing on it nervously. 'Of course not,' she said. 'What I mean is, I had sex with a client.'

'What, that architect fella?'

'Yeah, him. And his son.'

Lulu's eyes widened as she stared at Rosie. 'You had 'em both at once?'

Rosie nodded. 'In the garden.'

Lulu nodded too, then took a sip of coffee, smacking her lips in appreciation. 'Well, I got to hand it to you.

You got talent. Even if you are just a tad on the obtuse side.'

'What do you mean by that?' Rosie demanded, dropping the hank of hair in surprise.

'That Simon's been anxious to get into your pants for months,' Lulu pointed out, as if explaining geometry to a backward child. 'Well, fill me in, girl. What'd he do?'

'Well, it was so hot out that I took my shirt off and gardened topless. Lulu, I had no idea he was even in the house, but apparently he works from home on Tuesdays now.'

Lulu snorted. 'He tell you that? I bet he's been loitering in the house for weeks on Tuesdays, just to get a glimpse of your ass. Not much work getting done, I bet, and plenty of hand jobs. Anyway, go on.'

Rosie shrugged, feeling slightly less embarrassed since Lulu was being so matter-of-fact about the whole thing.

'There's not much to tell. He said he'd pay fifty pounds extra if I'd strip right down to the skin and, as I was halfway there already, I did, and one thing sort of led to another, and his son showed up too, and that was really sexy, two men wanting to get it on with me at once, both with enormous erections and both good-looking too, and before I knew it we were all fucking up against a tree in the garden.'

Lulu sat back and eyed Rosie with interest. 'You enjoy it?' she asked.

Rosie grinned shakily. 'It was great. I came like crazy.'

'Up against a tree?'

'Simon had me first, standing up with my legs around his waist. Then he held me up from behind while Jay had me. I have to admit, it was good.'

'Plus you earned fifty extra,' Lulu pointed out, looking thoughtful.

'And then I met that Countryman bloke outside the gate.'

Lulu leaned forward sharply. 'You met him?'

'He was waiting for me.'

'So he knew you were in there.'

Rosie looked at Lulu as a thought struck her. 'Do you think he saw us? In the back garden?'

Lulu gave a whoop of laughter. 'I bet that stirred his underwear if he did! Whew! That was one very hot scene there. So what's he like?'

'His name's Ben Hunter. He was pretty pissed off with me, and warned me off his clients.'

'Ha! That man sure has got some nerve, saying that to you. After Mrs Squires and all.'

The mention of Mrs Squires called instantly to Rosie's mind Ben Hunter kneeling there between the woman's thighs, the lazy slow pumping of his taut naked buttocks. She felt herself becoming moist and open again. God, this was really irritating. He wasn't going to get to her this way. She was determined about that. She'd screw every available man in London before she'd admit she had the hots for him. She decided not to tell Lulu about the humiliating incident with the T-shirt. Her nipples prickled as she thought of it. Those bright turquoise eyes on her skin, burning, the size of his hands, the obvious strength in his arms.

'What?' asked Lulu impatiently.

'Nothing.' Rosie shook her head to dislodge the memory and swigged down more coffee.

'He get to you?' Lulu asked shrewdly.

'Ha! He'd like to,' scoffed Rosie.

'He handsome?'

'If you like that sort of thing, I suppose so.'

'You tryin' to tell me you didn't like that sort of thing? Only you seemed sort of hot and flustered when you saw him shagging Mrs Squires. You get a look at his cock? Was it big? Circumcised or not? He got nice balls? What colour's his hair down there?'

'How the hell should I know?' snapped Rosie, that image swimming into her brain again. Yes, she had been trying to get a look at his cock. And failing. But she had imagined it, and was continuing to imagine it, and that was almost worse. Titillating. Maddening. Making her as horny as hell the whole time.

She looked up and saw that Lulu was watching her closely. 'He touch you today?' she asked quietly.

Rosie shrugged.

'Come on, give,' urged Lulu.

'OK.' Rosie got to her feet and paced around the kitchen. 'He pulled my T-shirt up and looked at my tits. Is that what you want to hear?'

'If it's what happened.'

'Yeah, it happened.' Rosie stopped her pacing in front of Lulu. 'And you're right,' she admitted. 'I did want him. But I hated him too. And anyway the bastard just walked away. After he'd got me at boiling point, by just looking at me for God's sake, if you can believe it, he just walked away.'

Lulu looked up at her friend and employer for a minute or so. It had quietened down in the next room, but there were sounds of laughter, of music.

'You still at boiling point?' asked Lulu softly.

Rosie swept her hands through her tangled curls, clutching at her scalp. She looked at Lulu. 'I think if a man touched me now, I'd go off like a firecracker.'

A broad grin pasted itself all over Lulu's face.

'Want a job, girlfriend?'

Chapter Five

Rosie stared at Lulu in confusion.

'A job? What do you mean, a job? I've got a job.'

'Yes, but look at it this way,' said Lulu with exaggerated patience. 'Your client list is way down due to Ben Hunter's poaching half the females away from you. So you have a free slot now and then. If you'll pardon the expression.'

'I don't follow.' Rosie frowned, plonking herself back down on her chair and staring at Lulu. 'What sort of a job?'

Lulu sat back and let out a huge sigh. She raised her eyes to the ceiling. 'You see what I mean? Obtuse. As in dull-witted, as in insensitive, thick, mentally challenged, and so on.'

'So what's the job?' insisted Rosie. She was used to insults from Lulu. It just went with the package.

'What do you think, carpet shampoo sales executive? Wake up and pay attention, Rosie, I'm offering you some easy money here. And I do mean easy.'

Rosie stared at Lulu. 'For God's sake,' she said suddenly, 'are you offering me a job as a prostitute?'

'There's not a thing wrong with working as a whore. It's an ancient profession; it's so old it's almost respectable. And besides,' Lulu eyed Rosie with interest, 'I need a redhead. I've had requests from my gentlemen for a redhead, and I do desperately need one. Preferably a redhead who is also a virgin, but I guess that's sort of a snag in your case. However,' said Lulu, brightening perceptibly, 'you could act that part, couldn't you? Act all coy and shy and alarmed at the whole shebang?'

'Lulu, I wouldn't have to act,' said Rosie with a half-strangled laugh. 'I *am* alarmed. There's no way I could do it.'

Lulu poured them another coffee. 'You're a woman aren't you? Sure you could do it. You could do it blindfold.' Lulu grinned as she stirred in sugar. 'Come to think of it, you might have to do that anyway. Some of the clients like a little bondage now and again.'

'I'm getting even more alarmed,' said Rosie, accepting a second cup and swilling it down. Suddenly she felt quite parched. And also excited. She could admit that to herself. Would she seriously consider it, though? Sex with strangers? Sex with men who saw her as the virginal redhead? She thought of Ben Hunter again, taunting her, turning away from her. Wouldn't it be a blast to be desired, lusted after, seduced by men who couldn't wait to get at her, who would pay for the privilege of fucking her?

'I couldn't do it,' she said after a long thoughtful silence.

'The hell you couldn't,' sniffed Lulu. 'Look, I'm expecting a client at three. Joanne, that's the brunette, was going to take care of him, but this particular client's a regular and he has asked for a redhead before now, so this would be the perfect time to get you started. Joanne won't mind this once. Do you know what she does in her day job? She's a lady who lunches, a real rich bitch. Her husband's big in conglomerates or some such damned thing. They've got a huge pile out at Marlow by the river, but she's bored. Wants a little spice in her life. The money's academic to her. She doesn't need it. She takes it, but it's the illicit sex she really wants. Her husband's a bit of a cold fish, so she wants to feel as if she can really light some man's fire, and everyone's happy.'

'What if her husband found out?' asked Rosie, fascinated.

'Who knows?' Lulu shrugged nonchalantly. 'I guess it'd put a bit of fizz back in their relationship. Or maybe he'd dump her for a newer, younger model. I can see you're thinking she's mad to jeopardise what she's got but, Rosie, the girl is *bored*, and the fear of discovery is all part of the excitement, don't you see that?'

Rosie looked unsure. 'She could take up pottery. Golf. Watercolour classes.'

'Whew!' Lulu sat back with a shout of laughter. 'You really know how to live, don't you? Pottery! For God's sake, do you think that's more exciting than being in a nice big warm bed with a nice big warm naked man?'

'Pretending to be a virgin,' Rosie finished with sarcasm.

'Hey, you could hack that. No problem.'

'Lulu, a man must *know* when he's having a virgin.'

Lulu made a dismissive gesture. 'Lie on your side, keeps you feeling tighter as he slips it in. Scream a lot. Hell, use food dye if you gotta.'

'What?'

'Virginal blood, idiot. He breaks the hymen, you bleed a little. If that's what he wants.'

'This is sounding more ridiculous by the minute.'

'Well.' Lulu shrugged. 'Your decision entirely, of course. But you need the money. And you'd like the work.'

'You seriously think I'd make a good whore?' Rosie guffawed.

'I think you'd make a *brilliant* whore,' Lulu assured her.

Rosie's eyes narrowed with calculation. 'But look, Lulu, there's got to be a premium on a virgin, surely. And there must be a limit to the number of times you could pull a stunt like that. I mean, word could get around.'

'We'd be careful,' Lulu assured her. 'And you're right, there's a premium for purity. Some men would pay very dear for a slice of your virginal ass, my girl, and why shouldn't we reap the benefit?'

'How much benefit are we talking here?'

'You're such a hot businesswoman, you take a guess.'

Rosie sat back, thinking. She turned her hands palm-upward and hazarded, 'Fifty?'

Lulu shook her head.

'Seventy-five then.'

'Way out, girl. *Way* out.'

'You're saying they'd pay a hundred pounds?'

Lulu held up two fingers.

'*Two* hundred?' Rosie stared in amazement.

Lulu nodded. 'I take fifty per cent of that.'

'That's robbery.'

'It's an hour's work at a hundred pounds, cash in hand. You can make that sort of money any other way?'

Rosie lifted a cynical brow. Lulu knew damned well she couldn't. She chewed her lip thoughtfully. 'This client who's coming at three, Joanne's client. *He* won't be fed this virgin line, will he?'

'Well, because he's already booked in, obviously he didn't ask for that specifically. He's a regular of Joanne's, and he's partial to her, but he has expressed interest in a redhead. If you can work the shy virgin spiel in there too, it'd give you a bit of practice.'

'Always supposing I'd do it anyway,' Rosie reminded her, because she suddenly realised that they were talking as if this was a done deal.

'Always supposing,' Lulu allowed graciously.

'What's he like? Is he ugly?'

Lulu rolled her eyes up to the ceiling. 'Ain't that just all I need, a picky ho on the staff? No, he's not ugly. He's fine. A bit lonely. Most of these guys we get here are just lonely, or looking for naughty thrills they're not getting with their missus.'

'And asking for virgins.'

'Well, some sure do. Enough to keep you in clover. Think of it. You take on a couple of clients a week, that's two hundred cash in your pocket, and for what?'

'For pretending to faint at the sight of a schlong?' Rosie suggested.

Lulu beamed.

'Oh all right,' said Rosie, sticking out a hand. 'I'll try it.'

'You won't regret it either,' said Lulu, shaking her hand.

But an hour later Rosie was regretting it already. Joanne the voluptuous brunette had taken the news of her replacement on the three o'clock job with every appearance of equanimity.

'I'll go up west and do a spot of retail therapy,' she said happily, eyeing up Rosie with interest. 'This is the redhead you've been searching for then, Lulu.'

'Found her right under my nose,' Lulu agreed happily. 'And a virgin too. You know how these guys of ours love a virgin.'

'Oh sure.' Joanne's dark eyes sparkled with suppressed amusement as they met Rosie's green ones. 'Hope you're a good actress, Rosie. You sure don't look like you've never had a man to me.'

And now Joanne was gone and Lulu had left her in one of the big downstairs bedrooms to get ready for the three o'clock appointment. Lulu had made some suggestions, laid out an array of tarty underwear on the big bed draped with purple silk (and God, she didn't even want to think about what was going to happen on that bed later) and told her to shower in the en suite bathroom and primp herself up a bit for the client.

So, Rosie had showered, and here she was like a good little whore doing a spot of primping. She had applied a very light dusting of translucent powder to her face and shoulders, just a hint of blusher to her pale cheeks, a lick of mascara to her lashes, a smear of berry-coloured gloss to her lips. Nothing overly dramatic, Lulu had cautioned. Keep it nice and light. She was a virgin, not a vamp.

She had brushed out her long red curls, leaving them loose on her shoulders, and had slipped off the wrap Joanne had lent her and trawled through the stuff on the bed. White, Lulu had specified. Virgins had to wear white, and they had to *appear* virginal as well as act the part.

Feeling suddenly very uncomfortable with all this, Rosie picked up a lacy white basque and started to fasten herself into it. Mega pulling-in of stomach here. Wow, these fastenings were snug! If this stuff belonged to Joanne, she was certainly of the hour-glass type. Rosie thought back to the sight of Joanne swaying down the stairs with her big naked dark-nippled tits bouncing and her hips moving so hypnotically; she'd had a really tiny waist. Much tinier and less muscular than Rosie's. God, it was enough to bring out any woman's latent lesbian tendencies, being confronted with a woman of Joanne's beauty. They'd been natural tits too – that sexy, heavy bounce and sway – not plastic and unmoving.

Rosie stared at herself in the dressing-table mirror when she had got the thing on. Her own full well-shaped breasts were threatening to spill out of the lacy see-through cups on the basque, her coral-coloured and suddenly quite violently hard nipples were now peeking over the top of the flimsy fabric as if to get a better look at what was going on. She hitched the thing up a fraction. Better. And better put some pants on with it? Her scarlet bush was brilliant beneath the basque's ice-white tube, and surely a virgin would keep that, her most intimate and prized treasure (oh, she was getting into it now!) well hidden from the beastly men who would seek to plunder it.

Beastly, beastly men! She hummed to herself, feeling happier, as she slipped on a white lacy G-string with side fastenings. She stopped to admire the effect. Now that looked good. She snatched up a pair of flesh-toned stay-up stockings with elaborately laced and embroidered tops, pulling them carefully up to the thighs. The bit of milk-white skin above the tops of the stockings was the bit men really liked, Lulu had told her.

She checked the clock on the dresser, then paused to survey the room more closely. A bit over the top, even by Lulu's wild standards. Purple everywhere. Purple velvet on the drapes at the window, purple sheets on the bed, fake leopard skin on the dressing-table stool and on the cushions and throws and rugs.

'It all suits Joanne's looks and nature,' Lulu had explained when she had shown her in and Rosie had laughed out loud. 'Maybe a bit intense for you but, hey, the darkness of the purple will show up the paleness of your skin and underwear. And it'll match your hair fine.'

Rosie had to concede that Lulu was right, but now it was three o'clock and she was beginning to wish she were somewhere, *anywhere* else, preferably digging a garden or mowing a lawn. For God's sake, she wondered in blossoming panic, what am I doing here? The man could be a maniac. He could be anything. Anything at all.

Calm down, she told herself. Just calm down. He's a man, OK, but you're a woman. A very intelligent and street-smart woman, and you can handle this.

But her mind kept tormenting her with unwelcome images. What if he was horribly fat, or lacking in personal hygiene? What if she simply couldn't fancy him at all? What if she closed up like a clam and couldn't even let him inside her when it came right down to it?

Calm, she told herself. Calm. She took deep breaths and sat on the bed. It was no big deal.

The doorbell rang.

Rosie sprang to her feet. Who was she kidding? Of course this was a big deal. This was prostitution, this was illegal, this was probably dangerous. No, she wasn't going through with it. Damn, now there were voices in the hall. She thought of running into the loo, getting out of the window, and was in the act of heading that way when the door swung open.

'Oh Rosie,' carolled Lulu sweetly, 'got a gentleman caller for you, sweetheart.'

I'll give her sweetheart, thought Rosie angrily. She rounded on them and stopped dead in shock.

'I believe you've met Ben Hunter before?' said Lulu with a smile.

Chapter Six

'I don't believe this,' said Rosie, fuming as she stomped around the purple-toned bedroom five minutes later. Lulu was, of course, gone, and Ben Hunter was now leaning against the door, arms folded over his chest, watching Rosie work herself into a state of near-hysterical fury. 'She set me up. My friend Lulu. How could she do this to me? She works for me!'

'Really?' Ben Hunter was looking hugely entertained by all this. 'I was under the impression that you were working for her.'

Rosie stopped pacing, and looked down at herself. And realised that of course Ben Hunter had been getting a good eyeful. She snatched up Joanne's robe and belted herself into it good and tight.

'I hope you're not forming any false impressions here,' warned Rosie irately.

'False impressions?' Ben stared at her blankly. 'What, you're not working here as a part-time prostitute?'

'No! Well, yes, I was going to, but that was before I

thought it through, and now she's set me up with you, the bitch, and you can both go to hell.'

'But Lulu said it was OK. She told me she had a delectable redhead here, and somehow, you know, I've been getting kind of hungry for a redhead.'

The turquoise eyes were staring into hers again. She could feel herself melting like ice in a spring thaw. It was uncanny how he did that. It was unnerving too.

'She didn't by any chance say I was a virgin too, did she?' snapped Rosie. 'Because it's a pack of lies.'

'No, she didn't say that. What she did say was that you were very tight and extremely passionate.'

'Very *tight*?' Rosie echoed incredulously, feeling herself starting to blush.

Ben shrugged. 'Every man likes a tight woman. It feels sexier on the cock.'

'Look, don't hold your breath waiting to find out about that,' said Rosie in fury.

'Think I might,' said Ben.

'*What?*'

'What if I told you I've already paid?'

'Well get a refund!'

He looked at her. Rosie pulled the robe tighter about her throat, feeling ridiculous and also trapped.

'No, I don't think so,' he said steadily. He pushed away from the door. 'Why don't you take the robe off and relax? It's going to come off one way or another.'

Rosie backed hurriedly away. How had she got herself into so ridiculous a situation? Really, it was farcical. Like an old French farce where horny men chased reluctant girls in and out of bedrooms and basements. She could feel a smile forming at the thought, and suppressed it sharply. If she started smiling at Ben Hunter, she was going to be flat on her back in bed before she knew it.

Instead, as she cautiously edged away from him she said, 'You know, I think it's pretty sad really.'

'What's sad?' he asked, coming ever closer.

'You – having to pay for it.'

'I haven't paid for it.'

'But you said you had!'

'I said what if I told you I had. But I haven't.'

Rosie backed away around a fake ocelot-covered love-seat. 'Well in that case, pal, all bets are off. You haven't paid and I'm not cooperating, so why don't you just leave?'

'You really want me to?' Ben asked curiously.

'Yes,' said Rosie, and was dismayed to find that she was actually lying. There was a new sort of excitement here in the games she was playing with Ben Hunter. Her sex life had been pretty dull for quite a long time, and now that she had dipped a toe in the waters of passion, so to speak, she found that she was really quite keen to take the full plunge. And if the plunge involved a guy who looked as good as Ben Hunter, so much the better.

'You're lying,' said Ben, advancing.

'Think you'll find I'm not,' said Rosie, retreating. She squinted at him with interest. Damn, he was so good-looking. And that clean animal strength that emanated from him, that was definitely appealing to the female in her. 'So you actually had to *pay* Joanne to have sex with you?'

He smiled. Oh, nice smile too. She hadn't seen that before. He'd been too busy snarling at her, accusing her of all sorts of shit. Which she had perpetrated, as it happens. She had hacked into his files, and she was going to steal his male clients. Just like he had stolen her female ones. Because all was fair in love, war and business, as he very well knew.

'I never paid Joanne for sex,' he said, skirting the loveseat carefully. 'She paid me.'

'What?' Now the laugh did escape, a hoot of incredulous mirth. Rosie almost forgot to back out of range of those long arms of his. Belatedly, she got moving. Ben Hunter made a wild snatch at her – goodness, quick reflexes! – but Rosie was fast enough to dodge and lunge across the bed, rolling to her feet on the other side with all the alacrity of a cat.

'Nice move,' allowed Ben.

'Thanks,' Rosie said graciously. 'Now you're telling me, right, that a whore paid you for sex. Now there's a novelty. You are *so* full of it.'

He smiled again and started back around the bed. 'Joanne's only on the game part-time, strictly for kicks. I've done her garden out at Marlow for some years. She approached me, gave me a little extra, and the rest is history. For discretion we meet here – she pays Lulu for the room and the time when we're together – and everyone's happy.'

'Seems like a neat deal all round,' said Rosie, busy

imagining Ben Hunter and the curvaceous Joanne together.

'It is.'

'And now here I am, upsetting the plan. Or rather *Lulu's* upset it. Because she's set me up. Now she may be happy with that. You may be happy with that. Joanne is probably happy with that too, since to her I guess shopping is the next best thing to getting screwed bandy. But I am here to tell you, *I* am not happy.'

Ben was rounding the end of the bed. Rosie looked to her left, and realised she had cut herself off by crossing the bed. The loo was on the other side. She'd have to lunge back across the bed, that was all she could do.

'Want me to work on that?' he offered sweetly.

'Ha! After what you said to me this morning? After you *threatened* me, actually.'

'I explained about that.'

'So you did. But not to my satisfaction.'

'I could satisfy you now.'

'I really doubt that,' said Rosie scathingly, and leaped for the bed as he came within striking distance. She got to the centre of it and scrambled for the other side, but irritatingly Ben Hunter leaped too, and he could leap a little further than she could, evidently.

Suddenly Rosie found herself pinned to the bed. He was smiling down at her, untaxed by their acrobatics. He was clutching both her wrists in one big mitt, not hard enough to hurt but certainly hard enough to keep her from trying to get them free. Rosie was further annoyed to glance down and see that the front of Joanne's robe was gaping open, and with her arms hauled up like this, things were sort of spilling out.

'You'd better let go of me, pal,' advised Rosie, panting as she writhed her lower body to break free. This only resulted in Ben throwing a leg over both of hers, stopping her in her tracks. Wow, he was strong. She had suspected as much, but now she could feel all the power in those muscles, those big hands, those wide shoulders. She was enjoying herself here. Just as Lulu had known she would. Damn Lulu! Lulu had seen the needle match that was developing between her and Ben Hunter, and thought it would be a blast to get them into bed together. Rosie just hoped Lulu didn't derive *too* much satisfaction from it, because as soon as Rosie got hold of her, that woman was going to be stone-cold dead.

Abruptly Rosie stopped moving. 'Satisfaction,' she said thoughtfully.

'Hm?' said Ben, nuzzling her neck in a way that sent shivers all the way from her toes to her scalp.

'God, don't do that! Let me up,' insisted Rosie.

'OK.'

To her surprise Ben released her. Rosie sprang off the bed and started pacing the room. Ben hitched himself up on an elbow and watched her with interest.

'Lulu's a manipulator,' Rosie explained, peering into every corner of the room. 'She's set me up for this quite carefully, and I think she'd want to see the results of her labours. Wouldn't you, Lulu?' she asked loudly.

Ben sat up on the bed. 'You think she's filming this?'

'I think she films everything that happens in these rooms, but yes, this especially. Wouldn't you, Lulu?' she added loudly to her unseen listener.

'You think it's bugged, too,' Ben said incredulously.

'I know Lulu,' said Rosie. 'OK, she can listen in if she wants, but I'm not having her gawping at my ass in close-up. Aha!' she said, and pulled a stool over to the far corner of the room. She scrambled up on to it. Interested, Ben left the bed and came over to where she was. 'Look at that,' Rosie said triumphantly.

There, almost hidden by the repeat pattern of rosettes in the wallpaper, was the tiny eye of a camera lens. They both stared at it for long moments, then Ben went into the loo and emerged with a can of shaving foam. Rosie took it, and squirted some of the contents carefully over the lens. She turned around on the stool and handed the canister back to Ben. He lobbed it on to the carpet and grabbed Rosie around the middle, carrying her back to the bed and flinging her on to it.

'You're really persistent,' Rosie gasped out, almost winded by her impact with the mattress.

Ben followed her down and started the business of nuzzling her neck again. 'Just think how annoyed Lulu's going to be when she can hear us but can't enjoy the floorshow,' he murmured against her neck, dropping small kisses there. 'If you were to moan a little, it'd drive her wild.'

Rosie grinned and obligingly moaned. God, this was *fun*. Lulu had been right about that much, anyway. She moaned louder, imagining Lulu in a state of extreme annoyance at missing all the entertainment. But was there going to be any? She didn't think that Ben Hunter would go ahead against her wishes and inflict himself on her if she didn't want him to – although she was, after this morning's threats and snarls, by no means sure about that.

But did she want him to?

Uncertain, she let him get on with the neck-nuzzling thing again, and oh, that was good, very good indeed. Her hands somehow strayed to his shoulders. Big shoulders. They made her feel small and feminine, quite a novel experience for a well-built woman of her fitness level. She kneaded them a little with her fingers, caught sight of the state of her nails, and wondered for one wild instant about a manicure. A gardener with a manicure. Now, that would have to be a first.

'You OK down there?' murmured Ben as he started work on her earlobe.

'You're a bit heavy,' Rosie complained mildly, but she found she kind of liked his weight on her. She felt small beneath him, and nestling, and cosy.

'You'll get used to it,' he said, doing very strange things to her nerve endings just by nibbling around her jaw line.

'You're talking like you think this is going to happen again,' Rosie pointed out, but it came out more mildly than expected. She didn't feel so irritated now – in fact she was more aroused than irritated. Just holding him so close to her had put her in a half-stupor of desire.

She felt one of his hands loosening the sash of the

robe, and then the silky thing fell open. Ben drew back a little, and Rosie could feel his eyes travelling over her semi-exposed body.

'You may be annoying as hell,' he said huskily, 'but you've got a stupendous body.'

'Well you just go ahead and *unhand* that stupendous body!' said an enraged voice from the suddenly open doorway. Lulu charged in and stood at the end of the bed, quivering with indignation, hands on hips. She glared at the pair of them.

Rosie struggled quite reluctantly out of Ben's embrace and sat up. Ben, looking very cool about the whole thing but with a noticeable erection springing up under the revealing line of his jeans, sprawled back on the bed and put his hands behind his head, observing Lulu with mild interest. Rosie cast a glance at him and felt the old irritation start growing again. God, the man was so damned casual!

Well, he was certainly casual about his sexual gratification, anyway, she thought angrily. Wouldn't most men have gone ballistic at being interrupted like that? But oh no, not Mr Cool here. The only thing that got him moving was his male clients being filched from under his nose. And wasn't that a bit insulting, come to think of it? He didn't mind being wrenched away from her nubile young bod, but tamper with his income and he was breathing fire all of a sudden. She couldn't stand mean men.

'I wondered how long it would take you to get in here, Lulu,' said Ben.

'Ha! Two minutes flat is how long it took, Wise Ass, because you know as well as I know, the video's part of the deal.'

'Part of the *deal*?' echoed Rosie faintly. She looked at Ben, then at Lulu. 'You mean the pair of you planned to film me being fucked?'

'Not *you* exactly, no.' Lulu backtracked hastily. 'Just anyone who uses the room – anyone in general. Ben knows that. Joanne knows it.'

'Oh well, that's all right then.' Rosie got to her feet and drew the robe around her, belting it up tight. 'Just so long as Ben knows. And Joanne knows. I wonder, would it have occurred to any of you, at some point in the proceedings, to inform *me* of just what was going on?'

'Well who'd think you'd mind?' Lulu demanded, looking both shamefaced and exasperated. 'Hey, most of the girls think it's a blast being filmed in the act. And the men love it. And it's for everyone's own protection too. No arguments over who did what to who, it's all there on film. Isn't that fair?'

'What do you do with the tapes?' asked Rosie icily.

'Nothing at all, well, nothing major.' Lulu squirmed.

'What's nothing major?'

'Nothing serious or dirty or anything. I sell some to a few select friends, that's all.'

Rosie's eyes widened. 'You mean if I hadn't suspected you were going to film us in here, your "friends" would very soon be enjoying a cosy little home video featuring us as a couple of porno stars?'

'Well, if you want to put it like that.' Lulu fidgeted.

'I don't want to put it any way at all, Lulu,' said Rosie, her voice oozing permafrost. 'In fact, I'm out of here. Right now.'

Rosie turned on her heel and strode over to the bathroom. She slammed the door behind her, too, and got dressed and left without another word to either of them.

Chapter Seven

Ben had a job on at five, so he left Lulu's shortly afterwards to cross town and battle with the rush-hour traffic. Fighting his way around the North Circular in his red flatbed, he thought about Rosie and how spitting mad she had been at Lulu. He laughed out loud. Whatever else she might be – damned annoying being top of the list – that girl was certainly good entertainment value. That was a real redhead's temper she had there. And she'd looked pretty magnificent standing there half-naked shouting down the majestic Lulu and making her look like a guilty schoolkid.

Yeah, she was gorgeous all right. He edged along in the traffic and considered how things might have gone had Lulu not made her entrance when she did. He spent long moments thinking about Rosie's cinnamon-tipped breasts, her well-muscled sweetly soft body, and the brilliant red filaments of pubic hair that he had seen escaping from those white lacy panties she had on.

Ben looked down at his lap; his cock was rearing up,

straight and true, at the thought of her. If Lulu hadn't come in, he'd have continued to make love to Rosie until she was wet enough and wild enough to let him inside her. His cock stiffened painfully at that thought. She was tight and very passionate, Lulu had said, giving him the sales pitch. But the thought of Rosie's tight little cunt, of her thighs spread wide open on either side of his waist, of her sighs and animal groans of satisfaction as he sank his cock into her, were driving him mad.

He should have stayed, as Lulu had suggested. Should have had one of the other girls instead. Now he was horny as hell and needing release. Glancing cautiously to either side as the traffic crept so slowly along, Ben reached down and unfastened the button at the waistband of his jeans. Checking again for outraged onlookers and finding none, he slid the zip down and eased out his naked cock. It was hugely erect and stirring restlessly as if scenting Rosie on the hot evening breeze.

Oh, that felt better. Sexy too, his dick up and ready while the other travellers around him were unaware of what he was doing. Getting bolder, he lifted his hips and pushed the encumbering jeans down on to his thighs. That felt even better. His balls, furred with golden hair, lay hot and heavy between his strongly muscled thighs. Lightly he touched a hand to his prick, wishing that it was Rosie's hand on him. The little eye opened and a glistening drop of seed oozed out.

He thought that it must be good to be a contortionist; if he was he could just lean down and fellate himself, suck himself dry, and imagine that it was Rosie's mouth caressing him instead of his own. He half-smiled as he eased the truck forward just a little more. Horns were blaring, people were getting impatient with the jam, but he was fine, just fine and dandy.

Well, a hand job was going to have to do. He placed his hand on the stem of his cock and started to rub up and down, up and down, thinking of Rosie's nipples and her naked thighs spreading out for him, revealing that fuzz of vivid hair she had down there and the pearly wet opening of her pussy, like a small pert mouth turned sideways.

He thought of touching his cock-head to that waiting mouth, parting the heavy concealing lips, pushing so, so gently until there was no resistance and his whole cock slid into her. His eyes were half-closed with the sweet sexuality of the situation, the rough tugging of his own hand pulling back his foreskin to expose the hot and hungry tip. In his mind's eye, Rosie cried out and her back arched like a bow. He kissed her tits, her ginger-tufted armpits, her neck, her open and gasping mouth, while he thrusted in and out of her with wild abandon, her pussy making soft sucking sounds against his cock as he worked on her.

Oh, so good. Nearly distracted by his pleasure, he eased the truck forward again and, glancing to the side, found a young blonde woman at the wheel of a white transit looking back at him. As her van had a higher wheelbase than his, she was looking slightly down on him, and was watching with keen attention as he pleasured himself.

Ben's brisk hand movements stilled instantly as he gazed back at her. God, wasn't this all he needed? Now she'd call the cops and he'd be arrested for indecent exposure, he'd be late for the job, he'd lose the contract. How embarrassing was this on a scale of one to ten? he wondered. Pretty damned embarrassing, actually. At least a twelve. Not wishing to offend, he covered his overheated cock with his naked forearm and saw that the woman was now – oh *no* – talking into her mobile. Jeez, he was in trouble. *Big* trouble.

His own mobile chose that precise, excruciating moment to ring. He cursed and snatched it up, leaving one hand on the wheel and his cock red and naked and bare to the woman's no doubt outraged eyes.

'Hi, is that Countryman Gardens?' said a light female voice.

'Yes, can I help you?' he asked a bit tersely, worriedly glancing at the woman in the transit.

The woman gave a little wave and a smile played about her mouth. Her eyes looked down at his lap. Oh, to hell with her! She was going to shop him to the cops anyway, so let the bitch look! He leaned back and let it all hang free. Let her get a bit of excitement. Why not? The breeze from the half-open window rushed over his glans like the brush of a silk nightgown. It did nothing at all for his self-control. He ached for release, and his dick twitched impatiently. The woman watched.

'Only I've got a job for you,' said the woman on the phone.

Ben sighed, annoyed at the interruption but

appreciating that work was money in the bank and should not, even in dire and provoking circumstances, be turned away.

'What sort?' he asked as pleasantly as he could, bearing in mind the desperation of his condition.

'That's what we ought to get together and discuss,' said the woman, and her voice was quite sexy now he thought about it. 'Um – I'm in the white transit.'

Ben's head shot round. The woman in the transit still held the phone to her ear. Her eyes met his, and she smiled and waved again. Then her eyes fell to his lap.

'I got your mobile number off the side of the truck. If you'll pull into the next lay-by, we can talk,' she said.

'Well, I'm already running late for a job,' Ben said slightly reluctantly. She was pretty, he was thinking. Blonde haired and blue eyed, and there was a suggestion of heavy curves under her pale pink T-shirt.

'How can I persuade you?' She seemed to ponder this for a moment. 'I know. If you meet me for a chat at the next lay-by I won't call the cops and tell them you've been flashing your cock at all the passing ladies. How's that?'

Ben looked at her incredulously. 'I *wasn't* flashing it at anyone. I was giving myself a hand job, OK?'

'Yeah, I saw.' She gave a merry little laugh; there was something smoky in the undertone, something intensely sexual. 'It always fascinates me, watching a man pleasure himself. I mean, you're so *rough* with it, you men. Is it your favourite way?'

Ben thought about this weird situation. He was

inching along in traffic with his dick hanging out, being ogled by an attractive blonde who was now wanting to talk dirty with him. But what could it hurt? He liked talking dirty.

'No, my favourite way of coming is in a woman.' There, that'd shut her up.

'Right. But there's a lot to be said for masturbation, don't you think? No one else to please except yourself. Be as rough or as slow or as fast as you like. No woman demanding a twenty-minute orgasm. No man wanting a two-minute fuck.'

'There's a lot to be said for a two-minute fuck,' Ben said with a grin. He was beginning to enjoy this.

'Is that all it takes you? Two minutes?' The woman nudged her vehicle forward beside his and eyed his crotch greedily. 'Go on then. Show me.'

It was a gauntlet flung down, a challenge. Ben tossed the mobile aside and put his hand back on his cock. His eyes locked with the blonde's. Then, slowly, he started to pump. He leaned back in his seat and watched her eyes widen and darken. She was wet, he'd bet. Just watching him. Women always loved his cock; it was big, in perfect proportion to the rest of his tall and well-muscled body.

He thought of driving not in thick London traffic but down a leafy lane with this hot, sexy blonde by his side, doing this while she watched from the passenger seat. And then he would stop the truck somewhere quiet and she would jump out, knowing his intention, and run teasingly off, and he would follow her with his cock sticking out of his trousers, and he would catch her in a fragrant meadow festooned with cranesbill and wild poppies and precious wild orchids. The air would be thick with birdsong and the heavy hum of bees, and he would push her to the ground, rip aside the fragile barrier of her pants and push himself inside her.

His hand moved faster. Thank God, the traffic was completely stationary now; it was getting hard to concentrate on practicalities when his whole being, every single nerve in his body, was centred on the heady stimulation of his hand as it moved up and down, up and down, on his straining prick. It was slick now, moist with its own juices. He turned his head and saw the woman was still watching.

His eyes held hers as he continued to pump his cock. He saw her tongue sneak out and moisten her lips. Wow, she was really getting off on this! Releasing his cock and wincing at the will-power required to do so, he snatched up the phone again.

'You still there?' he panted, and she was. She was still holding the phone tucked in against her jaw.

'Still here,' she said huskily.

'Like what you see?'

'Oh yes.'

'Well, I'm going to stop right now and tuck it back in my jeans unless you take your top off.'

Her eyes widened as if scandalised. He didn't think she was, though. More titillated than shocked.

'But my breasts are set a lot higher than your cock,' she protested. 'Someone might see.'

'What if they do?' said Ben. 'They'd love it and so

would you. Come on, let's have a little reciprocation here.'

'I don't know.' She looked uncertain.

'Shame. I'll put it away, then.' Ben reached for his painfully sensitised cock.

'No, wait. OK. You bastard. You want tits, you can have tits. Only don't stop.'

He saw her toss aside her phone. He watched with interest as she grasped the hem of the tight T-shirt and pulled it up over her head and off. Disappointingly, she was wearing a pink push-up bra and, although she looked good in it, very perky and curvaceous, he wanted to see the goods, not the packaging.

She picked up the phone. 'OK then?' she asked him. Then the traffic moved forward a bit in both lanes, and they moved both truck and transit on a few feet.

'No. Take the bra off.'

He caught the tail end of a swear word as she put the phone aside again. But she was a game girl. She reached behind her, unclipped the bra, and eased it down her deeply tanned arms and off. But she kept her arm over her naked breasts and grinned at him as she once more took up the phone.

'Take your arm away,' Ben said tightly, feeling she'd teased him quite enough. He was desperate for a sight of her tits now, and she knew it. His cock was so hard it was plastered to his navel by pre-come and sheer unadulterated lust.

She dropped the phone, turned a little towards him in her seat, and let her arm fall away. She revealed a delectable pair of very white and very plump tits, with dark-brown nipples puckered to tortured points by desire. The contrast between her white breasts and her brown arms was stark and exceedingly sexy; she'd been sunbathing wearing a bikini, keeping her breasts covered. Maybe they were too sensitive to the sun, maybe her nipples burned easily. He thought of rubbing soothing cream into those hard, prominent little nubs, squeezing those two fleshy mounds, and groaned aloud. When he thought of the skin of her crotch being white too, and that strip of white round her hips, and her nude buttocks as white as ivory against tanned brown legs, he almost lost control.

She knew it, too. He saw her laugh, glance around to be sure she was unobserved except by him, and then assume a provocative model pose with her arms behind her head. The pose stuck her naked, jutting breasts out even further. And then she gave them a sharp little wiggle that set them bouncing like beach balls. Still laughing, she took up the phone again.

'Now do *you* like what you see?' She half-laughed, half-panted; she was flushed with excitement.

'Definitely,' said Ben, ogling her freely.

'So do it,' she ordered. 'I want to see you come.'

Needing very little encouragement now, Ben once again clasped his cock and got pumping. As he pumped he kept his head turned slightly so that he could enjoy the sight of those plumptious breasts of hers while also keeping half an eye on the traffic's progress. She certainly had a gorgeous pair, but he was annoyed to find himself thinking that Rosie's had the edge. That mad redhead had better keep out of his way from here on in. No, concentrate on the blonde, he thought. He liked the intense chocolate-brown of her nipples against the pale cream skin of her tits. It was exceedingly sexy. And she wasn't covering them at all now; in fact she was pushing them up with her hands to accentuate the voluptuous curves. Lovely, lovely tits.

He pumped harder, gasping at the sweetness of the sensation. His hand movements became a blur, his balls lifted urgently, and then he let out a groan of release and came, hot and hard. Seed splashed up over his belly and on to the lower portion of his work shirt as his cock emptied in several long, satisfying spurts. He leaned back in his seat, panting, sated. He closed his eyes briefly, smiling with pleasure. There was a tinny sound and he realised the woman was talking on his mobile. Lazily he reached out and held the phone to his ear.

'So, do you have a window free sometime, to fit in another gardening client?' she asked suggestively, the fingers of her free hand stroking back and forth over one turgid nipple.

'Oh, I think I can squeeze you in,' said Ben with a grin.

'Good. Catch you later,' she said, and put the phone down. Much to his disappointment, she then pulled the T-shirt back on and down over her jiggling tits – she didn't bother to replace the bra, he noticed – and the traffic in her lane moved at last. Within a minute, the perky blonde was gone. Ben cleaned himself up with his handkerchief, tucked his deflating cock back into his jeans, and zipped up. Another satisfied client, he thought; and grinned.

By six o'clock he had finished moving a large rhododendron (easy to do, because they had tiny little plate-like matted root balls which were no problem at all to dig out), and relocated a struggling pieris Forest Flame to a more favourable position. He had pointed out to Sally MacGregor, his painter client, that as the weather had turned so warm this was by no means the ideal time to move either, but she had been insistent; so he told her to soak both the plants with water for days ahead of his visit, to lessen the shock of disturbance. Sally had dutifully done so, so their hopes of survival were good.

And now they were in Sally's studio, which was contained in a large wooden structure at the end of her lovely garden, and Ben was lying naked where she had her models pose, on a big sheet-covered open-backed couch just by the window to catch the best of the light. Sally was over behind her easel, sketching him with charcoal. She was naked too. It was peaceful down here, and Ben was tired from sex and work and the humid heat of the day, and he was very happy to lie back and let her work.

Not that he'd had sex with Sally yet, but Sally would expect it some time over the next hour or so. And watching her work was very stimulating, anyway. He remembered fondly the first time she'd shown him around the studio. He'd been distant with her then, unwilling to offend, willing to take up any invitations she might make but not wanting to make the first advance in case it lost him a job.

But Sally MacGregor had quickly got them over that first tricky time. After he had finished work in the garden, she had offered to show him round her studio and he had accepted. Once inside the snug and very private little building down the bottom of the garden, Sally had made her move. While showing him one of her seemingly mad abstract paintings – which apparently sold for even more mad sums of money – she had stepped in front of him with great aplomb, knelt down, and unzipped his jeans.

At first he had been limp with shock but, within seconds, his penis had filled like an elongated party balloon. With a grin Sally had leaned forward, clasped him firmly in both hands, and had taken him into her mouth and expertly sucked him off.

That had been a year ago, and they had been in here together many times since. Sally's favourite pastime seemed to be sucking him off, then leaving him lying spent on her couch so that she could draw him. And she liked doing it with her clothes off – which Ben didn't object to, not at all. Sally was a tall and well-stacked brunette. Her loose glossy long hair tumbled and rolled all over the place while she moved around the canvas, eyeing it, adding a scrawl here, a sharp line there. Her tits tumbled and rolled too, much to Ben's fascination. And her legs were seriously long and shapely, and topped with an enticing v-shaped forest of black hair at the juncture of her thighs.

'Your cock's standing up again,' Sally said in annoyance.

Ben's eyes travelled lazily down his body to see that this was true; then he transferred his gaze to Sally.

'Stop looking at my snatch,' said Sally, holding a hand in front of her dark bush. 'That's what's doing it.'

'I can hardly be blamed for that,' said Ben with a yawn. 'Cover it up if you don't want me to look at it. I *like* looking at it. My *cock* likes me looking at it.' He gazed at her, standing there with her hand over her bush. 'And don't go slipping a finger in or anything, not if you don't want me getting excited.'

'You mean like this?' Sally smiled, and slipped a finger in. 'By the way, the slugs are eating my hostas.'

'They do tend to.'

'So what should I do about it? I could put down some slug pellets, couldn't I?'

Ben held up a finger. 'Hear that?'

'What?' Sally had forgotten to fondle herself. Her hand dropped away from her crotch as she frowned at him.

'The blackbird on the eaves? The mistle thrush singing in the bushes over there? That male chaffinch in the background, calling to its mate? Oh, and that's a robin there – they sing beautifully. Probably got chicks hidden around the garden. Don't bother looking, you won't find them. They're speckled little things – perfect camouflage.'

'Yeah, I can hear them,' said Sally. 'So what?'

'If you use slug pellets, get used to *not* hearing them.'

'Why?'

'Why?' Ben shook his head in wonder. 'Because you'll kill them stone dead, Sally. You'll poison their food source – the slugs and snails – and if they don't eat the poisoned food they can pick up the pellets and ingest them. So don't use fucking slug pellets, OK?'

'OK, OK.' Sally held up a placatory hand. 'I'd no idea you felt so strongly about these things,' she grumbled, getting back to her sketching.

'What, about the natural world? I make my living from it; it supports me. I support it. Together, the natural world and I are a perfectly balanced double act. So sod slug pellets. And grit doesn't work. Forget it. Ditto eggshells. Slugs produce loads of mucus – you think an eggshell's going to be insurmountable to a creature like that?'

'So what the hell am I supposed to do?' demanded Sally. 'Let them eat the hostas?'

'Change the variety you've got,' said Ben patiently. 'Some hostas attract slugs, but others are extremely resistant to slug damage. That way, you solve the problem and you don't harm the environment in any way.'

'Oh.' Sally watched him with grudging admiration. 'Clever bastard. Will you fix that for me? Get some new ones? About six should do it.'

'Sure,' said Ben, and relaxed back on to the couch.

His anger at her poisoning suggestion had at least

made his erection subside for now. God, he hated the way people perceived their gardens – as their inviolate kingdoms, not part of the natural world at all, but able to be rigorously controlled by applications of chemicals and toxins that were lethal to wildlife and even more lethal to the long-term health of the soil.

Many of his clients asked him how to control aphids when their numbers rioted out of control in spring. 'Get a nest of blue tits in the garden,' he always said, to be greeted by hoots of derision and disbelief. And yet he was telling them the perfect truth; the fledglings would consume enormous numbers of the bugs, and if you weren't fiddling around with the natural balance with chemical fertilisers and weed killers and so on, other insects would thrive and help out too; ladybirds, and lacewings were voracious predators of aphids. Once they tried it, and fought against their panic and their stupid lust for total, impossible perfection in their gardens, his clients were always complete converts to the benefits of organic gardening – with the added advantage that they found themselves in touch with nature in a way they had never before found possible. No doubt about it, he thought, listening to the sweet singing of the blackbird on the eaves of the studio, organic gardening was *cool*.

But then he had always known that, long before the fashion gurus had declared gardening and cooking and DIY to be 'hot'. His dad, a head gardener on a thousand-acre Sussex estate, had always gardened the natural way; and he had inculcated in his son the practices that were kindest to nature.

Ben lay back in the drowsy heat and thought over his past. A couple of years as his dad's assistant had only confirmed his belief that gardening was the only possible job for him. Since then, he had worked for parks departments, landscapers, private estates – but he was a bit of a loner, averse to being told what to do by a boss, so he had finally drifted from the Sussex country village he called home and moved to London, where the new fad for garden design was cresting a wave, just as Janina, a friend from back home who was now a London-based lawyer, had told him. Here, there was money to spare for gardening enterprises and he had done terrifically well. City whiz-kids with plenty of cash and no time were eager to pay someone to form their idea of Eden in the back yard, regardless of cost.

The only trouble was, he hated living in Janina's spare room in London. Whenever possible, he escaped to the parks. But he was making huge amounts of cash. More than he had ever expected, because his female clients always paid him extra for the sexual services he was so happy to provide. His plan was to do this for five years, and then return to his Sussex cottage – he was currently letting it – and buy some land nearby to start his own nursery business.

He'd already been doing this for four years, and he was getting very anxious to quit the city and return to the country where he belonged. The fields of ripe yellow corn rolling like huge inland seas, the seagulls following a lone tractor across a brown expanse of earth, the spring buds bursting out in stunning profusion, the soft blue carpet of the woodland bluebells which were, he knew, in bloom right now – he loved it all. And God, he missed it. He was nearly, *nearly* there, though. Tantalisingly close to fulfilling his cherished dream. And nobody, not Rosie, not anybody, was going to stand in his way at this late stage. He couldn't afford to start losing customers now. Damn, he *wouldn't* let it happen.

'Don't lie there snarling like that, you look fierce,' complained Sally. 'I've told you, I'm not going to use slug pellets.'

'Sorry,' said Ben, and rearranged his face into more pleasing lines. 'It wasn't that. I was thinking of something else.'

'Oh? What?' she asked, genuinely interested, as she sketched on.

'Someone trying to filch my business,' Ben said.

'Really? Who?'

'It doesn't matter.'

Sally looked at him. 'Clearly it does. You looked like thunder for a moment there. Is he a better gardener than you or something?' she teased.

'*She* is an OK gardener. But she fights dirty.'

'And you don't?' Sally looked at him in disbelief. 'What's she like then?'

'Obnoxious,' Ben said flatly, but his cock stood up as he said it. And Sally was right; he was single-minded enough to fight dirty too. Fixing her up at Lulu's knocking shop, with Lulu's amused collusion, was proof of that. And if she kept on getting in his way, business-wise, then he was going to have to devise some drastic plan of action to remove her from his path. Maybe he'd have a word with Janina, see what the legal position was.

'Aha!' Sally laughed, witnessing this interesting spectacle. 'She's pretty then.'

'She's still obnoxious.'

'But still pretty,' said Sally, turning the easel so that he could see what she'd done. 'What do you think?'

Ben stood up and walked over to where Sally stood. His erection preceded him. He looked at the sketch; it looked like him, sort of. But not enough for his rather plebeian tastes. Modern art, he'd be the first to admit, was wasted on him. He liked cheesy old Monet and Renoir. You could keep Picasso and Dali as far as he was concerned.

'Good,' Ben said diplomatically.

'You hate it.' Sally smiled. 'But that's OK – someone else will love it, and pay the asking price.'

'You're a fiscal vampire on the quiet, aren't you,' said Ben.

Sally shrugged, making her breasts bounce prettily. 'How do you think I got this house, this studio? It's all very well loving your art, but poverty is *such* an unattractive thing, don't you think?'

'I do.'

'Which is why you're angry about this woman poaching your business,' suggested Sally. She put the sketch aside and reached out to run a finger lightly down from the tip of his cock to its base. Ben shuddered pleasurably as her fingers caressed his balls and tangled into the blond hair between his legs. She took his hand and led him back to the couch.

'I think you're ready for me now,' she said judiciously, in her no-nonsense way. 'What colour's her hair? Does she look like me?'

Ben shook his head. 'She's nothing like you. In any way.'

'Ah!' Sally pushed him down on to the couch. She lifted his leg so that it went over the open back of the couch, spread-eagling him there with his penis sticking out boldly. Ben, knowing how Sally liked to direct these matters, leaned back on his elbows and watched her broodingly.

'She's a blonde, then?' asked Sally, kneeling down between Ben's wide-spread thighs.

'Redhead,' said Ben, watching appreciatively as Sally hitched her knees over and above his thighs, then leaned back on the couch. Her breasts flattened a little as she did so, her taut nipples jutting louchely. Sally's tan was all-over, not like the sexy blonde in the transit. And Sally had a very nice, long-limbed, fit body, and he enjoyed her every time he had her because she was also, thank you God, very inventive.

She was being inventive now, reaching forward with one hand to part the dark fur between her open legs so that he could see the jewel-like redness of her inner lips, then she delved deeper, spreading the lips so that he could see the wet glint beneath.

'What's her name?' she asked, panting a little now as she saw the hot flush of desire spring up on Ben's face.

'Rosie,' breathed Ben.

'Rosie the redhead,' said Sally with a laugh. Her sparkling dark eyes held Ben's assessingly. 'She's got to you, this one.'

'Not this one, not any one,' Ben refuted coolly. 'Now are you going to fuck me, or what?'

Sally took the hint. She dropped what was obviously a prickly subject, and got down to some serious pleasure.

Chapter Eight

Next morning, the van came back fully repaired from the garage, which was nice. Sadly, it came back with a zonking great bill, which was not so nice. However, Rosie paid it, thanked the mechanic because he was good and she knew he could easily have charged more. Also, he had a nice ass. She was willing to forgive a man a great deal if only he had a nice ass.

She had just bid the mechanic goodbye, when Lulu showed up and fired up the computer and sat at the desk and unloaded her chocolate supply as if this was just another ordinary day. Rosie followed her into the sitting room and stood there watching, hands on hips, while Lulu settled in.

'Um, excuse me,' said Rosie when it seemed that Lulu was not going to acknowledge her presence.

Lulu looked up with a broad smile. 'You wanted something?' she asked, unwrapping her first treat of the day.

Rosie looked at her in perplexity. 'Um, do I know

you? I mean, from the way you're behaving it seems you think you might still have a job here, and actually I don't think you do.'

'Oh come on Rosie, you're not still mad, are you?' Lulu looked as if this would be a ridiculous way to be. 'So there was a little misunderstanding, so what?'

Rosie's eyes widened. 'No, Lulu, it was a *big* misunderstanding. In which I let myself be talked into becoming a part-time whore and in which you played a mean, cheap trick on me – setting me up with Ben Hunter who you *know* is a rival and a despicable man into the bargain, and trying to film me having sex with him.'

Lulu shrugged easily as she chewed the chocolate. 'Just thought it'd break the ice,' she said casually. 'See, I realised when you came back here yesterday that I *knew* this "Countryman" you were ranting on about. And I thought you seemed pretty attracted to him. So I thought I'd just put the two of you together and watch the sparks fly.'

'Well they flew all right,' spat Rosie.

'Sure did. Whew! Talk about chemistry.'

'I hate him, Lulu, and I don't want you ever, *ever* to try a stunt like that on me again.'

'As if I would,' Lulu said, feigning hurt.

'Oh yeah. As if.'

'So I've still got a job then? And *you* still got your job in my humble little establishment, yes?'

Rosie paused. Then she said, 'I must be crazy. But OK. Yes to both. For now.'

'Oh sure. Just for now.'

'So long as we understand one another.'

'I think we do.'

Rosie looked at Lulu uncertainly. God she'd never want to play that woman at poker, that was for sure. That big cheesy grin could conceal anything, up to and including incitement to murder.

'Got the list I got from the hacker? Countryman's male client list?' Rosie held out a hand.

Lulu retrieved the list from a locked drawer and held it out to her. When Rosie tried to take it, Lulu held on.

'What?' asked Rosie.

'You sure you want to go ahead with this? Poach his male clients? Really?'

'Sure I'm sure,' said Rosie blithely.

'Only I really should tell you that underhand business isn't Ben Hunter's style.' Lulu was frowning now. 'I'm serious, Rosie. He's ruthless in business, I know that; but I've never known him do a sneaky thing, not in the four years I've known him through his connection to Joanne.'

'So what are you saying? That I *dreamed* that little scene with Mrs Squires?'

'No, what I'm saying is, maybe he didn't pursue her, maybe she pursued him. Maybe she was bored seeing your female ass around her garden, maybe he sent round some flyers in all innocence, and maybe she got a look at him when he followed up and thought, woo! I could go for that. What I'm saying is, maybe Ben didn't know Mrs Squires was already a client of yours. Maybe she didn't tell him.'

Rosie looked at Lulu. 'That's a hell of a lot of maybes, Lulu. And I have to say that I doubt every one of them.' She snatched the list. 'I'm going ahead,' she said firmly. Then she left Lulu guarding the phone, and went to rob Ben Hunter – just like he'd robbed her.

She took the van this time, relieved not to have to risk besmirching her peachy little Beetle with chicken manure pellets and dirty grass-boxes. She checked the first client on the list and let out a snort. Mayfair! Wouldn't you just know that he'd get all the moneyed sorts, and she'd get people who haggled over the bill. Well, Rosie thought grimly, all that was going to change.

The house in Mayfair, just a stone's throw from the chic emporiums of Bond Street, was a delightful classical building on four floors, and there was a very well-tended huge wisteria draping itself over the facade. Grudgingly Rosie admired the way the plant had been looked after – pruning was always a wee bit tricky with wisterias unless you had the knack. And it appeared that Ben did have the knack, in spades. It was going to be beautiful when it flowered in a couple of months, dripping with lilac flowers – an absolute picture.

Heart sinking, Rosie steeled herself to ring the bell. She already felt upstaged and outclassed. He had that effect on her, damn him. No one seemed to be answering. Feeling rather more relieved than she would have admitted out loud, Rosie turned way. The door, with its lovely Regency fanlight, suddenly opened.

'Can I help you?' asked a brisk male voice.

Rosie turned back. 'Um – well – Mr Willard?' She looked at him awkwardly, feeling herself blush beet-red. He was fiftyish, with a head of steel-grey straight hair and a face that had once been handsome. Now it was arresting, patrician almost, and tanned from a recent holiday. He looked at her over half-glasses. Bright blue eyes, very piercing. This chap wasn't about to take any nonsense from anybody. He oozed authority.

It came home to Rosie, forcibly, just what she was doing here. Pinching Ben Hunter's customer. Fine, she could just about handle that because he had started it. But to offer the carrot, the clincher for the deal – her own quaking body – now that was something else. She doubted, all at once, that she could go through with this at all.

'Yes. Who wants him?' He didn't smile. He looked impatient, as if he was busy and she was interrupting his work.

She either had to bolt or go ahead with it. Rosie gulped a deep breath and stuck out a hand.

'Hello, Mr Willard. I'm Rosie from Coming Up Roses. We offer a comprehensive gardening service and as I happened to be in your area I wondered –'

'I've got a gardener,' he interrupted brusquely. He was already shutting the door. 'He meets all my needs.'

Rosie panicked and stuck her foot in the door. Mr

Willard looked down at it in disbelief, then back up at her flushed, desperate face.

'Young lady, either you take your foot out of my doorway this instant or I shall call the police,' he warned.

'I'm sure your gardener doesn't meet all your needs,' Rosie gushed quickly. 'I could. Mr Willard, please listen. I can match his price.'

'There's no advantage in that for me,' he argued logically. 'I'm happy with Countryman Gardens. Why should I switch to your firm for the same charge and risk disappointment?'

'You won't be disappointed,' she gabbled. 'Because I offer an excellent service. I'm fully qualified in all aspects of horticulture and, besides –' Rosie gulped again and spat it out '– I'll let you have me free the first time. Call it an introductory offer.'

That stopped him dead in his tracks. 'You'll do the garden for free?' he asked, wishing to clarify matters.

'Yes,' panted Rosie. 'And I can supply other services, too,' she continued, with a heavy accent on the word 'other' as she thrust her breasts at him, leaving no room for ambiguity. 'All for free, the first time. And very discreet. How's that?'

Mr Willard observed her closely. He obviously couldn't believe his ears.

'Let me get this straight,' he said after a moment's thought. 'You'll do the garden free, and allow me the use of your body too, free, the first time. And after that?'

'After that my rates are the same as Countryman

Gardens,' said Rosie, feeling as if she were about to spontaneously combust with embarrassment. 'Only the intimate liaisons are free. Every time I call, you can have me. If you want to.'

Mr Willard was still observing her with that piercingly birdlike gaze.

I am going to die, thought Rosie miserably. I am just going to curl up and *die* with humiliation.

'If I *want* to?' Mr Willard's face somehow rearranged itself into a smile and he opened the door. 'Young lady – Rosie – you had better come in so that we can discuss this further.'

They discussed it in bed. Mr Willard's first name was Sam, and he was a thriller writer, and he was a very leisurely and inventive lover, and he was simply thrilled to have this sudden bounty bestowed upon him.

'So it's a deal then?' Rosie asked as she lay gasping from the aftermath of an explosive orgasm. Sam Willard was kneeling between her wide-spread legs, still stroking her there, still making her shiver with sensation. It was becoming clear to Rosie that there was an advantage to taking an older lover; he had patience, and stamina. Even now, Sam's cock was hardening again.

'It's a deal,' agreed Sam, kissing the inside of her knee. His hands were resting on each of her knees, and he pushed them gently even further apart, staring intently into the moist recesses of her exposed sex. 'When can you start?' he asked, his lips moving up along the inner stretch of her thigh.

'Next Wednesday?' suggested Rosie, arching her

back a little as those inquisitive lips moved closer to where she wanted them.

'Perfect,' said Sam, and Rosie clutched his silver-grey hair with her fingers as he slipped his tongue into her.

Janina had rarely seen Ben angry. But he was angry now, pacing the flat and cursing this Rosie woman, accusing her of all sorts of heinous crimes.

'Calm down,' she suggested in a gap in the tirade.

'That *cow*. I've lost three more clients this week. She has got to go.'

'Ben, she's not going anywhere.' Janina tried and failed to suppress her amusement at her friend's wrath. She could just picture Ben squaring up to some plain spinstery sort of woman with dirty hands, each of them brandishing a trowel and flicking decorative pebbles at each other in a to-the-death contest.

'Oh, isn't she?' Ben stopped pacing and came and stood before the couch where Janina lounged, watching his fury with interest. She was a lawyer, but she would be the first to admit that the law was awfully dull and dusty most of the time, and any diversion from all that stuffy textbook reading was welcome. So Ben's anger was making quite a change.

For one thing, Ben – despite being what Janina called her 'bit of rough' – never normally got angry. He was so laid back he was virtually horizontal.

For another, he was angry with a woman. She had never seen him even faintly annoyed with a woman before. Ben was a walking magnet to females; women adored him and were very quick to jump into bed with him. But involvement had never been his scene. If a woman objected when he dumped her – and he always dumped them in the end, although never unkindly – he met the inevitable tears and recriminations with unfailingly equable good will. He simply was not temperamental.

But he didn't look placid now. What he looked like, Janina thought, was a bull that had been suddenly surprised by an intruder in his field. And it was *his* field. Ben had told Janina he had always been territorial. He was being territorial now, but he was also being angry, Janina pondered. Angry with a woman.

Hmm.

'She's an ugly old bat, I take it, this competitor of yours?' Janina prodded.

'She's not ugly and she's not old,' snapped Ben.

Well, well.

'You fancy her?'

Ben looked down at her. *'What?'*

Janina flicked back her blonde mane of hair and smiled sweetly. But despite the smile she was not placid and she was always inclined to goad, to dig, to provide the itch under the skin, the irritant. She was, after all, a prosecution lawyer. Provoking a reaction was what she did best.

'It's been a long hot day,' said Janina, leaning back upon the couch. She was wearing a short ice-white satin robe and nothing else. Ready to shower after a hard day's work, she had been downing her first gin and tonic of the evening and wondering what to watch on the telly. Then Ben had arrived, and piqued her interest.

'So what?' snapped Ben.

'So I'm getting a kink in my already stiff neck looking up at you.' Janina sat up, putting her glass onto the occasional table. She shrugged her robe down so that it was held by the waist tie, slipping her arms out of the flimsy thing. Her nude breasts spilled out heavily. Her pale pink nipples were very large. Ben watched them sway as she first knelt up on the couch and then lay face-down upon it.

'Do my shoulders, there's a love,' she sighed.

Ben sat down on the edge of the couch and applied gentle pressure to the knots in Janina's shoulders.

'Bliss,' she moaned. 'Does she have nice tits, this woman?'

'What?' Ben asked, wrong-footed.

'Keep doing that. And stop saying "what". You heard. Are her tits nice? I happen to know, Benjamin dear, that you are a tit man. You can't even keep your eyes off mine.'

'If you didn't always have them hanging out, perhaps I wouldn't look,' said Ben, massaging Janina's silky skin rather harder than was called for.

'But they're such good tits, aren't they?' she teased, grinning sideways at him.

'Yeah, they're good tits,' Ben allowed.

'And hers?'

'They're good tits too.'

'You've seen them? Naked, I mean.'

'Yeah.'

'So things are progressing along those lines, are they?'

'I'm sure I don't know what you mean.'

'You want her in bed.'

'She's a pest.'

'But you want her in bed. Ow!' Janina sprang up, her breasts swinging as she glared at him. 'Not so rough.'

'Ha! I thought you liked it rough,' Ben said mockingly, standing up. 'That's what you used to tell me, anyway.'

Janina rose gracefully from the couch and unbelted the little robe. It slithered to the ground. She stood there naked and stared at Ben defiantly. 'Do you know, it's so hot, I think I'll have another cool shower before Peter gets here.'

'Looks like you need it,' Ben said acidly, eyeing her puckered nipples, aware that the centres were erect now. Yes, Janina did like it rough. She liked to be whipped, and tied up. Handle her roughly and her arousal was immediately apparent, despite the fact she was being all haughty right now. He could see a tiny snail-trail of moisture just beneath her neat little triangle of blonde pubic hair. He wondered if rough handling would get Rosie in that state, and the thought made his cock twitch and grow.

'You know, you are in a very, *very* odd mood,' scolded Janina, sashaying off to take her shower. 'I'd like to meet this Rosie person. She sounds fascinating.'

And she was right. He was. He felt like ripping someone's head off and spitting down the neck. He felt *infuriated*. And frustrated. Despite Sally, and the blonde in the transit, he still felt as if he wanted to go out on the prowl. He wanted another woman. No. To be specific, he wanted Rosie: He wanted the very woman who was causing him such a lot of grief, who was standing in the way of all his plans. And why not? That was probably the best thing. Have the bitch and get it out of his system once and for all, then sort out the business side of things afterwards.

Why the hell not?

He went over to the bathroom door. The shower was hissing away, and Janina was singing tunelessly. He tapped on the door.

'Janina?'

'Yes, what?' she called.

'You really want to meet Rosie?'

'I said so, didn't I?'

'OK.' He went and picked up the phone, and dialled Lulu's number.

Chapter Nine

Janina had to reschedule a couple of appointments for the following afternoon, but she did it with surprisingly good grace because she really did want to get a look at Rosie. Ben and Janina's relationship was 'different', as she'd told him right from the off when she'd picked him up in a Sussex pub. She'd been down for the weekend after celebrating a success in court and he'd been the uncomplicated fuck that she'd needed. When he'd moved up to London she'd taken him on as a handyman in more than one sense – he provided muscle, practicality and sexual amusement for her. She was a polysexual being with a huge appetite for the more unusual practices and he was content with their arrangement, even if it did mean feeling like her pet doggie now and then. She was a regular source of sex during fallow times, and having almost free run of her apartment was a boon. Ben had explained to her that Rosie ran a gardening business like he did, but that she also worked for Lulu sometimes, mostly in the afternoons.

'You mean as a whore?' asked Janina in fascination as they drove over to Lulu's after lunch the next day in Janina's large Mercedes.

'You'll see,' said Ben, and Janina found that she could hardly wait.

Lulu met them at the front door, all smiles and welcome.

'Have you told her it's me?' asked Ben as they went inside.

'I told her it was a couple,' returned Lulu.

'And she still believes a word you say, after last time?' he grinned.

'Sure she does. We've mended our fences.'

'Lulu, this will bust them wide open again.'

Lulu's laughing dark eyes roamed over Ben and Janina. 'Baby, the only thing'll be wide open when she gets in the sack with you two is her legs.'

'So she'll forgive you?' asked Janina curiously.

'I think she will,' Lulu said more calculatingly. 'She wants Ben, even if she denies it. And she'll sure like the look of you, sweetheart.'

'Is she experienced with women?' asked Janina delicately, getting quite excited now at the thought of this 'Rosie'.

'I wouldn't expect so,' admitted Lulu.

'Even better.' Janina smiled, almost purring with anticipated pleasure. 'I take it you have some props to hand? For role playing?'

'No rough stuff,' said Ben, surprising himself. Last night he would have sworn that he would cheer if Janina tied Rosie to the bed and beat her with chains. Now, he was suddenly concerned about Janina's appetites and how Rosie might interpret them.

'Of course not,' Janina said, eyeing him with supreme innocence.

'We've got all sorts of dress-up stuff, I'll show you,' Lulu said obligingly, leading Janina off along the hall. She threw a smile at Ben. 'You go right on in, baby. Get started.'

'I'll join you later,' promised Janina with a wink.

Ben went into the room he had visited yesterday. Rosie was already there, dressed in white basque, white stockings, white thong and several huge ropes of pearls. She had fluffed up her ebullient red curls and had propped herself enticingly upon the bed, waiting for the door to open. When she saw who had opened it, the seductive smile dropped from her face like a discarded mask.

'What the hell are you doing here?' she demanded.

'I've booked a virginal redhead for two o'clock,' said Ben mildly, approaching the bed and running his eyes admiringly over her ensemble.

'Lulu said a couple!'

'That's right. My friend's with me. She'll be joining us soon. Lulu thought we might like a little time alone first. Enjoying being on the game, are we?'

'Don't take that tone with me,' Rosie warned. 'Anyway, I've hardly started.'

'No time like the present,' said Ben, sitting down on the bed. Rosie went to get off the other side, but Ben knew how fast she could move now, and was ahead of her, grabbing her wrists and pinning her down.

'Is she as obnoxious as you?' Rosie grimaced, trying to break free.

'Obnoxious?' Ben seemed to give this due consideration. 'You think *I'm* obnoxious? You pinch my clients and you call *me* obnoxious? You steal my livelihood and you call *me* obnoxious?'

'I'm just a better gardener than you, that's all,' said Rosie with a shrug.

'Oh really? What do you offer, cheap rates? Free plants?'

'None of the above,' Rosie said airily. 'I told you, I'm just a better gardener, and people recognise that. Ouch! You squeezed my wrist.'

'I ought to squeeze your throat, you cheeky little mare,' growled Ben, glaring down at her. 'I don't buy that. Better gardener, my ass. Gardens take time to mature, a gardener's work isn't a thing that's instantly apparent. So I don't buy it. No, you've got to be undercutting my prices or giving out freebies, so which is it?'

Rosie shook her head and grinned an infuriating grin. 'Trade secret, I'm afraid,' she sighed.

'I'm in the same trade,' pointed out Ben.

'You're a competitor, that's different.'

Ben stared down at her. 'One way or another, I'll find out,' he warned.

'Ha, I'm really shaking in my boots,' scoffed Rosie, rather enjoying herself.

'Bitch,' said Ben, and lowered his head and kissed her mouth.

'Are you talking dirty to me?' asked Rosie when she was able to come up for air.

'You'd only enjoy it,' Ben said accusingly.

'True.'

'Then I won't,' said Ben, and kissed her again, deeper this time. Rosie felt his erection stirring beneath his jeans and snuggled closer. Ben's eyes opened and stared into hers. Goodness, they were blue. Blue and clear as an ocean, and plenty deep enough to drown in. She returned his stare.

'I think you're going to do very well at this whoring game,' he said huskily.

'Well, I'm supposed to be a *virginal* whore, you know,' Rosie pointed out.

'Yes, what does that mean exactly?' asked Ben, kissing her soft white throat because he felt so drawn to it. It was irresistible. 'The two don't exactly go hand in hand, do they? How can a woman be a whore and a virgin at the same time?'

'With difficulty,' admitted Rosie. 'Also with fake blood and very tight inner muscles, and a convincing line in virginal screams.'

'You're joking.' Ben's lips were slamming over her collarbone. It was very nice, actually. It was a shame he was a competitor and such a rat in business as to start a fight with her, because really she suspected that he was very good in bed.

'No, it's serious,' said Rosie. 'Lulu gets lots of

requests from men wanting virgins. And redheads too. Apparently some men go completely ape for redheads.'

'So she's cornered the market. A virginal redhead. These men must be idiots.'

'Probably.'

'But a stiff dick overrules the brain.'

'And it has no conscience.'

'Yeah. Who said that?'

'Someone famous, and probably with a stiff dick.'

Rosie grinned. Ben grinned too. His own stiff dick was pressing very hard against Rosie's thigh. To his surprise, Rosie's hands went to his belt and unbuckled it. Then she freed the metal button.

'You're very forward, for a virgin,' observed Ben, leaning back a little so that she could work the zip free.

But Rosie was intent on unzipping him. She thought of him with Mrs Squires again, and how hard she had tried to get a glimpse of his cock, falling off the wall in the process. She pushed the zipper right down, and Ben's naked and aroused penis all but sprang out of the opening.

'I might have known you'd be the type to go commando,' breathed Rosie, admiring his cock with a rapt stare. It was very big, but in perfect proportion to the rest of him. It was lightly tanned, just like the rest of him too, but the glans glowed warm pink. She slid a hand inside the open front of his jeans and touched the sensitive skin of his belly, grazing her nails over it, making Ben shudder involuntarily.

'I might have known you'd be trouble,' returned Ben.

'Me?' Rosie gave him a wide-eyed stare. 'You steal my business, and you call me trouble?'

'I didn't steal anyone's business,' said Ben.

'Ha! And you're a liar too.'

'I'm not a liar.'

'I'm afraid you are.'

Ben gave her a glare and shrugged his light Chambray shirt off over his head. Goodness, but he was good to look at, thought Rosie. His chest was broad, his pecs clearly defined but not exaggeratedly so. He had a modest six-pack, a hard and flat stomach and a gigantic cock. Blond hair furred his chest, and feathered down like an arrow until it reached his balls, where it became thicker and slightly darker.

'You're not arguing,' Rosie pointed out, feeling breathless.

'There are better ways of passing the time,' Ben said maddeningly, leaning back on his elbows and casually lifting one knee, making himself thoroughly comfortable. 'Your turn now.'

Rosie sat back on her heels, looking mulish.

'Hey, I'm a virgin, remember? I'm far too shy to strip.'

'Then I'll help,' said Ben, straightening easily and kneeling up in front of her.

Rosie looked at him uncertainly for a moment. She suddenly remembered the threats and the brooding physical force he had displayed outside Simon's house. And she was in a much more vulnerable position now. Almost naked. Alone in a bedroom with him. Alone and *unobserved*, she remembered, because she had insisted to Lulu that the camera and mike be removed, and Lulu had agreed those terms. Furthermore, she had stood over Lulu as she removed the camera and the mike, just to be sure. Now, as he loomed over her, she was momentarily sorry that she had been so strident in her demands. After all, a watcher was a safety net of sorts. Instead of which, she was here alone with a man who was quite clearly angry with her, and who could very easily turn nasty.

Ben was examining the front of the basque. 'I think this thing hooks up, doesn't it?' His large hands were moving between her breasts, unfastening the long row of hooks and eyes that ran down the basque's front. She was amazed at how deftly hands that size could work. She was even more amazed that she was here like this, with this particular man, letting him strip her.

I must be mad, she thought with a sudden stab of real anxiety. I'm getting in too deep here!

'Stop,' said Rosie, putting a hand to her breasts to stop them spilling right out of the rapidly opening front of the basque.

Ben paused, looking up at her face with disbelief. '*Stop?*' he repeated.

Rosie nodded vigorously. 'That's right, I said stop.'

'No,' said Ben, and carried on unhooking.

'What do you mean, no?' demanded Rosie in outrage. He had reached her navel and was keeping right on going. The bastard! 'I'm not sure I want to go through with this.'

'Why? What's the matter? Got a guilty conscience?' asked Ben, still applying himself to the task in hand.

'No way!' Rosie shot back.

'I'll stop if you tell me what the deal is you're doing with my clients,' said Ben.

'No!' Rosie was trying to squirm away. Ben was keeping a firm hold on the basque, and the front was almost completely open now.

'Well, prepare to repel boarders, as they say in the navy,' he quipped, and got back to the hooks.

'All right, all right! I'll tell you, OK?'

Ben's hands paused. 'Make it snappy,' he said.

Rosie squirmed. 'Sexual favours,' she muttered. She could feel herself going bright pink.

'Sorry, I didn't hear that. Will you speak up?' Ben requested sweetly.

'*Sexual favours!*' howled Rosie at full volume. 'I charge the same rates as you but I sleep with them for free.'

'You do *what*?' said Ben.

'You heard! And why shouldn't I? After all, isn't that the deal you struck with my female clients?'

Ben stared at her. 'That's why only the male clients have been cancelling,' he said in wonder. 'What's up, Rosie, didn't you fancy any of the women?'

He hadn't denied it! So what was it with this angry outrage act of his? He'd done the same – worse, he'd started it. He could dish it out, but he sure as hell couldn't take it when it was lobbed back at him.

'How'd you know who they were?' asked Ben, his

face suffused with anger. 'How'd you get my client list?'

'I know a hacker,' threw Rosie in a temper. 'I got him to hack into your database.'

'That's industrial espionage or something. It's certainly illegal. You little cow.'

'So sue me,' shouted Rosie, trying to move away. But Ben held on. She squirmed harder, but Ben just tumbled her back on to the bed and held her there. 'You bastard!' she panted through clenched teeth. 'And let go of me, you sodding ape, you said you'd stop if I told you the deal, and I *have*, so just cut it out.'

'I lied,' said Ben flatly, and freed the last of the hooks.

'Ha! Why doesn't that surprise me?' shot back Rosie. She rolled sideways, away from him, but this only succeeded in parting her from one half of the basque. To get away, she had to whip her arm out fast, then roll, then the other arm. Success! But now Ben was holding the basque, and she was topless.

Never mind. She had effected her escape, that was the main thing, and while he was thinking about the view, she lunged across the bed and was halfway to the bathroom – which had a lock on the inside of the door – and was pretty pleased with herself when what felt like a ton weight hit her in the back and bore her to the Flokati rug.

All the breath left Rosie's body in a whoosh. She'd seen horses winded after a racing fall, and realised suddenly what it must feel like. She was flipped over so that she lay on her back gasping for air while Ben held each of her arms out crucifix-style. She couldn't even muster enough breath to swear at him. The turquoise eyes were now as cold as chips of glass as they stared down at her.

'You really are the most irritating little bitch I've ever come across,' he said succinctly, and lowered his mouth to hers even as her own opened to offer up a gasp of protest.

If only he wasn't such a good kisser, thought Rosie. If only he didn't look so good. If only he wasn't turning her on so much. The hair on his chest was brushing against her nipples, driving her crazy with lust. Ben let go of her hands and she automatically twined them about his neck, snagged them into his thick, gorgeous hair. His own hands snaked between their bodies and settled over her tits, teasing a moan of desire from Rosie. Her nipples felt as if they were on fire as he rubbed them, and then one of his hands was gone and she moaned again in protest.

A moment later, she felt him tugging down the G-string, pulling it over her thighs, over her calves, over her feet and off. She was naked now apart from the hold-up stockings and her string of fake pearls. Ben's mouth left hers and he looked down at her body, his hand trailing over her thigh and settling over her bright red bush. He smoothed his palm over it as if stroking an animal, then turned his body and, to her surprise, pushed her legs apart.

Rosie stiffened, wondering what he intended, and an instant later she found out. His head dipped between her thighs, and first his lips and then his tongue caressed her hard little clitoris.

'Oh!' Rosie gasped, as he delved deeper. She opened her legs wider, rolling her head from side to side on the furry rug, enjoying his touch rather more than she ought to. And right beside her head were his thighs and his rigid and reddening cock. She watched it with admiration for several seconds as Ben worked on her. Oh, it was big. And his balls. She adored his balls, and look, they were so high now, so prominent, he was ready to fuck her and yes, she was more than ready for that too.

Ben's tongue pushed inside her now, stabbing at her with deeply arousing movements. She reached out and fondled his straining cock. Ben paused for an instant as she touched him, then continued to lap at her cunt. Rosie applied both hands to the task, and she was so close that she could smell his musky, clean scent. Tempted beyond resistance, she shimmied her hips over a little and was then close enough to reciprocate.

Her lips closed over the tip of his cock, and she felt him start a little in surprise. Maybe he thought she intended to bite him? But she didn't. In a daze of lust, aware with every nerve-ending of his mouth and what it was doing to her, Rosie languorously pushed her lips down on to his penis, as far down as she could go without gagging, and gently sucked at him. His body stiffened again against hers, and she heard him groan.

Relishing the sound, Rosie grew bolder. She slid her lips back up to the tip, grazing the silky skin of his cock softly with her teeth as she did so. Ben hissed in a breath.

'That doesn't feel like anything a virgin would do,' he said huskily, coming up for air and sprawling back upon the rug. Rosie knelt up and carried on working at his cock as he lay there in a state of utter bliss.

Dropping a lingering kiss on to his glans, kneading his balls with her fingers, Rosie gave him a cheeky grin. 'I learn fast,' she panted and, still looking into his eyes, she pulled the skin of his shaft right back, exposing the ultra-sensitive head of his cock. She ran her tongue around it, then lapped the dewdrop of pre-come from the tip.

'Enough,' Ben said roughly.

'Why, are you going to come?' Rosie asked between bestowing tiny kisses right down the length of his penis.

'And that's not a very virginal question,' Ben pointed out. 'Come on, Rosie, mount me.'

Rosie let out a sigh. 'Men are always so penetration-focused,' she complained, but she was shivering with need now, greedy for him, her nipples rock-hard, her pussy dripping wet. She caressed his outrageously hard cock with her fingers, imagining it inside her, how it would feel, filling her and stimulating her. Oh yes, she wanted that. She wanted it right now.

'Just sampling the goods,' Ben said lazily. 'I'm paying good money for this, don't forget.'

'As if you'd let me,' said Rosie, moving her position so that she could straddle his thighs. Ben's eyes on her as she did this were quite enough to make her feel almost light-headed with arousal. Her pulse was rioting throughout her body; hottest and fastest of all was the beating between her legs as she stretched herself wide apart to take him in.

She clasped his cock delicately with her hands, and manoeuvred herself so that her slit was directly above the little open eye at the tip of his cock. She lowered herself, closing her eyes in ecstasy as he connected with her entrance and stretched it wider. Then she placed her hands on his shoulders and pushed voluptuously down, gasping out loud when he pushed up his hips and slid in, right up to the very base of his cock.

'Lulu was right,' murmured Ben. 'You do feel tight. Lean down here, I want to kiss your tits.'

Rosie obligingly leaned forward, dropping one engorged nipple into Ben's mouth. He took hold of her breast in his hand and sucked hard, and stroked her nub with his tongue. Rosie nearly went into orbit. Hopelessly aroused, she felt her hips move of their own accord, lifting and falling, exciting them both beyond the point of no return; and then someone grabbed a handful of her hair and jerked her head painfully back.

Rosie fell back with a shout of protest and found herself sitting on the carpet and looking up at a blonde Valkyrie clad in a white coat, a stethoscope slung around her neck. The coat was unbuttoned, revealing that blonde's nakedness underneath – and that she was a natural blonde.

'What the hell d'you think you're doing?' demanded Rosie, rubbing her abused scalp gingerly.

'Just checking on the patient,' said Janina, giving Ben a cursory look. 'And what do I find? That you are making him over-excited when he is in this delicate condition.'

Rosie watched Janina with something approaching awe. Wow, she was beautiful, with her luxurious mane of blonde hair and shockingly vivid blue eyes. Janina reached out a stiletto-clad toe and nudged Ben's turgid cock assessingly.

'Oh dear,' she sighed. 'You student nurses have no idea how to attend to male patients. Now, you see what you've done? You've got him into this state, and what are you going to do about it now?'

Rosie decided to join in the game. It was rather fun. And rather stimulating too. She liked the way the blonde's eyes dwelt on her breasts as she knelt there. She'd never had a woman before, and was wondering what it would be like. With any luck, she would soon find out.

'I was going to fuck him,' she said with a shrug. Her breasts bounced as she did so, and both Ben and Janina watched with keen interest.

'Show me,' said Janina.

Hesitatingly, feeling more than a bit foolish, Rosie once more took up her position across Ben's lap.

'Like that?' Janina inspected Rosie's position with a critical air. 'Go on, show me properly.'

Obviously the blonde wanted to see Rosie impale herself on Ben's still fully erect cock. She wanted the whole floorshow, and Rosie felt aroused enough to indulge her. She clasped the straining penis in her hands, and wiggled her hips down until its roseate tip touched her wet opening.

'Ah, I see,' said Janina, kneeling down beside the almost-joined couple so that she could more easily see what was going on. While Rosie crouched there, wanting desperately to push down and feel again the intense pleasure of having Ben inside her, Janina flourished her stethoscope and placed it against Ben's chest. She listened carefully. Rosie was prepared to bet that his heart was beating like crazy.

Then Janina straightened a little and peered between Rosie's widespread legs. With clinical coolness, she reached out a hand and, turning her wrist deftly, parted Rosie's furry red bush so that she could more fully appreciate the nature of the treatment Rosie was administering.

'We'll try it, shall we?' she murmured, as Rosie nearly expired with excitement when Janina's hand pressed firmly against her clit. 'Push down now.'

Needing no second urging, Rosie pushed. Ben's cock slid effortlessly inside her well-oiled portal. Oh, he was huge! She pushed harder, relishing the sensation of fullness. Janina's hand moved silkily against her stiff little clit, adding further sensations.

'Now lift up,' instructed Janina, 'and contract your inner muscles as you do so, to stimulate the patient more fully.'

Rosie pulled up, holding herself very tight. She paused, awaiting the next instruction, her breathing ragged.

Janina bent forward and peered again between Rosie's legs; Ben's cock was a slick column of reddened flesh, the tip of which was still imbedded in Rosie.

'Come off the cock now,' Janina said coolly. 'Before we continue, what the patient needs is nourishment.'

Reluctantly Rosie lifted her hips, and Ben's imprisoned cock sprang free.

'Straddle the patient's head now,' said Janina. Rosie gave her a look and Janina said, 'You have some objection to giving the patient nourishment?'

'I think he'd prefer just to fuck me,' ventured Rosie.

Janina swung the straps of the stethoscope and they connected, stingingly, with Rosie's buttocks.

'Ouch!' yelled Rosie in surprise. She rubbed the reddened flesh of her bottom and eyed Janina with hostility.

'I am the doctor, you are the student nurse,' Janina pointed out. 'So you do as I say, with no arguments. Now, straddle the patient's head, as I instructed.'

Rosie complied until her wide-open cunt was just over Ben's head.

'Now lower yourself just a little,' said Janina.

Rosie did so.

'Now the patient must drink your juices,' said Janina, and Rosie gave a gasp of pleasure as Ben's tongue started lapping at her. 'That's good,' Janina approved as Ben clasped Rosie's buttock in one hand and tongued her harder.

'Oh God,' moaned Rosie hopelessly. His tongue slithered over her clit, back and forth, back and forth, until it felt so hot, so swollen, so completely the centre of her being, that she felt it might well explode.

'Ah, you like the patient drinking from you?' Janina queried.

Rosie couldn't answer. Ben's tongue was driving her to a frenzy of lust, and his fingers had crept up between the crack in her buttocks so that now one of them was pushing easily inside her, and then two, and then, because she was so wet and so completely open, three. And all the time his tongue tickled and taunted at her clit, and suddenly it was too much and she was coming frantically, her hips pumping down on to Ben's fingers, her head thrown back in ecstasy, her back arching.

Janina watched all this with a critical eye, and when Rosie subsided, panting, she said, 'Good, now the patient has taken nourishment, we will return to the problem of *this*.' She tapped Ben's rigid cock lightly with her toe. 'Since you have been so careless as to get the patient into this disgraceful condition, it is up to you to resolve the situation. Stand up.'

Rosie knelt there a moment, trying to get her breath, feeling boneless and overwhelmed with the spent force of her desire. God, was she really doing this? Playing doctors and nurses with Ben Hunter and his scary lover?

A second stinging blow across her buttocks reassured her that she was. Wincing, she did as Janina said. Janina looked at Rosie's heaving breasts and sex-flushed face with interest.

'Now, before we relieve the patient of his unfortunate condition, I must examine you and reassure myself that you are suitable for the task. Kneel on the bed, please.'

Rosie knelt on the bed hastily, before Janina decided to lay into her with the stethoscope again. As she knelt there awaiting whatever Janina decided to do to her, she saw Ben get up from the rug with one strong graceful movement and come round to the other side of the bed. He sat down on it and turned sideways, leaning back on an elbow, watching the two women.

Rosie was momentarily transfixed by how beautiful his body was. His stomach muscles tautened as he lay back, and the long, strong muscles of his thigh were clearly visible. And his penis was still fully erect. Seeing her eyes on it, Ben looked down at it too. Carefully, he clasped it in one hand and pressed the tips of his fingers in beneath the base of his glans. He gave a little groan as he did this.

'Now you see, the patient is very experienced. He is slowing down his shameful arousal so that he does not spill over before he receives your treatment,' Janina told Rosie sternly. She pushed Rosie forward so that Rosie was now crouched on all fours.

Rosie felt Janina's hand slip under her arm. She squeezed Rosie's left breast, and her fingers briefly flicked at the erect nipple. Then Janina's hand cupped the breast fully, as if weighing it.

'Yes, I think these are very good for the purpose,' said Janina.

Rosie flinched as the stone-cold stethoscope was without warning attached to her nipple. Janina appeared to listen for a few moments, then the stethoscope was withdrawn and instead Rosie felt Janina's white coat brush against her side. Janina ducked her head and suddenly it was Janina's mouth that covered Rosie's nipple instead.

'Oh!' said Rosie in surprise, and the pleasure of that sucking mouth was very good indeed – until sharp teeth suddenly grazed her teat, and she stiffened and moaned – and then there was the sucking again, gentle and strong, so stimulating, and then the teeth again, pulling and tormenting at her most sensitive flesh.

'Oh, you bitch,' she groaned, wondering if she was going to expire from pleasure or pain, or both.

'Oh, you think so?' said Janina, pulling away from Rosie's left breast to give her full attention to the right one. Again, she sucked, and again she bit. But this time, an added refinement to this exquisite torture, she also slid the icy stethoscope down over Rosie's flinching stomach to her bush and then shoved the diabolical thing through the wet slit beneath, so that it covered her overheated clit.

The contrast was so stark, so unbearably stirring, that Rosie cried out. Janina pressed the stethoscope hard against Rosie's burning secret flesh, and then all at once the blonde's fingers were there in place of the cold metal, kneading and stroking, flicking and pinching.

Rosie came again, more slowly than the first time, but it was doubly intense.

'Good, good,' Janina praised her, drawing back a little. 'You are learning fast, and now I feel confident that you can administer treatment properly to the patient.'

She gestured to Ben. Rosie crouched there, panting, on all fours, her ginger curls falling in her eyes, her whole body aglow with sweat and sex. She saw Ben stand up and move around the end of the bed, saw Janina step back so that she was standing level with Rosie's hips.

Oh God, she thought, not more. If she came again she was just going to die. She felt light-headed with satiation, incapable of thought, certainly incapable of any more sex.

The bottom of the bed dipped. She half-straightened, about to protest, but Janina swiped her bottom again with the stethoscope.

'It's necessary for you to keep still now while the patient gets into the correct position,' said Janina sharply.

Rosie felt Ben's hands between her thighs, nudging them further apart. For an instant she had a vivid picture of what he must be seeing back there – her pinkened buttocks, her wide-open crack, her anus, her pearly-wet cunt, the sticky feathering of red hair all around it. And she found she didn't care. She was beyond caring. She was finished, exhausted. But as soon as his hands touched her inner thighs, she was shocked to find that she was ready again, ready and waiting – more passive now, certainly, but still eager to go on.

Not that she seemed to have any choice in the matter. Not with Janina standing guard over the proceedings. Ben's fingers were stretching her wider. His knees nudged between hers, pushing her legs further apart. She felt horribly exposed and at the same time totally turned on by this. She was beyond shame, beyond embarrassment, beyond any feeling at all other than the urge to fuck.

And now Ben's cock was hard and hot against her buttock. She felt the furry hair at his groin brush tantalisingly against her crack, felt the heated nudge of his balls as he positioned himself to mount her. She was panting again, mindless and powerless, and loving it. She felt him push his cock down between her legs, felt the slick, silky hardness of it pushing forward along her wide-spread crack. For an alarming moment, as his cock-head slipped over her anus, then paused and moved caressingly, she thought that he was going to enter there; but he moved on, and on – past the opening that was crying out for his entry, and on, so that he pressed hard against her clit. Rosie almost cried with need as Ben pushed lazily back and forth over it, massaging it, showing no sign of haste to penetrate her.

She opened her eyes and tears spilled down on to the purple bedcover. Her face was burning, her nipples so hard they ached, and she wanted only one thing now, and that was for him to be inside her. But still he caressed her. She looked down, past her dangling breasts and her heaving belly to her bush, and she could see the red and open-eyed head of Ben's dick surging in and out of the tangle of red curls at regular intervals.

Incredibly, she came again, screaming this time, unable to stop herself. And as she screamed and pushed madly back against him, Ben adjusted his position again and slipped inside her. Boneless with pleasure, it was all

Rosie could do not to collapse to the bed. And now he was pushing hard into her, concentrating on his own pleasure, his balls hitting her buttocks solidly every time he thrust in with quick, needy movements of his hips.

Oh God – was she going to come again? Ben's fingers were on her clit now, and she thought, oh no, I can't, don't, please don't, and then she came, weakly, almost drained, and when she was almost finished, almost done for, Janina peeled off her white coat and knelt up on the bed in front of Rosie's drooping head.

Janina grabbed her hair and pushed her head back. Being rocked by the violent motion of Ben's fucking, Rosie was suddenly treated to an unsteady view of a delectable blonde female body with cherry-red-tipped breasts that were gorgeously full, a slender waist and sweetly curving hips.

'Goodness, are you getting tired?' purred Janina sympathetically. 'Then you had better take some nourishment too.'

Janina pushed Rosie's head down between her open thighs, and obediently Rosie found herself lapping at the blonde with her tongue while Ben pushed at her with increasing desperation.

Had she ever had a man so big, so skilled as a lover, so absolutely to die for?

She knew she hadn't.

And he had to be her business rival. He hated her, and was, she was sure, only doing this to her as a form of punishment for her 'transgressions'. But oh, this was so good. When Janina's orgasm shook her, she clutched harder at Rosie's hair, almost to the point of pain. And as if Janina's satisfaction was the trigger he was waiting for, Ben came too, thrusting furiously and then pumping out his seed into her with a hoarse cry of pleasure. Up to this point Rosie had been sure she could not come again, but Ben's rougher movements against her G-spot and the hard pressure of his hand over her clit caused her to climax all over again.

'We'll rest now,' said Janina, sinking voluptuously back on to the bed with a happy sigh. Rosie flopped forward on to the bed, face down, and lay there panting. Ben lay down too, his cock subsiding now. Thank God, thought Rosie. They've done for me, but at least now they've finished.

'And in a little while we will start again,' said Janina, with a catlike smile.

Chapter Ten

Next day, as she drove out to Epping in the van to do a job, Rosie was convinced she must look as shattered as she felt. She was also convinced that she was walking as if she'd had her horse shot from underneath her. Ben Hunter and his friend seemed to be insatiable, and Lulu had practically had to evict the pair of them from the premises before they would leave Rosie alone. When Janina had suggested they pay for another hour of Rosie's services, she was quite relieved when Lulu said a very firm no.

'Listen, this girl's not a practised ho,' she told Janina. 'I don't want you ruining the girl before she's got the hang of things.'

After her session with them, Rosie felt that she had the hang of things. She felt sure that any sexual encounter after that one would prove a breeze. She also felt sure that it was the last she had seen of Ben Hunter. His parting shot had been, 'I don't expect we'll meet again, but it's been fun.'

And he had smiled at her.

Now what the hell had all that meant? What she *thought* it meant was, OK, I wanted you and I've had you, and now I'm going to forget you even existed, so good riddance. It'd been nothing more or less than a grudge fuck. Which she guessed was pretty much fine with her. Yes, he had a really good body; yes, he was great in bed; but no, she wouldn't miss his strong-arm tactics in business. She sort of felt, anyway, that they were even now. He had some of her clients, and she had some of his. It was only fair. Now, provided they just stayed out of each other's way – and Ben seemed keen to do that, she gathered – everything would return to normal.

Everything would be fine.

Rosie hummed along to the music on the radio as she battled against the traffic, and wondered with a slight pang of irritation why everything didn't *feel* fine. Why, for instance, didn't she feel that the chapter was closed on all that? Why did she feel not elated but, inexplicably, mildly depressed?

'I'm being stupid,' she told herself firmly. 'It's over, and thank God for that.'

'What I fancy is some camellias,' said her client when she got there. This was one of her own long-standing clients; she had worked for the guy for well over a year. But as they stood in his back garden – his very nice, well-tended, neat back garden – Rosie's heart gave a lurch as she recognised the beginnings of a conversation they'd had about a thousand times before.

Josh Fairley was a nice guy, with a nice family and

a good job in the city, but he had a blind spot about gardening and was forever leafing through gardening magazines and falling in love with totally inappropriate shrubs, trees and flowers, things that looked ravishing on the page but would die within the year in his very alkaline soil.

'Fine, we'll get some potted up for you,' said Rosie, cringing because she knew what was coming next.

'But I want some in that border,' said Josh, looking mulish.

'We can stand the pots in the border,' countered Rosie.

'I think they'd do better in the border,' said Josh.

'They'd die in the border,' said Rosie bluntly. 'The soil's too alkaline.'

'Yes, but you could redress the balance, couldn't you?' he asked hopefully.

'If I could perform magic, yes,' said Rosie.

'Yes, but Mrs Hopkins next door says that she had camellias, and they did very well here.'

'Has she got them now?'

'No, but that's only because she's gone minimalist and pulled all the shrubs out,' protested Josh.

'Not because they all died on her?' queried Rosie, knowing that this must be the case. There was always a gardening amateur who knew better than any trained gardener – it was a fact of life.

'Absolutely not,' insisted Josh.

He was so insistent that Rosie eventually had to agree to plant up some camellias in the border. Gloomily she left the house, knowing that it wouldn't, couldn't possibly, work and that when the camellias died, she would inevitably get the blame.

'I hate all gardening clients,' Rosie told Lulu when she got back to base.

'Mr Fairley after acid-loving plants again?' hazarded Lulu, busy with the invoicing and with chomping her way through another bar of chocolate.

'Um, did I say I was talking to you?' asked Rosie coolly, throwing herself down on the couch and closing her eyes.

'Well, pardon me for breathing,' said Lulu. 'You spoke, I was in the room, I just assumed you were addressing your remarks to me and not to the pot plants, that's all, girlfriend.'

'I am not your girlfriend,' snapped Rosie, straightening as if struck. 'I am not even your friend. I am your employer, so just get the hell on with your work, will you?'

'Whew!' Infuriatingly, this outburst only evinced a delighted grin from Lulu. 'Temper, temper. Still sore about yesterday afternoon?'

'What do you think?'

'I think you had a whale of a time, you got laid *and* you got paid. So what's your beef?'

'You deceived me, Lulu. Again.'

Lulu shrugged and started the printer. 'Seems to *me* like I did you a favour,' she said, raising her voice over the whirr of the machine. 'Got the man out of your hair, I guess.'

'What?'

'Well, I heard him say he doubted you'd meet again. And that's just what you wanted. So I guess that little episode is over, and perhaps now everyone will just get on with their work and settle back down again. He's got some of your clients, you've got some of his. You're even. So maybe now you can both just let the damn thing lie.'

Rosie glared at Lulu in annoyance. Yes, that was exactly what she had been thinking herself, but that didn't mean she wanted to hear the theory voiced out loud.

Why? wondered a tedious little voice in her head. Because you don't want this thing to be over? What did you expect? That he'd be so enamoured after romping round in the sack with you, that he'd swear eternal devotion, pursue you to the ends of the earth? The man's got a library, what does he want to get into book-buying for?

'Damn,' said Rosie out loud.

'What?' asked Lulu, frowning at Rosie.

'Just damn.'

Lulu turned back to the printer with a grin. 'I think he slept with you to get you out of his system,' she said over her shoulder.

'Well, he did. And I guess he has,' said Rosie morosely.

'You really think so?'

'Don't you?'

'Well, I think that was his *intention*,' said Lulu, busy shuffling papers now and stapling them together. 'I think that's why he got Janina involved, to sort of put you in your place, humiliate you maybe, cut you down to size. But the question is, has it worked?'

Rosie eyed Lulu suspiciously. 'Don't you think it has?'

Lulu winked and gave a little laugh. 'Not for one single damn minute,' she said. 'Coming to my party tomorrow night?'

'Absolutely not,' said Rosie.

But of course she went to the damned party, and of course she was sort of hoping that Ben Hunter was going to be there, although she would have denied it with her dying breath. But he wasn't.

Sternly telling herself that she was not in the least disappointed, Rosie grabbed a drink and circulated. Lulu introduced her to some friends of hers, and she chatted amiably enough to them, but she was only barely paying attention. Irritatingly, every time the doorbell chimed and a new arrival came in, she found herself glancing anxiously at the door, her heartbeat accelerating. And every time it wasn't Ben, she found herself less and less in party mood, and more and more gloomy.

Hell and damnation, what was going on? she wondered. She had spruced herself up and come out with the firm intention of enjoying herself. She was looking good. She had swept her red curls up on top of her head, and she was wearing a bronze halter-neck mini dress that clung to all her curves. She hadn't worn underwear, so no VPL. She was wearing a big bronze-coloured African necklet around her throat, and heavy gold-coloured beaten bangles on each wrist. Added to which, she was wearing sexy high-heeled sandals and carrying a glittery little bag she'd picked up for a song in the market.

She looked good and felt confident. Men and women alike were looking at her with interest. So why was she mooning about the place like a spare part?

Lulu, grandly bedecked in red and gold swathes of fabric, found her in the kitchen petting the cat.

'Turning into a party pooper?' she teased, getting more ice out of her big American fridge.

'I think I'm just tired,' Rosie said dismally.

'That's a shame,' Lulu said judiciously, 'because as you're out here you could have fixed up a few more of those little canape doodads for me. I'd do it myself, but I got flesh to press and some serious boogying to be getting on with.'

'What? Oh, all right.' Rosie decanted the cat on to the floor. He shot straight out through the flap in the back door.

'All the little bits and pieces should be in the fridge, just put them together on a plate,' said Lulu, hustling back off into the thick of the party with a bucket of ice clutched beneath one jewel-covered arm.

'Right,' said Rosie to the empty air. The beat was getting frantic in the next room, but out here it was cooler and quieter. Suddenly feeling like Cinderella when the ugly sisters had gone off to the ball, she sighed and hauled herself to her feet. She went over to the fridge and opened the door and looked inside. The noise level soared suddenly as the kitchen door opened again.

'Lulu, there's not much left in here,' she said, turning. Only it wasn't Lulu. It was – oh shit – Ben Hunter.

It was really weird, Rosie thought dazedly, how each time she saw him the physical impact of the man seemed just to bowl her over. He was wearing nothing special, just clean crotch-hugging jeans and an open-necked blue shirt, but she found herself eyeing him like a dog would a prime lamb chop.

'Hi,' he said, letting the door swing shut behind him. Turquoise eyes holding hers. Thick blond hair neatly brushed so that it gleamed beneath the overhead light. And the size of the man. And the scent of him, clean and fresh as new-mown hay.

Rosie caught herself inhaling, and stopped. 'Hello,' she said abruptly, and turned her attention irritably back to the contents of the fridge before it crossed her mind that she was bending over, and wearing an exceedingly short skirt and no knickers. She straightened, automatically brushing the dress down over her hips. She wasn't used to dresses; she nearly lived in jeans and T-shirts. There was a whole different way of behaving in a dress. You had to keep your legs together when you sat down, and not stretch up, and certainly not bend over from the waist and show the world you weren't wearing pants, and the whole thing was suddenly too tedious for words.

'Feeling peckish?' said Ben, and she heard him move across the kitchen to the table and sit down there.

This was ridiculous. She wasn't a teenager. For God's sake, she had been writhing around naked with this man and his friend yesterday afternoon. She withdrew from the fridge and shut it, then turned and looked him full in the face.

'What are you doing here?' she demanded, wishing her heart wasn't beating quite so peculiarly, and wondering if she could put the flush she felt on her face down to too much booze.

'Partying. You?'

'Wait a minute.' She approached the table and glared at him across it. 'Yesterday you said you doubted we'd meet again.'

'I didn't know you'd be here tonight, did I,' Ben said reasonably.

'If I'd known you were going to be here, I wouldn't have come,' said Rosie.

'Right.'

'I wouldn't, OK?'

'Fine. I think we've got that straightened out. We don't want to talk to each other. That's understood.'

'Good.'

'So come here and kiss me.'

'*What?*'

'You heard,' said Ben, and grabbed her arm and pulled her down on to his lap.

Rosie let out a yelp of surprise and pain. His thigh muscles were very hard, and Janina's stropping of her buttocks yesterday had left her slightly sore.

Rosie found herself staring into those mesmerising

eyes at close quarters. After a moment she regained her senses and started trying to disentangle herself, but it was too late. One hand went to the back of her head, and his mouth was suddenly on hers.

'You really are an audacious bastard,' Rosie gasped when he let her up for air.

'But you like audacious bastards,' said Ben, and kissed her again.

'I don't know what gave you that idea,' said Rosie when she could draw breath again.

'What have you got your hair up for? I like it down,' said Ben, and started pulling the pins out.

'Stop that!' said Rosie, squirming. She squirmed a little too vigorously and her hip grazed firmly against his erection. 'For God's sake, can't you keep that thing down for an *instant*?' she complained.

'Not around you, apparently,' Ben said huskily, and he kissed her again, deeply and sweetly and far too beguilingly, lingering over it, taking all the time in the world over it in fact, until she was a quivering heap on his lap, kissed senseless, boneless, clueless.

'Stop,' she said weakly, but didn't mean it.

She was already wet, already open, and he knew it. He was kissing her again, and his hands were all over her; on her breasts, on her hips, on her belly and – oh God – moving between her thighs which somehow opened of their own volition to let him in.

And wasn't this exactly what she had been pining for earlier in the evening? For him, for this wild and sweet rush of sensation that he conjured up in her?

Which probably any man at all could provide, said a cynical voice in her head as she reeled from more and more deep, drugging kisses.

But could they? *Had* they? Had Simon or Jay or Davey done this to her? Sucked the will right out of her like a vampire sucking blood and taken control over her senses this way? She didn't think so. And with that thought came another one: oh boy, am I in trouble.

But by this time she was kissing him back, pushing her fingers into his hair, inhaling the scent of his skin and his cologne, and her senses were saying, who cares? This is great. This is *wonderful*. Ben's fingers were up under the skirt of her dress, pushing hastily into her cunt as their mouths moved frantically against each other. His thumb was pressing hard against her clit.

What if someone comes in? wondered Rosie over the clamour of her hormones.

Someone did. It was Lulu. She said, 'Oops, excuse me folks,' and backed out again.

'No, that's it, enough, *stop*,' groaned Rosie against Ben's mouth. She pulled herself free of him with a gargantuan effort and stood up. Her knees were shaking. Her thighs trembled. Her cunt throbbed. Her clit twitched. Her nipples felt like someone had heated them up with a lighted match. Her heart was racing around in her chest like a sprinter in the hundred metres. I'm about to have a heart attack, thought Rosie. They will find me here stone dead on Lulu's kitchen floor, and the coroner will state that I have been shagged to death.

Ben came up behind her and folded his arms around her. It was like being embraced by a friendly grizzly. And it reminded her of what she had just turned down. Something that felt like a rifle barrel was pressing into her lower back.

'Come back to mine,' he said, nuzzling against her ear and sending shivers rioting down her spine.

'I've got my car here,' she said feebly.

'So what? Pick it up later.'

'I'll pick it up later,' agreed Rosie.

'Come on. My car's outside.'

'We should say goodbye to Lulu.'

'She'll understand.'

'Right.'

The galling part was, he obviously was doing better than her at the gardening game because he had a much more expensive car. A top-of-the-range Mercedes, for God's sake. No wonder he had no trouble at all snaffling her female clients. The leather upholstery folded around her like a fragrant comfort blanket. This thing was an orgasm on wheels. He flicked on the sound system and Schubert oozed out, caressing her ears. And he drove the automatic in that irritatingly cocksure way that men do, one hand lazily on the wheel, the other smoothing over her thigh.

But then, she had agreed to this, she reminded herself.

'Countryman Gardens must be doing well,' she said stiffly after a while.

'Hm?' asked Ben, glancing at her in the warm, enclosed darkness of the car's womblike interior.

'This,' said Rosie, twitching her thigh away from his hand.

'What, the car? No, it's Janina's. I just borrow it sometimes.'

'And what does she do, rob banks?'

'She's a barrister.'

'That's the next best thing. She got the brains, you got the looks, huh?' Ben gave her a tolerant smile. Damn, it was difficult getting a rise out of him. Well, the sort of rise she was after, anyway.

'We both have brains, Rosie. Don't you know that yet?'

Rosie looked out of the window at the sodium-lit streets they were cruising down and shrugged. 'I haven't taken that much of an interest,' she said cuttingly.

'Maybe you should have,' he said obliquely, and stopped the car. 'We're here.'

It was a very nice flat, set in a very up-market block; no change out of half a million for this baby, thought Rosie as Ben let her in, flicking on lights to show a huge cream-toned living room with floor to ceiling windows all along the far walls. At the touch of a button, oat-coloured curtains glided over to close out the night. Ben freed another button at the neck of his shirt, and walked across acres of wood flooring to a drinks cabinet.

'Drink?' he offered.

'Is Janina out?' asked Rosie, feeling unaccountably nervous.

'Away on business for a while,' said Ben, with a meaningful look.

'Just a mineral water,' said Rosie, wanting to keep a clear head if she could. She was dizzy with lust just from being in the same room as him; it wouldn't do to get smashed as well. God knows where she might end up. Or in what position.

'Take a seat,' said Ben as he fixed their drinks.

Rosie tentatively sat down on one of the big cream leather couches. Even if she hadn't known what Janina looked like, one glance around this apartment would tell her a blonde lived here. The soft creamy shades to complement her hair, touches of pale cool blue to offset her skin tones. Nervously she touched a hand to her hair. All the pins were gone, God knew where. He'd pulled every one out. She pulled her dress down over her thighs with a prim, anxious little movement as Ben came over and handed her a drink. He sat down and took a sip of his own. It looked like whisky with loads of ice. He leaned over and kissed her. Oh! Tasted like whisky too. Alcohol fumes flooded her mouth and shot up her nasal passages. It was delicious.

'Passive drinking,' she said a bit shakily, drawing her mouth away from his.

'Hm?' He was kissing her neck now.

'Like passive smoking.'

'Ah.' She felt him freeing the button on the halter-neck. The two halves of the bodice slipped down to her waist. Before she knew it he had put both their drinks down on the huge slab of granite that did service as a coffee table between the two big couches, and had turned back to her, kissing her again, placing both hands over the cool, hard-tipped fullness of her breasts. His hands were cool too, from handling the ice for the drinks, so that she gave a start when his flesh touched hers.

Smiling at her involuntary movement, Ben reached over and took a small mouthful of whisky, then scooped out a cube of ice. Coming back to her, he fastened his mouth over one aroused nipple, and the alcohol he held in his mouth washed over it, burning like fire. And the other engorged tip was rubbed firmly with the ice cube, so that the sensations were so shockingly different, so exceedingly delectable, that Rosie cried out with surprise.

'Oh, you bastard,' she moaned, sinking her fingers into his shoulders, just wanting him not to stop, never to stop, what he was doing to her.

Not lifting his head, Ben moved his mouth to the other nipple, and applied the ice to the one that had previously burned under the sting of the alcohol. Now it was icy, and her other nipple, frozen by the brush of the ice, was now aflame. Her eyes filled with tears of pleasure and pain as Ben flicked the ice cube away. She heard it skitter across the wood flooring and crack against the skirting board. He swallowed the whisky he'd been holding in his mouth, and now – oh God help her – he was staring at her breasts as his hands kneaded them, his expression openly lustful.

'Take the dress off, Rosie,' he murmured, his eyes

lifting to hers. His pupils were dilated. She suspected her own were, too.

There was very little left to come off. She pushed her thumbs beneath the flimsy fabric that was lightly bunched at her waist, and lifted her hips enough to slip the dress down over her thighs and off. Now she sat there wearing only her ridiculously high-heeled fuck-me shoes, her African necklet and her bangles. She was breathing almost painfully as she watched him watching her. She glanced down and saw that her nipples were reddened now, and tingling from his gentle abuse.

'Kneel up on the couch,' said Ben, leaning back against the cool leather to watch her move.

Rosie did so. She couldn't do anything else. She was like an automaton now, responding to every command he uttered. She was drunk and dazed and speechless with lust. She bent to take off the shoes, but he said, 'No, keep them on.'

So she left them on, and was careful not to damage the leather as she knelt up on the couch. Ben was behind her now, and she could literally feel those aquamarine eyes stroking over her back, gliding down caressingly over her buttocks. An instant later, his hand touched her there, and she gave a little shiver.

'Sore?' he murmured.

'Just a little.'

Even the soreness was welcome now; it heightened sensation as his hand moved over first one globe and then the other; then his fingers lightly traced down her crack and she nearly exploded.

'Please,' she whispered.

'Please what? Please do? Please don't?' Ben murmured against her ear. He bit the lobe quite hard, then traced a burning trail down her throat to her shoulder with his lips and his teeth. He nipped her quite hard on the shoulder and she gasped, her eyes closing.

'Do it,' breathed Rosie.

'Do what?' asked Ben tauntingly. He was close, burningly close behind her now, his hands coming up beneath her arms, cupping her naked breasts, his thumbs dragging back and forth, back and forth, across her overexcited nipples. Rosie whimpered.

'Say it.' He breathed against her neck, and she felt him move up on to the couch behind her, still fully clothed. She didn't want that, she wanted him naked too.

'Oh please,' she moaned.

'Say it,' ordered Ben, and she felt him much closer now, the heat and hardness of his body so clear to her even through his clothes. One hand left her breast and she heard him unstrapping his belt, the soft hiss of the zip on his jeans descending, the soft brush of material against her naked ass as he pushed the jeans down on to his thighs. Hopelessly she wiggled back, and his penis, naked and rearing up, was hot against her buttocks.

'Fuck me,' gasped Rosie.

'You want it?' asked Ben, his hands skimming down over her hips.

Rosie nodded frantically.

Suddenly she was spun around; she lost her balance

and fell back on to the couch, and Ben took the opportunity to pull her legs apart and up, so that her knees were on his shoulders and her buttocks were elevated to allow easy entry. Ben reached behind him and grabbed a sheepskin cushion, and lodged it under Rosie's ass. For a moment he hesitated, staring down at her as she lay there panting and open for him; then with great deliberation he unbuttoned his shirt and tossed it on to the floor. Then he leaned forward until his lips were against Rosie's and he said, 'Going to give me back my client list?'

Caught in a completely helpless position, Rosie wondered if she had actually misheard him. Where he was bending forward over her, her knees were bent right up. She could feel the hot bar of his cock against her wet opening. His hands were on either side of her head. He was pressing down on her in a way which almost made her feel claustrophobic.

No, she'd misheard him. Definitely. She twined her fingers into his hair and pressed madly against his penis, rubbing herself against him like a cat, feeling a delicious pressure on her clit.

'Did you hear me?' he asked against her mouth, and his lips opened, brushing tantalisingly against her. His teeth nipped at her lower lip, nibbled at her upper lip, then his tongue echoed the movements of his teeth.

'Oh God, please just do it,' she moaned, writhing against him.

'Going to give me back my client list?'

She heard him properly this time. The only trouble

was, she had stimulated herself so much by pressing against Ben's erect penis that her orgasm seemed imminent. She was breathlessly seeking release, rubbing herself dreamily against his cock until suddenly the pleasure came, intense and wonderful, and she cried out and pushed herself frantically down on to him. Panting, she came reluctantly back to earth, her clit still throbbing and more pleasure a distinct possibility if only he could forget about business for five damned minutes and just put it *in*.

She stretched her arms lazily above her head, aware of his eyes lowering to her breasts as she moved. Her nipples were hard, red and swollen. She was dripping wet, and he was holding her in a completely exposed position. What she wanted, *needed* now, was full, horny, penetrative sex.

'Fuck me,' she murmured, smiling dreamily.

'The client list?' Ben persisted, although she could see that he was in serious danger of becoming distracted now.

How was he holding back? wondered Rosie with niggling irritation. She decided the only thing to do was talk dirty to him until he cracked.

'You want to fuck me,' she whispered, trailing her fingertips down his side, brushing over his furred well-muscled thigh and zooming inward, between their hot pressed-together bodies, until she was clasping his cock. She pushed down voluptuously, dragging back his foreskin, increasing the pressure on his straining glans. Glancing down, she could see that the tip of his penis was very red now, inflamed with passion, wet with pre-come and with her own hot juices.

'I'm so wet for you,' she breathed against his mouth, pushing down again on his cock. She heard him take a long, shuddering breath, felt his hips move irresistibly against her pushing hand.

'Feel,' she said, and took one of his hands and guided it down beneath her bush, over her clit – oh, and that needed a lot more attention than it was getting! – to her opening. Growing bolder, and more desperate, she grasped his hand so that his fingers found her, and wriggled her hips down a little so that his fingers, at least, pushed up into her.

'Don't you want to put your cock there?' she said huskily, biting his lower lip. 'Your big hot naked cock? Feel how good that is?' Rosie groaned as his fingers delved. 'I wouldn't have cared if you'd taken me across Lulu's kitchen table tonight, you got me so hot,' she panted.

'Weren't you worried someone would come in?' murmured Ben, getting into the swing of the thing now, moving his fingers in and out of her in a hypnotically steady way that only increased her agitation.

'I wanted *you* in,' said Rosie with a sigh. 'And what if someone had come in? They'd only have enjoyed watching.'

'You like people watching?' murmured Ben.

'I liked Janina watching us,' admitted Rosie, her hand slipping down to the root of his cock to his balls. They felt like small cannon-balls inside their enclosing sac of flesh, standing up proud and ready. So why didn't he just get on with it?

'Did you like it when she did this to you?' He indicated his hand.

'That was extremely good,' said Rosie, remembering. 'But I'm just an old-fashioned girl, I guess. For me, there's no substitute for a cock.'

'Want it now?' asked Ben.

'Right now,' sighed Rosie, thinking yes, *yes*, at last.

'Tough,' said Ben, and removed his fingers. He dried them on her bush, and stood up. Rosie lay there, wrong-footed, splay-legged, amazed.

'Look at you,' he said, glaring down at her with hands on hips and prick waving in the breeze. 'You get a job as a whore, you offer sexual services to *my* clients, and now you're pleading for this.' He grasped his cock in one hand. 'Well, tough.'

As Rosie scrabbled up to kneel on the couch, feeling hot and throbbing with unfulfilled need, and totally bewildered, Ben started to do what only moments before she had been doing. His hand enclosed the reddened shaft of his naked cock and he began to pump it up and down.

'Have you seen a man wank off before?' he gasped at her.

Rosie shook her head dumbly, aware that she hadn't. Whenever she had been naked with a naked man with an erection, they may have touched each other, sure, but this? No way. They had all been too eager to get between her legs to waste time whacking off.

What added insult to injury for her was that he was looking her body over while he did it, obviously getting more and more aroused just by staring at her jutting sex-reddened tits, the vulnerable naked curve of her belly, the hot riot of curls at her snatch with the plump sex lips beneath, the long bare curves of her legs and feet accentuated by the high-heeled sandals.

Oh, he was really getting off on this, she thought angrily. Pumping like crazy. She was at once fascinated and irritated. Fascinated because she had never seen this done before, and it was arousing her so badly that she felt she might actually follow suit at any moment. And irritated because this wasn't what she wanted, what she *craved*, and he was punishing her, using sex as a stick to beat her with. Using his naked *cock* as a stick to beat her with. Showing that he could get his kicks without poking her, but using her, lapping her up with his eyes as he took his pleasure.

Rosie wanted to thwart him, so she angrily put a concealing hand over her red-curled mound. She covered her naked and heaving breasts with her arm.

'Don't cover up your tits,' panted Ben as he busily jerked himself off. 'I want to see them.'

'Well, tough,' said Rosie smartly, echoing his earlier words. Oh God, though, she wished he'd finish. It was incredibly erotic having him stand right in front of her, wanking. And it seemed to be going on for ever. She couldn't believe how violent he was with his prodigious organ, pulling and pushing at it with wild movements; but those movements were constant, and they were stimulating. Rosie could see that. His penis had grown so big, so red. With a hollow feeling of realisation she thought, that if he were inside her now she would be climbing the walls.

He was huge. Massive. He would fill her totally. His hand movements were almost a blur now. There was nothing she could do but watch, heart racing, pussy emptily throbbing, feeling the hot press of her own nipples against her concealing arm, feeling that she hated him for denying her what she wanted.

Men were so petty, she thought angrily, and then she was watching again, in rapt admiration, listening to his panting breaths, the way his strongly muscled chest rose and fell in agitation as he worked on his cock. He couldn't go on much longer. He just *couldn't*.

And he didn't. In the instant that she thought he had to come, he came, exploding like some fabulous Versailles fountain, his seed spurting and spurting – and falling hotly on to her stomach, on to her arm, on to her thighs. Ben groaned in satisfaction as the last of his seed was spilled.

Rosie looked down at herself in amazement. Then she looked up at him, standing there with his head thrown back in the languorous aftermath of sexual release, his hand still on his penis, still pumping a little, wringing the last ounce of enjoyment from the experience.

'You bastard,' Rosie shot out furiously. 'I'm covered in come.'

Ben exhaled luxuriously and looked down at her. 'Come into the shower and get cleaned up,' he said, and pulled her – somewhat roughly, she thought – to her feet.

Even the shower room in Janina's flat was the last word in designer chic. It really was a shower *room*, a large tiled area with so many showerheads and such a bombarding avalanche of water pressure that half a dozen people could easily have used it at once. In fact, thought Rosie, they probably had. She couldn't imagine the innovative Janina letting such a blissful excuse for group sex go unexplored.

But she was pleased to get cleaned up. As Ben switched what looked like Niagara on and stepped beneath the flow, Rosie went to remove her necklet and bracelets, but Ben said, 'No, keep them on. They suit you when you're nude.'

The cheek of the man. So she kept them on, and applied herself to soaping his come off her body, aware that he was watching her as the water slicked down over her skin and pummelled it into pinkness. She watched him too, but more furtively. The gloss of the water only heightened the beauty of his well-muscled body, and she noted with some considerable interest that even when quiescent, his cock was still pleasingly big.

And of course it didn't stay quiescent for long. Showering together was so sexy, and she couldn't help but see that after about ten minutes of this he was getting visibly aroused again, his cock first jutting out as it lengthened and stood up, and then coming fully erect again so that it was nearly flat against his well-toned belly. By the time he got into that state, he had finished washing and was leaning against the tiles, the hot water shrouding him in steam and buffeting at his big body. His attention was fixed on Rosie.

She cleared her throat nervously and carried on soaping her body, although she was perfectly clean now.

'I want to soap your breasts,' said Ben after watching her for some minutes.

Rosie looked up. The turquoise eyes held hers. She shrugged, feigning indifference, but there went her heart again, breaking into a gallop.

'If you really want to, I don't see how I can stop you,' she said coolly.

She wasn't so cool when he came close up against her and took the soap from her hand. Rosie stared as he worked a lather up on his palms. She forced herself to keep looking into his eyes, but what she really wanted was to look down at his body, his lovely hard chest, his flat belly, his rearing and endlessly enticing penis.

Ben placed both his hands over the full curves of her tits and started to massage them. Rosie nearly liquefied on the spot. He rubbed them slowly and deliberately, very firmly, enjoying the feel of them beneath his hands as they rolled beneath his palms. Her nipples were stiff with excitement, the soft plump flesh warm from the shower.

But then he drew back, and watched intently as the water washed the soap away from her breasts and down her quivering body. Abruptly he reached out and turned the shower off. He grabbed a huge soft mint-green towel and handed it to Rosie, then took another for himself.

'Let's go on into the bedroom,' Ben suggested huskily, his eyes sparring with hers. 'There's something I want to do to you.'

And about time too, thought Rosie. She nearly knocked him down in the rush.

Chapter Eleven

Rosie awoke next morning feeling a faint sense of annoyance. Her next feeling, when she opened her eyes, was one of total disorientation. She was not in her rather shabby little bedroom in her rather shabby little flat. As she blinked into wakefulness, she realised that these surroundings were a great deal more expensive and certainly much more grandly set out.

There was cream watered silk wallpaper on one wall, vast opaque glass doors all along another, muslin-draped floor-to-ceiling clear glass doors that seemed to lead out on to a balcony on another and, as for the other wall – Rosie looked up, straining with the effort – well, it sported a frankly lewd painting of a copulating couple, and the head of the bed, which was brass and actually rather lovely, was pushed right up against it.

Really, you had to admire Janina's taste. And her earning power.

Rosie strained to look at the painting more closely, but she found that she couldn't move her head very freely and wondered why. And then she remembered why, and she let out a bellow of rage.

She was tied to the bed. Her legs were splayed out and each of her ankles was secured by one of Janina's expensive scarves to the bottom of the bedstead. Her arms were pulled out to either side of her head, and her wrists were tied to the bedhead with more scarves. And there was another scarf looped through her necklet and tied to the all too solid-looking brass bedhead so that she couldn't, under any circumstances, break free.

That bastard!

'You bastard!' she yelled, in case he was still in the flat. She doubted it. He was probably off shafting one of *her* female customers, which was what he obviously did best.

He certainly hadn't shafted *her*. She thought back to last night, to her frankly unseemly haste to get in here from the shower room so that he could fuck her. But he hadn't. He had just said, 'So, are you going to give me my client list back?'

Laughing, almost teasing, thinking this was all part of the same delicious game they had been playing together for most of the evening, Rosie had said, 'Nope,' and grinned at him.

'Then you leave me with no choice,' said Ben, and he'd started kissing her and shoving her back on to the bed, which was fine, and then he'd started tying her up, which was also fine, she supposed – a little light bondage was always acceptable – but he'd just tied her up and then he'd left her there.

So, here she was. Stark naked. Tied to the bed. *Sans* shag and *sans* her erstwhile lover, and feeling extremely belligerent. For one thing, she badly needed a pee. Really, this was not funny.

'Really, this is not funny!' she howled at the top of her voice.

Her voice seemed to echo off the walls. The flat sounded totally empty. That ill-natured, fat-headed, grudge-holding son of a bitch! He'd buggered off and left her like this. Didn't he know better than that? Didn't he know, didn't *everyone* know, that you never, ever, left a person tied up alone after a bondage session?

And what was she thinking of? *After* a bondage session? This bondage session, apart from the tying-up part, had never even started. He had tied her to the bed and left her. She remembered that she had shouted a bit after a while, but he had obviously left the flat, and she had grown tired, and eventually she had fallen asleep. Now she felt stiff and angry, and she needed to go to the bathroom.

'You asshole!' she wailed, full-volume.

'You called?'

She looked down. Beyond her pink-tinted toenails (she had painted them especially for Lulu's party) she saw Ben standing in the open doorway. He looked fresh and clean in faded Levis and a lumberjack-type shirt. His hands were in his pockets. He was watching her with amusement.

'Yes, I called,' spat Rosie. 'Untie me. I need to go to the bathroom.'

'That's OK,' said Ben easily. 'I've got something for that.'

And to Rosie's horror he went to one of the cupboards behind the opaque glass panelling and drew out what looked like one of those blue-and-white porcelain piss-pots, the sort that eighteenth-century ladies took into church with them. If the sermon went on for too long, they just put this long hollow oblong container under their voluminous skirts, and peed.

'Look, joke's over. Just untie me, OK?' Rosie asked in a fury.

'I told you, there's no need. Not unless you've decided to give me back my client list, and – oh yes – to stop importuning my male clients?' Ben approached the bed with the little pot and looked down at her stretched out there.

'No way,' Rosie said hotly.

'Sure about that?' asked Ben.

'Positive.'

Ben nodded as if this came as no surprise.

'Then you can use the pot. Oh, and by the way, I'm going to watch.'

Rosie writhed against her bonds and glared at him. 'You complete, total, utter *bastard*,' she roared.

'Here, let me help you,' Ben said sweetly, and he bent over the bed and lifted her hips. The freezing cold porcelain stroked against her buttock and Rosie nearly went through the roof. Then he settled it between her wide-spread legs.

'I hate you,' said Rosie, incandescent with rage while her bladder screamed for release.

'Like I care,' said Ben, and stood there with his arms folded.

He was looking at her naked tits, she noticed in abject fury, because every time she strained against her bonds, they were thrown into prominence and wobbled enticingly. God, he really was going to watch her take a pee! She wasn't only angry with him, she was angry with herself too. Because she was getting a little turned on by this. And her nipples were standing up now, darkening and hardening, so that it was obvious to him that the situation was arousing her.

'It's something I've never done before,' Ben said almost conversationally. 'Watched a woman peeing. It's sexy.' Rosie noted that the front of his jeans were now sporting a healthy bulge.

Oh, to hell with him! She had to pee, *needed* to pee, and it was only a normal function, she told herself, no big deal. But could she relax enough to do it, with him watching? With her bladder full to bursting, she felt that she could. She relaxed, and a trickle emerged to tinkle against the porcelain base of the pot.

'Wow, that *is* sexy,' said Ben, his eyes nearly burning a hole between her legs.

Rosie let the flow commence. Eyes tightly shut so that she shouldn't have to see him witnessing this, she peed copiously into the pot and a wave of blissful relief swept over her. The flow thinned to a trickle, and then to a drop or two. Then she nearly screamed as something touched her exposed crotch.

Her eyes flew open. It was Ben. He was dabbing her dry with a tissue, his movements firm and far too enjoyable. With the deftness of a male nurse he lifted her hips once again, and removed the full pot. He went off into the bathroom with it. She heard the loo flush as she lay there, cringing, wondering if she had really just done that, if he had really *made* her do it.

But he had. He came back with a moistened, soapy sponge and a towel.

'Oh Jesus,' Rosie said hopelessly as he soaped between her legs to clean her up.

'Nice?' asked Ben with a smirk.

Nice? Oh, he knew how nice it was! And then when he'd soaped her, he went and fetched a warm moist flannel and removed all traces of soap from between her legs; then he dried her very thoroughly with a towel. By which time Rosie was completely aroused and wanted nothing more than for him to stop this charade, get his clothes off and screw her. Which, of course, he had no intention of doing.

'You're disgusting,' she said shakily. She was annoyed that her voice shook. It shook because she was, despite all that washing and towelling he'd done, getting uncomfortably wet and hopelessly turned on by him sitting there beside her on the bed, idly staring at her body like she was an interesting insect caught beneath a microscope.

'I don't think Janina's going to be very pleased when she comes in and finds out what you're up to in her flat,' she said, sounding ridiculously prim to her own ears.

Ben looked unworried. 'Janina's away for the rest of the week on business in Strasburg,' he pointed out. 'And actually I think she would be pleased. Are you kidding? She'd be all over your naked enticing body like a cheap suit.'

'And why aren't you?' snapped Rosie, then wished she hadn't. She didn't, after all, want him thinking she was desperate for it. She had some pride.

'Because you want me to,' said Ben.

'Don't flatter yourself.'

'You want me to,' he repeated, 'and it's driving you crazy that I'm not doing it to you. And Rosie.' He leaned confidingly over her and flicked one of her turgid nipples with his finger. 'I'm not going to fuck you again until you give me back that client list, and stop balling my male clients. That's the price for the use of my dick, OK? You toe the line.'

'You can go and fuck yourself,' seethed Rosie.

'Anatomically impossible, I think you'll find,' Ben said equably. 'Now let's see – are you wet yet?'

To her outrage, he trailed a finger down over her navel to her bush and then down on into her cleft. Her flesh jumped at the contact. Of course she was wet. She sometimes felt that she'd been wet ever since she first had the misfortune to set eyes on him.

'Oh yes,' he breathed in satisfaction. 'So you are.'

'Not that it's going to do *you* any good,' snarled Rosie.

'Oh, I don't know,' said Ben. He reached down and opened the door to the little circular cabinet on his side of the bed. When he straightened he was holding something monstrous in his hand.

'What the hell!' Rosie burst out.

'Don't tell me you've never seen a vibrator before?' he said, waving it tauntingly under her nose.

It was horrible. Bright shocking pink and ten inches long, it roughly approximated an erect penis. She had a terrible feeling that she knew what he was going to do with it. He flicked a switch on the ghastly thing, and it started to purr and vibrate.

'Don't you *dare*,' said Rosie, fighting her bonds like fury now.

'God, that's very sexy,' Ben said appreciatively as her wild movements caused her breasts to swing like church bells.

'Look, you've had your fun,' Rosie pleaded. 'Now just untie me and we'll say no more about it.'

'You mean you don't want to know what this feels like?' he offered with a glinting smile.

'It'll feel like ten inches of rubber,' said Rosie.

'So you *haven't* used a vibrator or dildo before.'

'All right, no, I haven't. And I'm not exactly over-eager to start now.'

'Ah, but you've got an advantage over other first-time female users.' Ben rested the tip of the thing against her belly. It shook and trembled; so did her belly. It felt kind of odd, kind of outrageous, kind of stimulating. He touched the thing to her nipple. Oh dear. Her nipples were alarmingly sensitive. She stifled the groan she felt building in her throat.

'You've got a man here to slip it up you,' said Ben, and reached down and untied one of her ankles. Just one. It seemed an ominous sign; and instantly she realised that it was. Because now he was placing one hand under her free thigh, was in fact now pushing that thigh up and open, exposing her and rendering her wide open to any exploratory moves he might choose to make with the hideous plastic doodad in his other hand.

'Men are experts at slipping things up women,' said Ben, when she gasped and squirmed. His hand tilted her pelvis a little to the left, getting the angle just right. Her leg was over his shoulder. She was trapped here and starting to get very panicky indeed. He pushed the tip of the damned thing lower, so that it quivered against her bush, penetrated her sex lips, seriously and all too briefly pulsated over her clitoris, then homed in on the target.

'Bastard,' choked Rosie, tears springing into her eyes as he pushed the tip into her. Tears of extreme pleasure and humiliation and hatred and arousal. She was so wet, so open, that the vibrator's entry was smooth and easy. Ben eased it in until the thing was fully lodged inside her, where it pulsed and maddeningly aroused and tweaked at her sensitive innards until she started to pant and writhe against his hands.

'Oh God,' she moaned, as he moved the thing around in there. Her G-spot was getting an awful lot of attention. Too much. 'Oh!' she whispered, as his fingers moved silkily over her hard little clit. It was an excess of riches by anyone's standard, his caressing hand and this huge, monstrous thing filling her.

'No,' she groaned, but it was no use at all. She couldn't fight it. She felt her climax start to build like an avalanche, and seconds later it had knocked her flat and swept her away and she was screaming and trying to get that horrible thing even further up inside her, thrusting her hips down on to it, on to his fingers. Her back arched crazily as sensations hit her again and again.

And then she was coming back to her senses, panting and cursing weakly at him as he pulled the plastic monstrosity out of her with a wet slurp. He switched off the little motor. She watched in horrified fascination as he propped the ugly thing between his thighs and used tissues to dry it off. It looked like his own erection, standing up like that. Oh damn, his erection. She thought about it and was suddenly very hot again, even though she ached from the penetration of the vibrator. When he was satisfied that the thing was dry, he put it on the side table.

'Thought again about that client list?' he asked.

'Yes, I've thought,' said Rosie, trying to get her breath back.

'And?' he prompted, his eyes holding hers.

'And you can go straight to hell.'

'Well, save me a seat, Rosie. Because I haven't finished with you yet.'

And to her rage, he stood up calmly, retied her ankle, and left the flat again.

*

'Rosie?'

She awoke groggily to find him standing over her. How long had she been asleep? The angle of the sun that slanted through the windows told her it must be early afternoon. She was hungry. She thought that very soon she would have to pee again, but not right now, thank God. And thankfully her bowels were behaving themselves for the moment. She didn't like to think about what was going to happen when she really needed to use the bathroom in earnest.

'The list?' he said.

'Up yours.'

'That's an unfortunate choice of words, under the circumstances.' Ben smiled tolerantly. 'Because it's not going to be up mine, is it? It's going to be up *yours*.'

'You started this, not me,' Rosie told him.

'Yeah? Well I'm certainly going to *finish* it, you can be sure of that.' He turned to the half-open door. 'Guys?' he called.

And to her horror two more men came into the room. The first was older than Ben, shorter and stockier and with a lustrous head of white hair that had once been, she was sure, pitch black. His face was strong and ruggedly attractive. His dark eyes were out on stalks when they saw her spread out naked on the bed. After him, dressed in jeans and plain shirt like the other two men, came a younger man. He looked no more than eighteen or nineteen. He had soft straight floppy brown hair and nice blue eyes and a good physique. They looked like manual workers, she thought. She noticed that the younger man was blushing hotly and trying not to stare at her nudity. Well, at least one of them had a shred of decency! The thought didn't help her much; the youngest member of the trio might have decency, but like his two pals he sported an uncomfortable-looking bulge beneath his jeans.

'What the hell are you playing at?' Rosie asked indignantly.

It was bad enough Ben leering at her while she was stuck here legs splayed and tits on parade, but to bring his friends along to share the show really was beyond a joke.

'Whatever I want, since you won't see sense over that client list,' said Ben. He turned to the older man. 'Daniel, this is Rosie. Rosie, Daniel.'

For God's sake! thought Rosie. Was there nothing he wouldn't stoop to, to get his own way? And here he was making introductions like this was a social event, like she was not tied to the bed naked and being ogled by three men.

'She's gorgeous,' said Daniel, as if she were a prize heifer.

'She's beginning to lose her sense of humour,' snapped Rosie. 'Rapidly.'

'And this is Luke. Luke, this is Rosie.' Luke was still blushing, but he was staring at her breasts, enthralled. And the bulge, noticed Rosie, was getting bigger.

Ben put a friendly, paternal hand on Luke's shoulder. 'Luke and Daniel work for me at Countryman Gardens,' Ben explained.

'How completely wonderful for the three of you,' Rosie said acidly.

Ben ignored her. 'Now what I want you to do, Luke,' he went on to the younger man, 'is get your kit off.'

Luke looked bewildered, but he nodded. He quickly unbuttoned and shucked off his shirt to reveal strong arms and a well-developed chest covered in a light fuzz of darkish hair that narrowed as it dipped down to meet the waistband of his jeans.

'All of it?' he asked, pausing.

'All of it,' Ben assured him.

Shrugging, Luke kicked off his trainers and then unzipped and kicked off his jeans. Unlike Ben, he wore underpants. They were creaking under the strain right now, but he wore them. Or something approximating underpants, Rosie thought, staring. It was a thong. A black thong. It covered very little – just the triangle over his crotch – and it looked as if his straining cock was going to rip the material at any second.

'That too,' said Ben.

Luke, still blushing charmingly, hooked his thumbs into the thong's sides, yanked it down and stepped out of it. Seeing Rosie getting an eyeful as he straightened, he decorously placed both hands over his modesty.

Ben came to the bed and untied both Rosie's ankles. Oh, the relief! She stretched her legs luxuriously, aware of Daniel watching her like a dog eyeing up a piece of meat, aware of Luke's fascination with her pale naked body. Aware too that she was finding this both alarming and exciting at once.

'Now what I want you to do, Luke,' said Ben, returning to the staring young man who still cupped his manhood as if he had the crown jewels down there, 'is get on the bed and mount her.'

'Jesus!' breathed Luke.

'*What!*' shrieked Rosie.

'Shut up, bitch,' Daniel said quietly, surprising her.

'Really?' asked Luke, eyes shining like a child's who had been promised a visit to a theme park. 'What, you mean really do it? But she's tied up.'

'Her legs are free,' Ben pointed out. 'So you can get in as deep as you want. In fact –' he glanced at Rosie '– I *insist* you get in as deep as you want.'

Oh no. He really meant to go through with this. He was going to let this, this *boy* have her, and then – she just knew it – he was going to let this other, older one with the cruel eyes and the women-as-meat attitude let rip too. And she was tied up. Helpless. If she screamed, would anyone hear? Someone in the next flat, maybe?

But she doubted it. She'd been screaming quite loud in the throes of orgasm since Ben brought her here, and no one had raised the alarm.

'You're such a bastard,' she said to Ben.

Daniel, she noted, was fondling his crotch as if he couldn't wait for the action to begin.

'Get on the bed and stick it in her, right?' Luke asked, anxious to clarify the situation. He was now less cupping his cock and balls and more rubbing at them in glee. In fact he was nearly hopping from one foot to the other in anticipation.

'Right in her,' said Ben, his eyes on Rosie's. 'Right in,' he added reflectively, clearly giving it some thought. 'Up to the hilt.'

'Right.' Luke was obviously keen to get started, the little perv. He came around the other side of the bed and Rosie kicked at him.

'Feisty little bitch,' said Daniel from the sidelines, groping himself busily. 'She wants it really.'

Luke more cautiously grabbed Rosie's flailing leg. Ben helpfully came to the other side of the bed and grabbed the other one. God, are they going to make a wish? wondered Rosie with an edge of manic humour. Between them Ben and Luke managed to hold her still enough for Luke to get into a kneeling position between her wide-stretched thighs. Rosie saw that his cock was uncovered now, bobbing around merrily like a ship's bowsprit on a stormy sea as he fought to subdue her. It wasn't as big as Ben's, but the sight of Luke's fine brown upstanding cock towering against its backdrop of gingerish hair, and his work-toned body with its muscles moving smoothly to wrestle her into position did odd things to her.

'Look at her tits,' said Daniel, narrow-eyed as he stared. 'Look at those puppies. Big and fat and bouncing all over the place. Nipples as hard as acorns she's got. She's gasping for it.'

And the most humiliating part of it was, he was right. And she was still very wet from Ben's earlier incursion with the vibrator, which was bound to smooth Luke's path.

'Come on,' panted Luke, bending over her as he fought to achieve penetration. 'Open up, you know you want to.'

His seed-slippery cock connected with her clit, sending arcs of pleasure shooting up to her nipples. He slid down a little on the bed, and abruptly found her slit with the tip of his cock, and thrust mightily with his hips with a yell of pleasure more befitting a cowboy on a bucking bronco than a man on a woman.

He was in!

Oh, and it felt so good. Better than the vibrator, she thought, if a little smaller. Livelier and warmer. She felt herself getting flushed with excitement, hotter and hotter. Ben and Daniel watched from the sidelines with keen interest as Luke pumped away at her like a madman, still gripping her wide-spread thighs with his hands, bruising her a little, not that she cared right at this moment. All she cared about was that he just kept going, grunting heavily as he thrust his hips back and forth. She writhed against him, wishing that someone – anyone – would at least rub her clit, because it was crying out for attention.

Oh, but this was intended as some perverted punishment, she reminded herself. But it was bliss. It was lovely, that big pulsing thing pushing and shoving at her. And then Luke came, very noisily, and she felt him grow bigger inside her and then the wild spasms of his orgasm, which seemed to go on and on. And then he slumped over her, panting. And then he drew his cock out of her and knelt there between her legs, looking happy and triumphant as he got his breath back.

'The list?' Ben asked her again as she lay there feeling completely liquid with pleasure, and badly wanting more.

'No way,' she gasped out.

'Daniel.'

Daniel was keen to get started. As Luke moved off the bed and started drying himself off with the tissues on the side table, Daniel threw off his shirt. Goodness, he was hairy! And the hair was white, like the hair on his head. Rosie found it sexy. She found his hard uncaring eyes sexy too. She knew that even if she didn't want it – and she did, she did – Daniel was the one of the three who would just plough in anyway.

He was unzipping his jeans, kicking his legs free of them. Gardening work did wonders for the male body, thought Rosie, admiring his tanned and toned belly. His bush was very thick and startlingly white, and his erect browny-purple cock, tanned to a turn like the rest of him, had the look of a dark fetish thrown down on to white silk. God, he was attractive. And hard. His whole body was hard, like Ben's, like Luke's, and his penis was very hard indeed.

Aware of Ben watching while fully clothed, and of Luke standing there stark naked now he'd dried himself off, eager to see the rest of the show, Rosie felt almost ridiculously turned on. She couldn't seem to catch her breath at all. Every breath was a shallow pant. Her nipples were achingly erect, their tips hard as acorns.

Ben was staring at them. Luke was too. Oh, this was so sexy! By the time Daniel hoisted himself up on to the bed, her defensive kicks were nothing but a token, and having seen Luke cope with them, she realised Daniel would have no trouble at all.

He grabbed her behind the knees and pulled her down the bed so that her knees were draped over his hard-muscled shoulders. Kneeling between her open legs, Daniel gave her a frankly unpleasant sneery smile and put both hands on her full white breasts, which had been fascinating him ever since he came into the room.

'Oh yes,' he breathed. 'These are real, aren't they? I hate those plastic titties that don't move when you rub them.' Daniel rubbed hard at Rosie's tits, pushing them up like a balconette bra, watching the nipples spill above his hands. They were rough from gardening work and chafed her delicate skin in a way that hovered tantalisingly between pleasure and pain.

He held her tits up like that for long moments, enjoying the view while Rosie lay there panting like a landed fish and wishing – God help her! – that he'd just get on with it, do it to her. He was going to very soon. When his cock brushed between her legs, accidentally stimulating her, he couldn't resist pressing it against her a little. She felt its rigidity, its heat, its moist tip, and groaned and pushed helplessly back, trying to get her clitoris against it so that she could rub herself to release.

'Hot bitch,' said Daniel, and took her turgid nipples between his thumbs and forefingers, squeezing vigorously.

Rosie yelped as her nerve-endings made a lightning connection from nipples to crotch. He laughed softly and squeezed again, harder. Rosie's head thrashed on the pillow as though she was a fever victim. Her eyes opened dazedly and she was suddenly looking into Ben's eyes. Daniel squeezed again, and she pushed down wildly against his cock. Her eyes slipped down Ben's body and she saw that he, too, was very hard. She rubbed herself restlessly against the hot cock between her legs. Was Ben going to have her too, when Daniel had finished? Or was he going to go out into the street and grab a passer-by and invite him up to sample her wares?

The thought of it made her even hotter. And Luke, she saw, was getting hard again, his cock stretching and standing up like a blow-up doll. He saw her looking at it and, ridiculously coy, put a concealing hand over its length.

'Oh God, don't hide it,' moaned Rosie, and Luke shyly took his hand away and let her look.

Daniel squeezed again. Oh, her nipples were sore! Why didn't he bite them and have done with it? She squirmed and tried to rub herself furiously against Daniel's erection, her eyes going from Luke's naked cock, to Ben's concealed one, to Daniel's looming grey-furred body crouched over her, and suddenly she was coming like crazy, over and over, sensations ripping at her. Seeing her in the throes of her orgasm, Daniel laughed again and pinched at her nipples with a quick, painful rhythm as if he was milking her.

'You want some cock, baby?' he muttered, and then he let go of her bruised breasts and used one hand to guide his now purple and engorged tip down into her wetness. He pushed quickly, very businesslike now, intent on coming inside her before her writhing and panting excitement brought him off without penetration.

One huge thrust, and he was in. Weak and hot and pliable from her climax, Rosie lay back and let him take his own pleasure – not that she could have stopped him doing so anyway. And suddenly she felt supremely sexy, like a female goddess, with three men paying their tribute at her altar of beauty and feminine allure.

She lay back. She *surrendered*. Daniel, intent on his own pleasure, humped her mightily, almost pulling out with every thrust and then slamming himself back into her. Again and again he did that, until his breath was coming in short fierce grunts that kept perfect time with his thrusts.

'God, you'd think it'd hurt her,' murmured Luke in awe.

But Rosie was too wet, too steeped in pleasure, to feel pain from Daniel's wild movements. Relaxing into this somehow elemental experience, she watched Luke come even closer to the bed so that he could see more clearly Daniel's huge member stoking Rosie's boiler. Luke groaned, horribly aroused once again by the sight, and started to jerk himself off while watching the couple on the bed.

The two men came simultaneously, Daniel grunting as he pumped out his tribute to her, Luke groaning and catching a waterfall of come with two hastily grabbed tissues. And then it was over. Daniel pulled out and stood up, and Rosie lay back, sated, and waited for Ben. Surely, now he'd do it? She didn't even care if the other two watched any more. She was too hot to give a damn.

'OK guys. Thanks,' said Ben to his two employees.

Looking almost sheepish now, Daniel and Luke gathered up their scattered clothes and left the room, closing the door after them. After a few moments of tense silence in the bedroom, both Rosie and Ben heard the outer door to the flat close. They were gone.

'Well, did you enjoy it?' Rosie taunted her tormentor lazily. She was flushed with sex, incredibly alluring, and she knew it. He couldn't possibly resist her now.

'Well, *you* certainly did,' observed Ben, coming closer to the bed. He had his thumbs hooked into the waistband loops of his jeans, and was staring down at her with a brooding intensity.

'It was great.' Rosie shrugged. She could just about shrug with her hands tied up like this. She somehow knew that her casualness would sting him, and she saw fleetingly that it did before he carefully made his face expressionless. 'But hey, enough's enough. I've got clients lined up for this afternoon, so although it's been fun, I've got to run along.'

'My clients – or yours?' queried Ben grimly.

'Mine,' said Rosie, although the garden she was supposed to be tending right now (roses to tie in, lawn to mow, couch grass to dig out of border) was one that she had filched from him. Mr Prendergast. A nice man. Only twenty-five and into commodities. Into redheads in a big way, too. He *had* been Ben's client. But now he was hers. Possession was nine tenths of the law, so sucks to him.

'I wish I believed that.' Ben sighed.

'Suit yourself.'

'Oh, I will.' He stood there, staring down at her. Her heartbeat, which had been slowing down, speeded up again. He bent forward, leaned over her. He was going to kiss her!

But he didn't. Rosie's heart sank. He was only untying her wrists, and the scarf that was looped through her necklet. But hey, that was good. Surprised, Rosie swung her legs round so that she was sitting up on the edge of the bed. She rubbed lightly at her wrists, but the scarves had been very soft. Apart from a little stiffness and a bit of after-sex soreness around her pussy and on her nipples, she was fine. Disappointed, but fine.

'You're not going to give that list back, are you,' said Ben, watching her thoughtfully as she stretched her arms above her head. She saw his eyes dip to watch her breasts rise perkily with the movement.

'No,' Rosie said sweetly. She looked down at her red and swollen nipples and raised her hands to brush lightly over them. It was a gesture designed to drive him crazy. 'Ow, they're sore,' she complained mildly, taking a leaf out of Daniel's book and lifting the two white globes with her hands. Her nipples rose dark and still hard above her fingers, pooched out and inviting.

She looked archly up at Ben. 'Have you any lotion I could rub into them?' she asked hopefully.

Ha! She was going to get him. Ben went off into the bathroom and returned with an expensive lily-of-the-valley-scented moisturiser. He sat on the bed beside her, nipped up the lid on the plastic bottle, and squirted peach-coloured creamy fluid into his palm.

'I'll do it,' he said, reaching over. 'Just keep holding them up like that.'

Rosie adjusted her grip on her breasts a little to expose even more of their beauty. It was amazing, she thought, almost swooning with delight as Ben started to anoint her tits with the soothing cream, how she had never really paid her breasts that much attention before. Now she was very conscious of them every day, of their potent allure, of their almost infallible ability to render men malleable. She was aware of them swaying beneath her T-shirts, she was aware of their sensitivity and sexy pulchritude when she soaped them in the shower, and right now she was aware that Ben could hardly take his eyes off them for an instant, and that his penis was still very erect under his jeans, and that his hands felt incredibly good on her outrageously hard nipples.

Oh, this was sexy. She was still holding them up for him, and he was rubbing them with his big rough hands, the cream sinking into her skin, his palms grazing over her nipples again and again. He was going to give in at any moment. His breathing was heavier now, his concentration on her tits intense.

But abruptly he drew away and stood up. He yanked

a tissue from the box on the side table and wiped his hands dry, then took the bottle of lotion back into the bathroom. Then he came back in and stood at the foot of the bed.

'Get showered and dressed, Rosie,' he said coolly. 'There's something I want to show you.'

Oh *yes*, she thought, and almost scampered off into the shower room. Mr. Prendergast's couch grass was going to have to wait.

Chapter Twelve

To her disappointment Ben did not join her in the shower room. He waited in the kitchen, drinking coffee until she was ready, then fed her toast and marmalade and fresh coffee from the cafetiere.

'Ready?' he said at length, having tidied away the dishes. A very methodical man, thought Rosie, watching him. Very single-minded too. Boringly so. Gallingly so. What the hell was he up to now?

'Ready, yes, but I'm not dressed right for anything but an evening bash, am I? So ready for what?' Rosie replied guardedly. She looked down at her completely inappropriate bronze party dress, her – in the cold light of day – ridiculous shoes.

'Wait and see.'

Half an hour later they were out of London in his red pickup truck and shooting off down the motorway to the south. Something he wanted her to see, he'd said. Well, what? She hated mysteries. Couldn't he come right out and tell her what this was all about? Was he taking her on a date? It didn't seem likely. She asked him what this thing was he was so keen to show her, but all he had to say was, once again, 'Wait and see.' And then he switched on Radio 1 full blast so that further chitchat was not an option.

Anyway, thought Rosie, sitting back and casting her fate to the winds, it was a nice day. The sun was hot, all the trees were in bud, they had the windows wound down and Ben was a very competent driver. As she had guessed he would be. Here was a man who did everything steadily and with forethought. Here was a man, she thought, who *planned*, and who would plod along relentlessly and see that plan through to the end.

She'd never before considered steady determination an attractive factor in a man's make-up. In the past her dates had been young and a bit foolhardy, student pals from Sparsholt mostly, out for a few beers, a few laughs, and some good times. Which had always seemed pretty much OK to her.

Until now.

Ben Hunter was different.

Ben Hunter was, with the fingers of one hand tapping on the steering-wheel as they sailed along, and an arm leaning casually on the open window, exceedingly sexy. If a bit of a grouch.

A *lot* of a grouch, actually.

And now they were driving through country lanes, through what looked like a forest, actually. The sun lanced through the overhanging trees, dazzling her.

She could hear birdsong over the roar of the music and the engine. Not many other cars down here. Blissful. Not like London, where the car was king, dominating all roads, clogging up the city like a horde of termites clustered on a single mound.

'Where the hell are we?' shouted Rosie to make herself heard over the garage beats.

Ben flicked the music off and shot her a grin. 'Ashdown Forest.'

'Oh?' Rosie stared at him in bewilderment. 'Terrific,' she said dryly, but she thought it was beautiful.

'I have this fantasy about driving along a country lane with a beautiful woman,' said Ben.

'Oh yes?'

'Yes.'

As they approached a small crescent-moon passing place in the lane, Ben pulled in, slapped on the hand-brake and switched off the engine. Total silence. Well, thought Rosie, not quite total. The birds were singing wildly. The breeze was shimmying through the trees and hedgerows, making the white foaming drifts of cow parsley that frilled the lane dance and billow.

'So?' Rosie looked at him, effecting a bored expression.

Ben turned a little toward her. 'Don't you want to know what the fantasy is?'

Rosie shrugged, but she was deeply curious. 'Go on. Surprise me.'

'She jumps out of the truck and runs off into the bluebell wood. I follow. We make love.'

Rosie raised her eyebrows at him. 'Actually that sounds a bit tame for you.'

Ben smiled that infuriatingly fetching smile, leaned across her and threw the passenger door wide open. His turquoise eyes held hers.

'I'll give you a ten-second head start,' he said generously.

Rosie looked at the woods that led off darkly and seemed almost impenetrable, and then at his face. 'But you said this was just a fantasy.'

'It was. Now it's for real. One.' Ben paused a beat. 'Two.'

'You're such a bastard,' said Rosie, outraged, not for the first time that day.

'Change the record, Rosie. Three.'

Rosie took the hint. She quickly slipped off her high-heeled fuck-me shoes and bolted barefoot out the door.

'And remember,' he called after her, 'if I catch you, I can have you.'

'Eat my dust, sucker,' Rosie threw back over her shoulder.

'Four.'

She heard no more counting. She was running. She could run like a deer, barefoot. She just hoped no careless asshole had dumped glass or nails around. But she doubted it. This was too far off the beaten track. Even running full pelt through the trees, she could admire the beauty of her surroundings. Lunging through a tunnel of ivy, she came out on to a big dell full of bluebells. It was breathtaking. The azure of the flowers was made doubly intense by the dark shade that was cast by overhanging trees. It was completely, totally gorgeous, and the smell was just heaven. It was almost, she thought, a sacrilege to run through this carpet of blue, to trample some of it underfoot. But she did. And she was about halfway across the sweetly scented carpet of shimmering blue when Ben caught up, bringing her down with a flying rugby tackle.

'Not fair,' gasped Rosie, rolling and writhing to escape his clutches.

Ben hung grimly on. 'In what way not fair?' he demanded, working his way up her body with his arms.

'I'm barefoot and you're wearing trainers.'

'That's a pretty sorry excuse,' said Ben.

'We'll crush the flowers.'

'That was my intention,' he said, and pinned her whole body neatly beneath his and kissed her.

'I wish you weren't such a great kisser,' sighed Rosie when he stopped.

'Why?' He kissed her again.

Rosie came up for air. 'Because it makes me do things I shouldn't.' She smiled.

'Like?'

'Oh, like this.' Rosie pushed him back so that she could sit up. She unfastened the halter top of her inappropriate dress and let the bodice fall to her waist. Then she plucked up a couple of handfuls of bluebells and teasingly held them to her breasts to cover them.

'Oh, I think we can do better than that,' said Ben, pulling the dress down still further so that it was draped around her knees as she knelt there. He picked some flowers and bent over her bush, weaving the bluebells into the bright red strands of crinkly hair. Rosie flinched with growing sexual excitement as his big hands brushed so titillatingly against her mound. He sat back on his heels and admired the effect.

'You look like a wood nymph,' he said after a moment's reflection.

Rosie looked down to the front of his jeans. 'So now what? You've caught me. What happens now?'

'I told you. I fuck you bandy.'

'You said "make love" back in the truck,' complained Rosie, clutching her bluebell bra cups against her nipples to stimulate herself. The flowers were very cool and fragrant.

'Well,' said Ben, reaching out to slip an arm around her waist and pull her in against his body, 'now I'm saying I'm going to fuck you bandy.'

'What if I scream?' asked Rosie.

'I'm counting on it.' He grinned, trying to wrest the armfuls of bluebells from her.

'Not like *that*,' said Rosie in exasperation. 'I mean in terror at what you are about to inflict upon my cringing body, you vile man, you.'

'What, a thorough fucking?' He kissed her naked shoulder, making her shiver in the shade of the trees. 'You can take it.'

'Maybe I don't want to take it.'

'Yes you do. God, Rosie, get those tits uncovered, will you? I'm desperate here. I've been watching you get shagged by a vibrator and two men today, and now I want to get at you.'

'That was your own fault,' Rosie pointed out.

'Actually it was yours,' said Ben, tossing bluebells aside with abandon as he fought his way through to her breasts.

'Whatever.' Rosie teasingly held a single head of bells over each rampant nipple. 'Look. Blue.' She indicated the flowers. 'Bells,' she said, and gave a delicious little shimmy that sent her tits swaying.

'Rosie, that's more than flesh and blood can stand,' groaned Ben, rubbing agitatedly at the bulge under his jeans.

Rosie took mercy on him and tossed the remaining flowers aside. She put her hands up under her breasts, lifting them louchely. 'What do you want to do?' she asked beguilingly. 'Kiss them? Bite them? Take them in your hands and feel them? Take them into your mouth and – oh!' She gasped as he did exactly what she was suggesting. Within a split second his hot open mouth was on one engorged nipple and he was sucking at her like a very large baby. 'Oh God that's good,' said Rosie, clutching at his head. 'Keep doing that.'

'Try and stop me,' muttered Ben against her swollen teat, before transferring himself to her other breast. He nipped at her nub with his teeth, pulling it out, then using the suction of his whole mouth to increase her pleasure when he had sensitised her nipple almost beyond endurance.

'I love your tits,' he moaned against one of them,

before tonguing the other with circles and laps and sucks that nearly brought her to boiling point right then and there.

Nearly.

But not quite.

Ben's fingers then slid down her hip and over her richly decorated bush, pushing in beneath to find her clit. Rosie gasped again and parted her legs to allow him easier entry. The cold, grassy flowers beneath her prickled at her wet cunt and her bare ass and her thighs in the most delicious way.

Enjoying his caresses, her tongue twining and battling with his, Rosie pulled his shirt up and out of the waistband of his jeans. Fiddling beneath the soft material, she found the button, freed the zip, and lustily pushed both hands down inside the gaping front of his jeans. Cool, hard, flat belly. Crisp curling hair, very thick. Ben's hips pushed forward against her hands and there, oh there was his cock nuzzling lewdly against her hands like a vibrant horny animal, so silky, so hot. Jesus, so *hard*.

She wanted to kiss it like a worshipful acolyte. More important, she wanted to see it. Kissing his lips, his cheek, his ear, she tore at the buttons of his shirt, pushed the damned thing off down his arms, saw him now naked to the waist, his fly undone, his erect almost shockingly naked penis waggling triumphantly at her.

'That's so gorgeous,' groaned Rosie.

'Thanks,' said Ben, grinning.

'I want this so much. You bastard. You've made me wait ever since last night.'

'But that's increased the desire, hasn't it?' suggested Ben, and Rosie knew that it had.

There seemed no need now to prolong the mutual agony further. Ben pushed her back onto the scented carpet of blue and spread her thighs and pushed his cock down between them. Finding the spot, he thrust up and, with one smooth and easy movement, he was there. Enfolded in silken wetness, and fighting for control. Had he ever before, before *Rosie*, lacked control? It had always been a source of pride to him that he could hold on and on, drawing out his own pleasure and the pleasure of the woman he was with.

But then – and this made him pause as nothing else would have done – had he ever really *engaged* with any of those women? Oh, in the physical sense, sure. But Rosie was, well, disconcertingly different. When they were together the conversational ball was batted back and forth as fast as anything that happened on Centre Court at Wimbledon. They spoke, he realised belatedly, the same language, the language of the earth and growing things, of the entire natural world. Their sex drives were similarly high. Their horticultural knowledge – and it pained him to admit this even to himself – was on a similar level.

He hovered there, uncertain suddenly, lodged inside her while she lay there gasping, arms above her head in complete abandon, her breasts moving with each laboured breath, her ribcage rising and falling shallowly, her glowing green eyes staring up into his. Damn it, they *were* alike, he thought. Even their fitness level, honed by manual toil and not Pilates, was on a par.

Ha! Am I looking at my soulmate here? wondered Ben. And the thought was unnerving. He'd always told himself that his goal was everything. Living here in the country, running his own nursery business, had hogged his attention for the past few years. He had indulged in sex with a variety of willing London women, finding their polished and cynical city ways a little alarming at first, and then a novelty.

But Rosie wasn't a London woman. She was a *country* woman, just as he was a country man.

'Do you like it here?' he asked her, and the effort to keep his voice steady while he was inside her was considerable.

Rosie smiled deliriously. 'I love it,' she murmured, shifting a little against him. 'Oh Ben, please do it.'

So he did it. It was no hardship at all to fuck Rosie. But he wondered how much of a hardship it would be to let her go.

They lay there afterwards, side by side on their backs, not touching, both staring up into the glinting green canopy of trees, both relaxed, content. Rosie chewed idly on a bluebell stem and listened to the stillness all around. Wood pigeons were cooing high up in the trees. A blackbird was sounding a mild warning call nearby – they were close to a nest, she thought.

'We ought to move,' she said idly.

'We're not close enough to really worry it,' said Ben sleepily.

God, he'd heard it too. And *understood* it. She smiled to herself. Now this was amazing, wasn't it? To meet a man in London who not only listened to the natural world, but understood its meaning? But he didn't belong in London, she thought. She turned her head and looked at his profile. Handsome bastard, she thought. Women must fall at his feet like ninepins. His eyes had closed, and his chest rose and fell with every deep, steady breath. He was completely relaxed, and she suddenly realised that she had never truly seen him relaxed before; in London, even though he gave a very good impression of being laid back, he wasn't really.

It's being here, she realised. It's being in the country, where he belongs.

'So what was this thing you wanted to show me?' she asked, propping herself up on to her side and looking down at his face. His eyes flickered open, intensely blue even in this subdued light. She wiggled her eyebrows at him like Groucho Marx. 'Or have I just seen it?'

'No, but I was good, wasn't I?' He grinned.

Rosie nodded. 'And endearingly modest, too. So what is it then? Is it this place? This bluebell glade?'

'Nope.'

'We're really irritating that blackbird,' she said as the noise level increased. She leaned closer to him and brushed his lips with her own. Her breasts pressed pleasurably against the hard wall of his chest.

'Yeah, let's go,' said Ben, and he reached a hand up

to the back of her head so that he could kiss her more easily.

'We really should,' said Rosie against his mouth, not exactly fighting to get free.

'Soon,' said Ben, and pulled her on top of him and kissed her more deeply.

It was nearly an hour later when they finally made it back to the truck. They were both starving from making love in the open air, and stopped in a village pub to eat pie and chips. Rosie drank sweet cider, and Ben, ever careful, ever cautious, stuck to pineapple juice.

'Am I ever going to get to see this mysterious something you wanted me to see?' asked Rosie as they piled back into the truck.

'Right now,' said Ben, and they went roaring off along the lanes again, stopping briefly to allow a herd of black and white cows to cross, and even more briefly to let a tractor turn. When Ben steered the truck off the lane and on to an unmade-up track, Rosie grew extremely curious. Maybe he was kidnapping her. Not that she gave a toss. She yawned, feeling weary after the long day's exertions. She actually believed now that gardening was a whole lot easier than whoring for a living. She felt lulled by the movements of the flatbed's suspension as it lurched over the bumps.

'Rosie? You asleep?'

She jerked her head up. She had been asleep for a split second, but now she realised that he'd stopped the engine and that the truck was parked outside a cottage. There was a little white-painted picket fence all around its borders, and woodland crowded darkly at its back. It looked very old, but was neatly whitewashed and just about crawling with climbers – big rambler roses, Virginia creeper, honeysuckle. A golden hop was creeping its tendrils up and over a trellis archway over the gate. There was a sign on the gate that said Pond End Cottage.

'They really shouldn't put honeysuckle up near a thatch like that,' said Rosie, her keen gardener's eye drawn immediately to the lushness and beauty of the planting, searching for flaws in what looked like an otherwise faultless layout.

'I know,' said Ben, jumping out and coming round to her side of the truck as she climbed stiffly out, stifling another yawn. 'But I love honeysuckle, particularly that one. It's the old-fashioned hardy Woodbine, not great on flashy form or colour, but the scent's amazing.'

'Yeah, but it's called Woodbine because it binds wood. Throttles it. That's how they make those barley-twist walking sticks – get some honeysuckle creeping up a branch, and there you go.'

Ben opened the gate for her and gave her a tolerant smile.

'You knew that, didn't you,' said Rosie, hesitating beneath the trellis arch. 'What, are we going in here?'

Ben nodded.

'Is this what you wanted me to see?'

He nodded again.

'Well it's wonderful. But so what?'

'It's mine. I've been letting it out while I was working in London, but the tenants have moved on and at the moment there's no one in residence.'

Rosie digested this. She looked again at the thatch. It looked old, like ripe netted compost. 'Except for a few bats, I'd guess,' she said thoughtfully. 'And the odd collared dove or two. And maybe a few mice.'

'They come in every October,' said Ben with a smile. 'The mice. That thatch is their winter quarters.'

'Don't the tenants object?'

'They did a bit. I said I'd sort it.'

'And did you?'

'No. I like having them up there. I like listening to them when they scamper about at night. And they don't exactly outstay their welcome. By the spring, they're outside again.'

'I never had you down as soft-hearted,' said Rosie in some surprise.

'I don't suppose I am,' considered Ben. 'But why hurt something that isn't hurting you? Doesn't make any kind of sense.'

'Do you think that a winter sharing the thatch with rodents caused your tenants to flit?'

'Possibly.'

'Aha. Then you *are* soft-hearted. Those mice cost you money.'

'There'll be other tenants.' He shrugged. 'Short-term, preferably.'

'Why, are you thinking of moving back down here?'

'I'm going to do that, yes. And I'm going to buy that

field over there. The farmer who owns it, Bill Harris, and I, have an agreement. He'll sell it to me so that I can open my own plant-growing business, providing I can meet his price, and the price is non-negotiable.'

'And what is the price?' asked Rosie, fascinated.

Ben named a figure.

'Jesus! And are you getting close to it yet?'

'Close enough. With what I can raise and a bank loan, I'll get there. Or I was getting there.' Ben gave her a pointed look. 'Then you broke into my database and filched half my customers.'

Rosie's jaw dropped. She looked from Ben's suddenly set face to the cottage and back again. 'I didn't know,' she said lamely. Then defensively she added, 'How could I have known?'

'You didn't know, and you didn't care,' said Ben.

'That isn't true. I didn't know, right, that's true. But I thought you were pinching *my* business, remember? And I thought, OK, then, I'll pinch his. Tit for tat.' She scuffed her shoes and glanced down uncomfortably. Then she looked up at him. 'Look, I didn't know.'

'And now you do.'

Rosie shrugged awkwardly. 'I didn't know,' she repeated in confusion. One moment he had been the enemy, and now he was, well, what the hell was he? A very good lover? More than that? Less? She couldn't get her head around all this.

'Well.' She indicated the cottage and smiled her best, most winning smile. 'Aren't you going to invite me in for a cup of tea?'

Chapter Thirteen

Inside, the cottage was dark with ceiling beams and cool from the thickness of the walls. A big old-fashioned grandfather clock ticked somnolently in the hallways. Rosie preceded Ben into the sitting room. It was comfy enough, with its big open fireplace and chintzy chairs, but it had that sad vacant look that properties often get when they are uncared for by their occupants, or left empty.

'You know what you ought to do in here, according to feng shui principles?' said Rosie as she walked around the room. 'Ring bells in every corner, burn incense, make a helluva lot of noise. This place is too yang.'

'Too what?' Ben flopped down on the sofa.

'Yang. Too dark, too cool, too female. In other words –' Rosie came over and sat down next to him '– it needs doing up.'

'Oh damn!' Ben shot her a pained look. 'Don't tell me you're one of those tedious women who want to move the furniture round and distress the walls every six months?'

'Me? Distress walls?' Rosie guffawed. 'Listen, the only thing that'd get distressed if I took up decorating for a hobby would be me. I'd rather dig the garden.'

'Right.'

Silence fell. The clock ticked on.

'So,' said Rosie with a wide-eyed look, 'what's the bedroom like? Are you going to tell me there's a four-poster up there?'

'You guessed.'

'Really?' Even as a little girl, Rosie had dreamed of one day sleeping in a four-poster bed.

Ben nodded and gave her a look. 'Want to come and see?'

Ben gave Rosie a thorough tour of the rest of the cottage – which didn't take long, because it was tiny – and then escorted her to the bedroom, where they thoroughly road-tested the four-poster bed that nearly filled the little room.

'I didn't know, OK?' said Rosie as they lay tangled together in the big and absurdly comfortable bed. The four posts at its corners looked like very old oak, beautifully carved with corbels and laurel leaves and flying buttresses, all stained by age to a deep chocolate brown. Ben was on his back with his arm around her and she was lying half across him, one of her legs flung across his thighs. She felt that she could just about stay here for ever.

'So you said,' Ben murmured sleepily.

'I honestly didn't.'

'I know, you said.'

'It's the truth.'

'Uhuh.'

'Are you falling asleep on me?' asked Rosie, outraged.

'No, I'm falling asleep *underneath* you,' replied Ben, opening one eye to peer at her.

'Well, don't. We ought to discuss this.'

'I'm done with discussing, Rosie. Actions speak louder than words.'

Rosie let out a yell as he rolled, taking her with him. She pitched up at the end of the bed, her head inches from one big corner post. Ben crouched above her. They stared at each other for long moments, then he lowered his head and kissed her, and then he kissed her breasts, and then he kissed her belly, and pushed her legs open and kissed her clitoris, his tongue snaking out between his lips and licking the little bud.

Rosie watched him in rapture as he knelt between her legs, the fading daylight from the tiny cottage window staining his tanned skin to amber. Wow, he's so beautiful, she thought, watching the muscles moving under his skin, watching him grow flushed with arousal, watching his penis becoming erect again. Ben's mouth left her clit and she gave a little moan of protest, but his mouth came back to hers, and that was nice too. She could taste herself on his tongue. Oh, that was very nice.

She reached down and gave his cock a friendly squeeze with both hands. Encouragingly, she lifted her hips and twined her legs firmly about his waist. She kept on squeezing at him, stroking him, relishing the silken feel of his skin, dipping down further to feel the growing jut of his balls then slipping her hands up higher to feel the hot moisture at his tip.

'God, that's enough,' Ben groaned, and pushed his cock down between her wide-apart legs. He lingered for long aching moments over her clit, massaging it very firmly with his penis until Rosie was in a turmoil of lust.

'Hurry,' she panted, and Ben moved his hips back a little and dipped lower so that his glans came up against her cunt. He pushed in just a little, lodging his cock into her, then stopped again, panting and fighting for control.

'You want it right up?' he taunted through gritted teeth.

'Yes,' snarled Rosie, and took the matter out of his hands by lunging forward and down with her own hips and impaling herself upon him.

'Hot little bitch,' he murmured, closing his eyes in ecstasy.

Remaining kneeling between her legs, Ben leaned forward a little and grasped the bed's sturdy post in both hands to steady himself and give leverage. Taking a tight grip on the post, he started to thrust in and out of her. He pushed against the post when he pushed up, leaned back from the post when he drew nearly out of her.

'Oh, that's nice,' moaned Rosie, her eyes open,

watching him as he moved over her, watching the strong flex of his pectorals and glutei as he pushed and pulled against the post, watching his hips pistoning, watching his thick wheaty bush and the rhythmic flash of his thick sex-reddened cock she was being treated to every time he pulled back.

Oh, and the feel of him as he slammed back inside her! So hot, so full. His balls grew more and more prominent as his excitement mounted, slapping hard against her undercarriage with every thrust. This was wonderful. She lay back and felt like Nell Gwynn in a Restoration drama, being rogered by the horny king. And that made her think briefly about how many other women had been serviced in this old bed, how many children had been born in it, how many husbands had brandished erect cocks, pulled up nighties, whispering of their lust in the country darkness, parted soft female thighs, searched for that magical entrance to bliss, bared coyly covered breasts and squeezed them and kissed their nipples, sucked milk from them if the woman hadn't yet weaned the latest child.

She thought of Ben sucking milk from her breasts, thought of her breasts heavy and blue-veined and dark-nippled, transformed by child-bearing, her teats standing out very large and hard like a feeding-bottle for a baby.

Her mind went back again to those horny sons of toil, pushing the nighties aside, oh, yes, and then pushing the thighs open, and their cocks standing up ready – oh Jesus! Rosie pushed a desperate hand down into her bush, and rubbed her clit luxuriously as Ben pumped at her with growing franticness. Then they would spit in their rough hand and use that to moisten their cocks for easier entry, and then cocks and cunts would connect, and there would be that breathless, beautiful shove of male flesh, the hot pumping of blood as the lovers writhed and panted, the equally hot pumping of flesh in flesh, the spilling of milk from breasts as emotions and hormones rioted, the quick indecently hasty thrusting of hips until seed spilled and a new harvest was sown.

'Oh *God*,' wailed Rosie, and came like crazy, pushing herself down against Ben's lunging hips until he too could hold out no longer. He came and came and came, and then knelt there, head lolling against the post, panting heavily.

'You're such an animal,' Rosie complained mildly when she was able to think straight again.

'You weren't thinking of me at all, were you?' He was staring down at her in a peculiar way.

'What? Oh, well.' Rosie flushed guiltily. 'Just a little fantasy that kind of took over.'

'What sort of fantasy?'

'I can't tell you.' Now she was embarrassed.

'Another man?' He had that peculiar almost guarded look on his face again; she couldn't think what the hell was going on in that brain of his.

'Men,' she corrected ruefully.

'What men? Daniel? Luke? Someone else?'

'*Imaginary* men.' Rosie was getting a little tired of

this. She suddenly felt less like a Restoration heroine and more like a victim of the Inquisition.

'What the hell does that mean?'

Rosie sat up, frowning. He was actually *angry*.

'Look, it was no big deal,' she said irritably. 'It was the bed, that's all. I started thinking about all the other couples that must have had sex in it, and it, well, it turned me on rather a lot. As you could tell.'

'Oh.' Ben sank back on to the bed beside her.

'And then when you started using the bedpost, I lost it completely.' Rosie glanced at him. Suddenly the atmosphere was distinctly awkward between them. 'I wasn't thinking about any other man specifically,' she explained. 'The ambience of this place just got to me, that's all.'

A smile tugged at the corner of Ben's mouth. He lay back against the pillows. 'Tell me about it,' he ordered.

Rosie shook her head.

'Come on, tell me.'

'You only want me to talk dirty to you so that you can get your rocks off again, admit it,' said Rosie, as he dragged her down beside him.

'I admit it,' Ben said graciously. 'So tell me.'

'I fantasised I was Nell Gwynn.'

'I don't look anything like Charles the Second.'

'That isn't the point, this was a *fantasy*. And then I started thinking about this bed and women having babies in it, and women being fucked in it, and it all got rather graphic.'

'How about the men?' said Ben against her hair, his

hand whispering down over her shoulder to cup her breast. Rosie felt her nipple expanding like a flower.

'They were hard-working sons of the soil,' Rosie said sleepily.

'Oh, you go for that, do you?'

'I think we both know the answer to that one.'

'Did you know that until the nineteen thirties this was a gamekeeper's cottage?'

'Nope. Was it?'

'Yes. From talking to people in the area, I've found out that a family of eight lived here in Victoria's time.'

Rosie squirmed pleasurably as his hand stroked her breast. 'What, you think, in this bed?'

'It's probable. This fantasy.'

'Hm?'

'All these horny men.'

'Mm.'

'Give me a few more details.'

'You're such an *animal*,' said Rosie delightedly.

Chapter Fourteen

They stayed overnight, then drove back to London early the next morning, stopping at a service station to get an execrable all-day breakfast. Ben dropped her at her door, and Rosie crept inside in her ridiculously inappropriate party dress and fuck-me shoes. Sometime yesterday she had crammed her necklet and bangles into her little gold bag, so she was spared at least the humiliation of being caught out in broad daylight in full party gear. But she was pleased to get inside her flat and shut the world out. At least she thought she was shutting the world out, until she saw Lulu sitting there in front of the computer.

'Hey!' Lulu's grin of welcome was as warm as toast. Her eyes grew wide with incredulity as she saw what Rosie was wearing. 'You been wearing that ever since the party?' she demanded.

'Didn't have time to change,' Rosie said breezily, edging toward the bathroom.

'You get it on with Ben Hunter, you lucky girl?'

'Yes, I suppose you could say that.'

'Ha! I knew you two would hit it off eventually.'

'I wouldn't go that far.'

Lulu leaned forward confidentially. 'Seriously though, he's a great lay, isn't he? Everyone tells me what a great lay that man is. He is, isn't he?'

'He's very good in bed,' admitted Rosie, feeling herself blushing. Which was pretty absurd, considering what she'd been getting up to over the last twenty-four hours.

Lulu lowered her voice and leered engagingly. 'He's big, right? He's real big, would you say?'

'All right!' Rosie burst out angrily. 'He's massive. He's hung like a *mule*, is that what you want to hear?'

Lulu sat back, surprised. 'Just making conversation, that's all.'

'Well don't. I need a shower, so please just excuse me!'

To Rosie's annoyance, Lulu followed her into the bathroom and stood outside the shower cubicle, watching her while she soaped herself.

'Your first appointment's at eleven,' said Lulu.

'Right.'

'Mr Marriott.'

'Oh.'

Mr Marriott had been one of Ben's customers.

'Something wrong?'

'No.' Rosie soaped more vigorously.

'Is that a bite mark on your tit?' asked Lulu.

'Quite likely.'

'He likes that, huh? That man is some stud muffin, I'm telling you. He bite you when he's putting it in?'

'Yes,' said Rosie, to shut her up. Daniel had bitten her tit, not Ben.

'Wow.' Lulu had her arms crossed and was listening avidly. 'And?'

'What do you mean, *and*?'

'He like any other little things like that? He bite your ass? Bite your clit when he's tonguing it?'

Rosie closed her eyes. She had forgotten how casually detailed Lulu could be about the sex act. She opened her eyes. 'You really want to know? He tied me to a bed.'

'Hey, bondage. That's cool.'

'Then he refused to fuck me.'

'Restraint heightens pleasure,' said Lulu.

'But he fucked me with a vibrator.'

'Nice. That feel good?'

'He would have felt better.'

'But it was good anyway.'

'Lulu, the man made me piss in a pot right in front of him. He watched. And he said it was sexy.'

Lulu shrugged. 'Hell, that's nothing. I got one client, likes the girls to piss on *him*.'

'Then he brought in two of his workmen and ordered them both to have me.'

Lulu's eyes widened with interest. 'Phew! And did they?'

'They couldn't wait.'

'Which is understandable,' said Lulu, eyeing Rosie

sagely up and down. 'They get naked to stick it to you, or they just unzip?'

'Pass me that damned towel.' Rosie turned off the water. 'They got naked. I was naked and tied up, and they got naked too.' Rosie felt her clit twitch at the memory.

'So they were all three in the room, all having you one after the other?'

'Ben didn't. He just watched.'

'Was he naked too?'

'No, he was dressed.'

'Damn! That man looks so good naked. Those shoulders, those hips. That cock. His butt ought to be preserved in aspic. God, I'm getting horny. And then what?' Lulu passed Rosie a big pink towel and Rosie wrapped herself in it.

'Then he took me down to show me his place in Sussex.'

'Took you to meet his folks?'

'Hardly. He chased me into a bluebell wood and had me there.'

'Screwed you good, huh?'

'All right, I admit it, it was great.'

'And then?'

'He took me to the cottage he owns down there.'

'And then let me guess. More screwing? He get you through the door and drop his pants and play hide the sausage?'

'Yep.' Rosie was drying herself off.

'And?'

'There was a four-poster bed. Honestly, Lulu, by the time I got out of it this morning I could barely walk straight.'

'Whew!' Lulu took the wet towel from her as Rosie marched off nude into her bedroom. 'I gotta say, you are justifying all my faith in you. I just *knew* you'd make a good ho. Speaking of which, I gotta client for you at three today. Wants the full works. The cringing red-haired virgin. Think you can manage that, after all you've been up to, wringing poor Ben Hunter's cock dry, you naughty girl?'

'I can manage it,' said Rosie dryly.

'Well good for you. Now if you'll excuse me, I am off to the bathroom to have a quiet little fiddle, OK?'

'No! Wait Lulu.' Rosie looked awkward. 'I'm going to give him his client list back.'

Lulu let out a low whistle. 'He really got to you then.'

'No, he didn't get to me,' Rosie said hotly, stepping into clean jeans. 'It just feels like a dirty trick, that's all. Under the circumstances.'

'Yeah? And what circumstances are those?'

'He's trying to buy a plot of land in Sussex next to his property. He wants to start a nursery business. That's the only reason he's in London, to get enough cash together to make it all possible.'

'He got to you.'

'He did not.' Rosie tugged on a pink T-shirt. 'But I've got to live with myself, haven't I.' She snatched up a comb and started hauling at her red locks with it. 'And how could I, if I felt guilty about Ben all the time?'

'You're such a soft touch,' tutted Lulu.

'What, you think I should hold on to the list?'

Lulu shrugged. 'I think you may as well, now things are pretty much straightened out between you anyway. As insurance.'

'Insurance against what?'

'Against Ben pinching any more of your clients.'

'But I don't think he actually pinched any of them in the first place,' said Rosie, tossing the comb back on to the dressing table. 'I think you were right. I think he put round some flyers, and maybe those flyers had his photo on them, and Mrs Squires took the bait. And you know what? I don't even blame her. I would have done the same.'

'He got to you.' Lulu smiled. 'You going to see each other again?'

And then Rosie remembered that he had said nothing about that when he'd dropped her off here. Nothing at all.

'Well, I expect so,' she said casually. 'Of course we will.'

But a week later Ben still hadn't called. He hadn't phoned, he hadn't sent her a text, or a fax, or a fucking *e-mail* even, and her guilt over his client list had long since turned to seething resentment.

How could he? she wondered as she drove out to a job in Marlow. How the hell could he do that? Use her and then dump her? And how *dare* he do that. When they had been – well – so close. So intimate. She had thought they were sort of in tune with one another. She had thought they were getting along fine. But for him, obviously, the whole thing had been no more than one massive grudge fuck.

'Despicable bastard,' she muttered as she got her gear out of the van.

'Asshole.' She cursed him as she trotted around the side of the big mock-Tudor pile that backed scenically on to the river.

'Loser,' she snarled as she slapped the mower down on to the lawn.

'Who is?' asked an amused female voice behind her.

Rosie spun around, and was surprised to see the lovely dark-haired Joanne from Lulu's place standing there. She was wearing white slacks and a sugar-pink clingy top, short enough to show her tanned midriff and the little gold ring in her navel. Tan-coloured mules completed the ensemble, and made Rosie feel instantly dowdy. How Joanne looked, in her obviously expensive designer clothes and with her polished nails and flawless make-up, was *rich*. And of course she was. She remembered Ben telling her so.

'God, Joanne, you made me jump,' complained Rosie, slapping a hand to her chest. 'Is this – I mean, do you live here?'

'Yep.' Joanne said it with a small wistful sigh. She lifted an eyebrow at Rosie. 'I suppose Ben's told you about our arrangement?'

Clearly Joanne was referring to her clandestine meetings with Ben at Lulu's place. She nodded.

'Oh: Well, that's a relief. As you can see, my husband's very wealthy.'

'Yeah,' said Rosie.

'And I don't want to upset him.'

'No, of course not.' And lose your platinum credit card?

'Good. Glad we got that out of the way. More to the point, what are you doing here?'

'Well, a Mr Renwick contracted me to do the garden.'

'That's my husband Colin.' Joanne frowned. 'But why'd he do that? He usually leaves all the domestic arrangements to me. And the arrangement for the garden is that Ben from Countryman Gardens does it.'

'Well, he did,' Rosie said awkwardly. Mr Renwick had been on Ben's client list, and it had been Mr Renwick she'd approached – catching him in one evening and putting a proposition to him that he had eagerly taken up right then and there – and she'd had not the slightest idea that Joanne was *Mrs* Renwick. She hadn't realised that it was Joanne's husband she had seduced one evening in his conservatory, and really, this was terribly embarrassing, because she had intended to give the damned list back to Ben, but he hadn't called, and she had gotten good and mad at him, thus forgetting her resolution to do the decent thing and return the list, and this was all exceedingly awkward, and she now saw, with a sinking heart, that it was about to get even *more* awkward, because there was a red flatbed truck coming up the drive, and it looked worryingly familiar.

'Oh, here comes Ben now,' Joanne said calmly. 'We'll

soon get this straightened out. I'm sure it's all been nothing but a misunderstanding.'

'Sure,' muttered Rosie as the flatbed stopped on the gravel. Ben emerged, looking tall and tanned and every bit as edible as when she'd last seen him a week ago. He also looked pretty angry as he came around the side of the building to where the two women stood.

'What the fuck are you doing here?' he asked Rosie, confirming her suspicion that he was fuming.

'Doing the garden,' Rosie said stonily.

'Doing *my* client's garden,' corrected Ben. 'Do you know, I really thought you might have listened to everything I said, but you didn't take in a word of it, did you? You're still using my client list.'

'Look,' wailed Rosie, 'I spoke to a Mr Renwick.'

'So? Mr Renwick pays the account, so the account's in his name.'

'Well, I didn't know Mr Renwick was married to Joanne.'

'Does that matter?' Ben's eyes were frosty as they glared at her. 'The fact remains you are *still* poaching my clients, and I want it to stop.'

Well I would have stopped it, if you'd phoned me, you bastard, thought Rosie furiously. His angry stance was making her feel defensive and angry too.

'Well tough tit,' she shot out.

'You *what?*' roared Ben.

'Children, children.' Joanne stepped neatly between them, holding up placating hands on which glittered a great many expensive gold rings. 'Come along now, play nicely. Can't we resolve this amicably? Or at least discuss it like adults.'

'She isn't capable of behaving in an adult fashion,' Ben said tightly.

'*She?*' shrieked Rosie. 'What the hell am I? Something the cat dragged in?' Right this instant, standing beside the cool and immaculate Joanne while they talked over her head as if she were an idiot, that was certainly what she felt like.

'Well, you said it,' said Ben, looking at her scathingly.

'Bastard!'

'Bitch!'

'Ah.' Joanne pointed a stern finger at the air. 'Enough. Come on. Either you two behave, or I'll have to severely punish you both.' She looked at Ben reflectively. 'Actually, I think I'll start with you.'

To Rosie's surprise – and no small amount of outrage – the beautiful brunette twined herself around Ben and kissed him. And Ben didn't exactly beat her off. With a last glare at Rosie, he concentrated on Joanne, pulling her in against him and kissing her very thoroughly back.

Rosie turned away from them and folded her arms angrily, tapping her foot. If they wanted to play silly buggers, let them get on with it. She was here to cut the grass, not watch those two playing tongue-hockey.

'Come on,' said Joanne behind her. She felt a slap on her butt and whirled around irritably, suspecting Ben. In fact it was Joanne standing right behind her, still with her arm around Ben's waist. Joanne smiled at her warmly. 'Come *on*, Rosie. Lighten up.'

Freeing herself from Ben, Joanne grasped the hem of her sugar-pink top and in one swift movement pulled it off over her head and dropped it on the grass. Rosie's jaw dropped. Joanne wasn't wearing a bra. Rosie felt renewed awe as she looked at Joanne's gorgeous figure, at her very big but firm breasts, at their chocolate nipples crinkling a little in the cool breeze. Through each prodigious nipple there was a small gold ring.

'I didn't know you had nipple rings,' said Rosie in surprise.

'They're new.' Joanne looked down at her bountiful breasts proudly. 'They're still a bit sore, but they look great, don't they.' She looked up at Ben, then reached down and gave his burgeoning jeans-clad erection a playful tweak. 'Come on you two. Last one in the river's a sissy.'

And she ran off down to the water's edge, peeling off her slacks as she went. She wasn't wearing underpants either. Her pearly buttocks bounced alluringly as she charged down to the water. She kicked off her tan mules at the water's edge, and waded in.

'For God's sake,' mumbled Rosie, uncomfortable with the entire situation. Would her body stand comparison with the delectable Joanne's if she stripped off? She didn't think so. She ought just to pack up her equipment and get out of here and leave them to it, she thought. And yet her clit was twitching with interest at Joanne's display. Joanne's tits were wonderful. Was she turning into a lesbian or something?

'Terrific tits,' said Ben, echoing her thoughts as

Joanne turned, waist-deep in water, and waved at them, making her breasts swing heavily.

'If you like that sort of thing,' Rosie said coldly.

'Oh, come on.' Ben gave her a slight smile. 'You couldn't take your eyes off them. Admit it. You'd like to get your hands on them and see what they feel like. Kiss them. Rub your tits against hers. I bet that's a real turn-on for a woman.'

'What, like you rubbing your cock against another man's?' snapped Rosie.

'Hey, don't knock it 'til you've tried it.'

'You mean you *have*?'

'When I was in secondary school. In the showers after football. Sometimes someone would get a stiffy, more often than you'd think, actually, and we'd tease them.' He shot her that glinting smile again. 'Sometimes there was more than teasing, and things got a bit hot. There was this very good-looking boy called Nigel, and he got an erection, and I was at that unruly-hormones stage that teenagers go through.'

'I thought you were *still* at that stage,' Rosie said acidly.

He gave her that maddeningly tolerant smile. His turquoise eyes surveyed her calmly. 'You want to hear this or not?'

Rosie did, so she kept quiet.

'Anyway, it was the first time I'd ever seen another boy erect, ready for sex. My parents were the old-fashioned sort, all closed doors and no naked parading around the house. I'd seen animals, growing up in the country, but never another boy. I was amazed at how different his penis was from mine. He'd been circumcised as a baby. He was a roundhead, not a cavalier like me. And mine was sort of pink and red, but his was brown and mauve. His wasn't as big as mine, not his cock and not his balls either. I was pretty well-developed by then.'

'And?' prompted Rosie. Joanne was splashing about in the river now, she noticed.

'Well, I got excited looking at his cock, and soon my cock, much to my embarrassment, was in the same condition as his, standing up like fury. All the other boys noticed and started teasing us both, and then there was a lot of joking about how did men *do* it to one another, and before we knew it someone had posted a guard on the door and the other boys had grouped round us to watch, and we were getting ready to do it right there in the communal showers.'

Rosie was now listening in fascination. And feeling distinctly horny.

'Did he, um, put it up you?' she asked.

'No, I was the one eager to try getting it up another boy, not him.' Ben smiled, remembering. 'Nigel was sort of passive. He wanted to be fucked, not to fuck me. And I was happy to oblige. Hell, I was so highly sexed at that age, and no girl had yet agreed to have sex with me, I think I'd have covered a nanny goat if I could have got hold of one.'

'Go on.'

'One of the other boys found an old pot of Vaseline. I put a smear of it around Nigel's anus, poking my finger into him a bit, and he got extremely excited then and had to clutch at his cock to keep from coming off too quickly. I would have liked him to spread the Vaseline over my penis, but he was too far gone for that so one of the other boys did it. It was like a ceremonial anointing, and we were all naked as the day we were born, and there were more than just two stiff cocks in the room by then.'

'And?' Rosie was feeling flushed and aware of warm moisture seeping from between her legs. Just the thought of him as a horny teenager was enough to make her cream for him.

'Well, finesse went out the window after that. Nigel bent over a bit. I was surprised to see that his anus was sort of winking at me – he was very excited. I'd never done it before, so I pushed it up him as gently as I could, and I was amazed at how far in I could go, and how Nigel braced himself against the shower wall with one hand to take the impact of my thrusts, and I can remember even now how his shoulder-muscles bunched up, and how tight he was down there, and how he moaned and moved against me, and the water was falling down from the shower head on to his hair, plastering it to his skull, and one of the other boys was leaning in and jerking Nigel off, and all the rest of them were jerking *themselves* off. It was a highly sexual situation.'

'How about the poor chap keeping watch?' asked Rosie.

'Oh, he had his cock in his hand too,' Ben laughed. 'So as I say, don't knock one-sex sex. It's great. Speaking of which, I suppose you're aware that Joanne wants to get into your pants?'

I want to get into hers too, thought Rosie. First hers, then yours.

'Does she? Well, I might let her.'

'I want to watch.'

'Why, Ben!' Rosie affected a scandalised look. 'What on earth could you hope to see? Two sets of naked bouncing titties? Would you like that?'

'I think you already know the answer.'

'Well, why not?' Affecting sophisticated disdain, Rosie pulled off her T-shirt. Ben's eyes instantly went to her breasts, like filings pulled by a magnet.

'They're not as big as Joanne's,' he remarked. 'But I think they're a better shape. Higher and firmer.'

'Listen, do you think I care about your opinion?' she asked, coolly unbuttoning her jeans and quickly unzipping them.

'No, I don't.' Ben's voice was edged with permafrost.

'Good.' Rosie gave him a brittle smile. She kicked off the jeans, toed off her trainers, and then she was standing there stark naked. She put her hands on her hips and stared at him. 'Coming in?' she asked archly, and turned and strode down to the water.

'It's lovely, come on in,' called Joanne encouragingly from about twelve feet out.

It wasn't exactly lovely, thought Rosie as she braved the water. The current was quite fierce and the water was cold, but she didn't want to look like a fool by loitering palely on the bank while they had all the fun, so she gritted her teeth and waded deeper. When the water hit her groin, she gave a yelp, but kept going until it just brushed the tops of her nipples.

'God, it's *freezing*!' she complained to Joanne, aware that her teeth were chattering uncontrollably. The river bed felt horribly slippery, too.

'It takes some getting used to,' admitted Joanne. 'I swim in here most mornings.'

And she turned and swam strongly off parallel to the riverbank. Cursing under her breath, Rosie braved the water up to her shoulders and kicked off, following Joanne. She was a strong swimmer too, and she soon caught up with the brunette. There was a splash behind them and soon Ben was crawling level with them. All at once they were racing out to the small island in the middle of the river, and Rosie did her best to keep up, but she knew she was outclassed. As Ben got into his stroke, even Joanne had to accept second place.

Well, at least the exertion had warmed her up, thought Rosie as she watched Ben trudge out of the water and on to the little island. Really, the man was ludicrously good-looking, even from the back. *Especially* from the back. Such broad shoulders, such narrow hips, and those buttocks. She was enthralled by all of him.

Joanne crawled out next, laughing and streaming water, her long dark hair sleek to her head and slicked down her back.

'God, you two are slow,' teased Ben, giving Joanne a hand up the bank and on to the grass.

Rosie was the last to arrive, and she obstinately

turned her head away when Ben would have helped her out too. Shrugging, he sat down on the grass beside a panting Joanne and let Rosie struggle out as best she could. Rosie tried to ignore their eyes on her body as she joined them. If they could be cool, so could she. She collapsed on to the grass beside Ben.

'Blimey, you two are fit,' she complained.

'It's easy to be fit when you're rich,' said Joanne offhandedly. 'You can afford personal trainers, your own personal gym, massages, anything you need. Money's the key to it all.'

'But you could get fit without it,' Rosie said mildly. 'Ben doesn't put in any gym time – do you?'

'Nope.' Ben lay back on the grass. Rosie tried – and failed – not to stare at his cock. Even after immersion in the chill river water, it was still a good size. She looked up, and her eyes met Joanne's. Joanne smiled a secret co-conspirator smile at her.

'Neither do I. The gardening keeps me fit.' Rosie shot Joanne a grin as Joanne carefully wrung out her hair. 'Hey, Joanne, this is the answer to all your problems. Fire your gardener and do it yourself. You'd be saving a packet and getting free fitness into the bargain.'

'Ah, but I don't *want* a bargain,' Joanne said sweetly. 'I like all my indulgences. I like the fact that I'm expensive to run. My husband likes it too. I am the outward evidence of his success. Like his expensive car and his big house.'

'Is that why you do the whoring on the side?' asked Rosie, interested. 'As a sort of rebellion against him?'

Joanne laughed throatily. 'No, I don't. I just like whoring, that's all. It's fun. And you have to admit –' she glanced down at her ample charms '– I'm perfectly built for it.'

'Are they real? Not plastic?' asked Rosie, riveted by Joanne's awesome naked breasts.

'See for yourself,' invited Joanne, leaning over Ben so that Rosie could grab a feel.

Rosie put out a hand and stroked it down over Joanne's left breast. The nipple ring caught at her fingers, and the nipple was puckered from the cold water. Joanne's breast felt very cool. Experimentally, Rosie squeezed the big orb and then pushed at it lightly, so that it swung.

'Feels real,' she admitted.

'Feels good too,' said Ben, lying back with his eyes closed.

'Ben loves my breasts,' Joanne said confidingly. 'Sometimes he likes to have me fully clothed, with just my tits naked.'

'They are beautiful,' Rosie said admiringly, still stroking at Joanne's left breast.

'There are *two* of them,' Joanne said encouragingly, so Rosie knelt up, leaned over Ben, and fondled both Joanne's breasts.

'Does that feel good?' she asked tentatively, as Joanne leaned into the caress.

'Lovely. A bit harder. Rub your thumbs over my nipples. They're sore and it's made them very sensitive.'

Rosie obliged. She noticed that Ben had opened his

eyes and was watching them. She looked down at his crotch. His penis was stirring and standing up. Her eyes went to his face, and his eyes locked with hers. Joanne let out a sigh and her head fell back, her eyes closing in rapture. Ben reached up and grasped Rosie's breasts in his hands, echoing her movements as she attended to Joanne.

'I know,' said Joanne, after a small amount of pleasurable time had elapsed. 'Let's take turns on Ben, Rosie.'

'Fine by me,' murmured Ben.

'You first,' said Joanne.

Rosie was certainly wet enough. She let go of Joanne's breasts while Ben kept both hands on her own. She flipped one leg over Ben's hips and put both hands down on to his straining penis, rubbing it to even greater hardness.

'Oh,' said Ben, squirming up against her.

'Easy, Tiger,' breathed Rosie. She pushed his cock until the tip connected with her entrance, then she pushed vigorously down on to him, wriggling her hips hard on to his. She crouched over Ben, gasping a little because it felt so good holding him inside her. He was squeezing her breasts. She lifted up, preparing to push back down and take them hurtling along the path to climax.

'No, not so fast,' warned Joanne. 'Get off him now.'

With a sigh of regret Rosie lifted her leg like a rider dismounting. As she did so, Ben's cock came free of her body.

'Look at that, isn't that the most gorgeous erection you've ever seen?' Joanne cooed admiringly as she now flung a leg over Ben's hips. His cock, wet from Rosie, gleamed slickly and quivered with need.

Joanne sat down on Ben so that her bush tickled his aroused organ tantalisingly. Ben moaned. Chuckling excitedly, Joanne grabbed his penis and hovered for one long moment above it before plunging her hips down so that he pushed up into her.

'Oh, so good,' she groaned. 'Come on, Rosie, do it to me.' She guided Rosie's hand to her moist dark bush. Rosie sank her fingers beneath the thick curls and found the little nub of Joanne's clitoris. She rubbed it. Its skin was soft, its substance hard.

'Is that good too?' Rosie asked.

'Mm,' said Joanne.

'Well tough, get off him, it's my turn.' Rosie pushed Joanne aside.

Ben's cock came free of the lovely brunette and instantly Rosie fell upon him like a harpy and bundled his cock eagerly up inside her. She pushed merrily up and down. Oh, he was huge. It was wonderful.

'Enough,' said Joanne, and Rosie was unseated. Joanne took her position on top of Ben, and skewered herself like a kebab on his reddening penis.

'Jesus, what are you two doing to me?' groaned Ben, writhing beneath their ministrations.

'Fucking you in tandem,' grunted Joanne, lunging down on to his cock quite violently until she was abruptly replaced by Rosie.

'Gang-banging you,' added Rosie, and plunged down on to his dick. Fearing that Joanne was about to push her off, she went at it with gusto, thrusting down on to him very fast, pumping at him like fury. Her breasts bounced madly as she pleasured him, hands on her own thighs, her concentration upon the task absolute.

But again Joanne insisted on her share. She nudged Rosie aside and reclaimed her seat on Ben's penis. She too now thrust faster, panting as she did so.

'Oh, he's getting bigger,' she murmured, flushed with delight.

Rosie reached behind Joanne's pistoning buttocks and grasped Ben's balls, squeezing them encouragingly. Ben gave a loud moan and his hand snaked down, grabbing Rosie's thigh, then creeping around to her buttock. He found her crack, and then infiltrated it, shoving a finger up into her. Rosie shuddered as his thumb pressed firmly on to her clit, and she quite forgot that it was her turn to mount him. They continued just as they were, Joanne pleasuring Ben, Ben bringing off Rosie, until both Ben and Rosie came with shouts of delight. Then Joanne lay back and let Ben bring her to orgasm.

Exhausted, they all slumped on to the bank, Rosie on Joanne's left, Ben on Joanne's right.

'This is heaven,' murmured Rosie.

'Mm,' agreed Ben.

'You see?' said Joanne, stifling a yawn of repletion. 'You two *can* get along.'

There was a silence.

'I don't hear anyone rushing to agree with me.' Joanne tutted.

Still silence.

'I tell you what.' Joanne lifted Rosie's hand, and Ben's too; then she put them across her body and joined them together. Both Ben and Rosie turned their heads and looked at her curiously. 'How about this for a terrific idea? Instead of all this aggravation between you two, how about a little harmony for a change?'

'Meaning?' asked Rosie.

'Use your head. Instead of fighting over the clients, why not pool your resources? Why not combine your two businesses into one, and both reap the benefits?'

Rosie sat up. 'What, you mean work *together*?'

'Why not? The female clients adore Ben. The male clients lust after you. Doesn't it make perfect sense?'

'No,' said Rosie, scrabbling to her feet. 'No way. Not ever. My business is *mine*.'

'Ditto,' said Ben, sitting up and glaring at her.

'Look, it's just an idea,' Joanne said defensively.

'It's a stupid idea,' Rosie told her, and turned and waded back into the river. 'I'm going to get on with the lawn,' she flung back at them.

Chapter Fifteen

So now you're *not* going to give him his list back,' said Lulu as she and Rosie sat comfortably sipping coffee in Lulu's kitchen a couple of days later. 'Is that right? Just so I can get the situation clear in my mind.'

'He hasn't called me,' said Rosie, as if that were explanation enough.

'So? This isn't exactly a standard boy-meets-girl dating scenario we have here, unless it's escaped your attention.' Lulu poured more coffee for them both from the cafetiere. 'This is not a "oh should we kiss on the first date and maybe grope on the second and maybe, *maybe*, get into bed on the third" type of thing.'

'What?' Rosie took another chocolate digestive.

'Whoa on those biscuits, girl, I don't want no fat ho servicing my clients, thank you so very much,' Lulu chided her. 'No look, what we have here is *passion*. What we have here is *fireworks*.'

'All right, I'll admit to that,' said Rosie.

'You might fight him, but you want him too, am I right or am I right?'

'You're right.' Rosie dunked her biscuit.

'And he's mad as hell at you, but he wants you in bed every time he sees you.'

'Yeah,' said Rosie. Half her biscuit fell off into her cup. She stared at it dismally. 'But Lulu, he hasn't *called* me.'

'Will you stop with this calling business? Who gives a fuck either way? He hasn't called you because what he has here is a major conflict going on. You're standing between him and his life's ambition. But he kind of *likes* the fact that you're presenting an obstacle. He admires you for standing up to him, even while he'd like to kick your sorry ass for doing so. He thinks you're sexy as hell. Whether he'd admit to it, or not, he's relishing the fight. And he took you back to his home in Sussex, didn't he.'

'Yeah, so what?' Rosie was fishing around with a teaspoon, trying to rescue her biscuit.

'Home's a special place to a man like Ben. You think he'd take just *anyone* back there? Because I am here to tell you, he wouldn't.'

'So where does all this leave me?' sighed Rosie.

'With half a biscuit, sticky fingers and a ruined cup of coffee,' joked Lulu, trying to get Rosie to smile.

Rosie didn't smile. 'Joanne suggested we work together,' she said.

'Joanne's one very sensible girl,' said Lulu. 'Why don't you two hotheads follow her advice?'

'We'd kill each other within the first week,' Rosie predicted gloomily.

'Oh, probably,' allowed Lulu. 'But what a way to go!'

'I really, really hate that man,' said Rosie, slapping the teaspoon down on the table.

'Just keep saying it,' said Lulu, standing up and taking the cups to the sink. 'Sooner or later, you'll start believing it.'

'I hate that red-haired bitch,' Ben told Sally as she painted him in her little garden studio the following week.

'Sure.' Sally looked at his naked and tumescent groin. 'Is that the reason you've got an erection?'

'No, the reason I've got an erection is because you always paint in the nude. And it gives me ideas.'

'Right.' Sally daubed a little chrome yellow on to the canvas from her palette. Her naked breasts – rather less exuberant than Joanne's, and certainly smaller than Rosie's – jiggled prettily as she applied the brush. She squinted at him. 'Happily it doesn't matter for this canvas. I want you erect for this one.'

'Oh good,' said Ben dryly.

'Did you bring me those hosta plants you promised?'

'They're in the truck.'

'Thanks. Can you just think about Rosie for a second?'

'Why?'

'Because you get harder.'

'Ha. Ha. Ha.'

'Not amused, huh? She's really got to you, hasn't she.'

'Someone actually suggested we work *together*. Can you believe that?'

'Ha!' Sally let out a shriek of laughter. 'You'd both be dead in a week,' she predicted. 'And not from digging borders.'

'It's a ridiculous idea,' said Ben, settling back a little on the sheet-draped chaise longue.

'No, don't move for God's sake,' complained Sally.

Ben tried to settle down. He felt unusually agitated, and acutely irritated at the way Rosie kept sneaking unbidden into his head. What was going on here? Was he actually *falling in love* with Rosie? The very idea horrified him. At the same time, it had a sort of lunatic appeal. He kept having this mad vision of her meeting him at the door of the cottage in Sussex, with a blond baby perched on her hip. The fact that it was a *blond* baby alerted him to the fact that this was obviously *his* baby. He had never before even considered the idea of children. He had certainly never before considered the idea of a specific woman bearing his children, or occupying the place he thought of as exclusively *his* home. But here he was, and here this vision was, this funny little daydream, and what frightened him shitless was that it kept drifting into his mind more and more often, and he wondered if he might be going mad.

'What I need,' Ben said thoughtfully, 'is to get my mind off her. Distract myself.'

Sally said, 'Good idea,' and since he was looking

dreamily out of the window, she allowed herself a secret smile and a small pitying shake of the head. Poor sap. He was in love, and he didn't even have the sense to realise it.

It had been a busy day for Rosie. A Thursday. A day of morning gardening, giving a large pond its spring clean, furnishing it with new plants: bog iris, a pink water lily, some trendy zebra-striped horsetail. Candelabra primulas on the pond margins, and skunk cabbage for foliage appeal, and shoring up the shelf so that wildlife could get in and out easily. Then shagging Mr Copeland, the pond's owner, in his summer-house, and spanking him with her muddy trowel, which he seemed to enjoy a great deal.

The afternoon was taken up at Lulu's, ostensibly in entertaining a sixteen-year-old whose father had come to Lulu to get the boy 'a good start in life'. Nudge, nudge, wink, wink. Lulu said she had just the thing, a real lady, (not a virgin, Rosie noted with some amusement, because what good would a virgin be to a boy who needed showing the ropes?) and red haired too. Did the boy like red hair?

The boy *loved* red hair, that much was obvious right from the outset. When he was admitted to Rosie's boudoir, where she was reclining on the bed in her usual white-basque-and-pearls-and-lacy-stockings get-up, he closed the door behind him and just stood there and stared.

Rosie gave him an encouraging smile. Well, at least

he was an attractive boy. He was at that delicious stage of development when he almost, *almost* had the look of a man. But not quite. Big-boned and almost six feet tall, he had that gangly awkward look still, which he would lose over the next couple of years.

Really, he was going to be a very handsome man indeed. She liked his clear pale skin, his short-cropped curly dark hair. His eyes were a deep navy blue and they were keenly intelligent. He was wearing jeans and a blue open-necked shirt worn loose outside his trousers.

'Well, come in,' said Rosie, smiling. 'I don't bite. Unless you want me to.'

Flushing, he came nearer to the bed. This, thought Rosie, was going to be a doddle. He was going to be putty in her hands. He was going to be – and then he took a flying leap at the bed, and landed half on top of her. Winded, Rosie was about to try to draw breath for a shout when he started kissing her furiously and fumbling at her G-string, trying to yank it down.

For God's sake! Some doe-eyed innocent *this* was. She felt her rope of fake pearls give way and the beads went twanging off in all directions.

'Slow down,' she managed to gasp out when she could get some air.

'Shut up, hooker!' snarled the boy.

I'm a rotten judge of character, thought Rosie, and brought her knee up sharply. The boy let out a heartfelt cry and finally stopped what he was doing. Instead, he curled into a foetal position and clawed, groaning, at his wounded balls. Rosie got up, slipping and sliding on escapee pearls, and marched over to the door, flinging it wide.

'Lulu!' she yelled.

Lulu came at the gallop, and took in the scene at a glance.

'You OK?' she asked urgently.

'Still the resident virgin,' said Rosie, feeling, now that her moment of fright was over, that the whole thing was hilarious.

'Little fucker,' muttered Lulu, descending on the bed and grabbing the boy's ear, yanking him off her furnishings and out the door. Rosie toed the door shut behind them, hearing Lulu and her captive moving off along the passage, Lulu cursing, the boy saying he'd tell his dad.

What on earth am I doing here? wondered Rosie. I'm a gardener, not a whore.

When Lulu had dispatched the boy out the door, Rosie sauntered out to the kitchen and said to Lulu, 'That's it. I quit.'

'What, because of that little toad?' demanded Lulu.

'No, because I'm not cut out for the work. I can't take it seriously. I can only take gardening seriously, as a matter of fact.'

'Well.' Lulu sat down at the kitchen table and ran her eyes over Rosie. 'I'll sure as hell be sorry to lose you, girl.'

'Yeah, but I won't be sorry to go,' said Rosie, and she went to get changed back into her normal clothes.

*

On Friday, Ben called her up on the phone. She was in the office with Lulu and was so surprised when she snatched the phone up and heard Ben's voice on the other end that she almost dropped it.

'I thought I'd give you a call,' said Ben, sounding not particularly enthusiastic to be doing so.

'Hey, don't bust a gut, Hunter,' said Rosie, while Lulu watched her keenly. As Lulu heard Ben's surname, she started waving her hands around and making urgent 'don't-say-that-for-God's-sake' mouthings at Rosie, who paid her no attention at all.

'Look, are you going to be civil about this or not?' snapped Ben.

'That very much depends on what you've got to say.'

'Come to dinner with me.'

'What?' She had expected insults, threats, anything, but not that.

'Come and have dinner, if you feel you can manage a whole evening without snarling at me.'

'I wouldn't swear to that,' muttered Rosie, feeling almost light-headed with shock. 'Dinner where exactly? Because I'm not coming to Janina's flat, no way. You'd tie me to the bed again or some such damned thing.'

'Dinner in a *restaurant* is what I meant before you charged in with both feet,' Ben said tightly.

'Which restaurant?' asked Rosie, determined to be difficult. 'Only I'm a fussy eater.'

Lulu raised her eyebrows at Rosie. Rosie would eat a barn door between two bits of bread, if it tasted nice. Fussy she was not.

'Box of Delights in Camden Town,' said Ben. 'I've heard they've got a new chef there, Micky Quinn, and he's red hot. Married the owner, Venetia Halliday, and moved in just recently, apparently.'

'Well, OK,' said Rosie.

'Hey, don't bust a gut,' Ben said sarkily. 'I'll pick you up tomorrow at eight, how's that?'

'OK,' said Rosie.

'See you, then.'

'Yep.'

Rosie put the phone down. Then she threw her arms in the air and did a wild little dance around the room.

'So you're not that excited about the idea then?' Lulu observed dryly.

'He asked me out! He asked me out on a real, one hundred per cent real, ordinary date! Can you believe that?' Rosie screeched to a halt. 'What the *hell* am I going to wear?'

'Your bronze party frock's nice.'

'And my hands, look at the state of my hands.' Rosie was staring at her digits as if a surgeon had removed her hands and replaced them with those of an axe murderer. 'No, I can't wear that old bronze thing again. He saw it just the other day. I need a new dress. I need a manicure. I need new shoes.'

'You need to calm down,' advised Lulu, rising and steering Rosie kindly into her own vacated chair. 'Cool it, Rosie. He's phoned, and that's what you wanted. Deep breaths now. D-e-e-p breaths.'

Rosie inhaled deeply. Then out. Then in. She felt a

bit calmer, but it was worrying how her face kept trying to arrange itself into a manic grin of delight. At this rate she'd throw herself straight into his arms tomorrow night, and she wanted to be sophisticated, cool, hip. She wanted to knock him bandy with her poise and chic. She didn't want to be the gauche blushing Rosie he knew, with dirt under her fingernails and grass stains on her butt.

'I've got to go up west,' she said after a few relaxing minutes.

'Want some company?'

'Hell, yes. No. Wait. Am I free this afternoon?'

'As a bird.'

'Then let's do it. The works. I want to knock that arrogant bastard flat on his gorgeous ass when he sees me.'

Lulu gave a conspiratorial grin. 'You're the boss.'

Chapter Sixteen

When Rosie opened the door of her flat to Ben the following night, it was hard to say who got the bigger surprise. Ben was wearing a navy suit and a shirt and tie. He looked like a prosperous businessman instead of a gardener, and he was holding a bouquet of two dozen ginger-toned and sweetly scented Whisky Mac roses edged with white fronds of baby's breath and tied with apricot silk ribbons.

'Hi,' he said, eyeing her up and down and sending her heart stampeding about like a wild mustang.

'Hello,' Rosie said coolly.

She knew she looked cool. She knew she had succeeded in surprising him. Lulu had guided her around the shops yesterday like a woman with a purpose, which is exactly what she was.

'I have a plan here,' Lulu had said, steering Rosie past anything even faintly loud. 'We are talking Audrey Hepburn. Something simple and stylish and black. With your colouring you'll look just fantastic in black, with some of those ravishing black kitten heeled shoes, and lots of big pearls around your throat, and your hair up on top in a French pleat, and those nails, my God, we are talking disaster, but nothing a manicurist can't fix. Opalescent polish. Very restrained, I think. And you've gotta wear some make-up. Coral lipstick, toffee-toned blusher. Eyeliner too, just a thin line with a little flick-up at the end, accentuate those pretty green eyes.'

Very little input had been required of Rosie. She just nodded, or sat still, or followed Lulu as she cut a swathe along Oxford Street. And now she stood here greeting Ben at the door, a svelte and stylish goddess, and she could see by the look on his face that all Lulu's efforts had not gone to waste.

'You look different,' said Ben, in massive understatement.

'So do you.' She took the flowers and went through to the kitchen, filling the sink and plunging their stems into water. 'Lovely roses,' she said.

'They're the same colour as your hair,' said Ben.

'I noticed.'

'Ready to go?'

Rosie picked up her terracotta wrap from the sofa, and her little black beaded bag, which had cost enough to make her gasp. Then she followed Ben out of the door and down to where he had parked the Mercedes.

She loved Box of Delights. The building was ancient and thick with atmosphere, and the staff there were both knowledgeable and friendly. They both started with pan-seared scallops, and the food turned out to be marvellous. But the atmosphere between them was not so good. It was stilted. They hardly spoke. Through pepper-crusted lamb with samphire, and apple charlotte with vanilla cream, there was a distinct chill in the air. When coffee and chocolates arrived Ben said, 'This isn't working, is it?'

Rosie shrugged uneasily. 'I don't know what you mean exactly.'

'This. Us trying to act like a normal couple. Because we're not, are we?'

'Hardly,' snorted Rosie.

'So shall we stop all this pretence and cut to the chase?'

Rosie looked at him. His light-blue eyes glittered like ice in the candlelight. The soft light accentuated the depth of his tan. His hair gleamed. Her stomach flipped slowly over. Wow, he was so good-looking. Lots of other women in the restaurant had looked at him with interest, but she noticed that he had not returned their interest in the slightest. He seemed to be brooding over something. At which point in the evening to throttle her, probably.

'Suits me,' she said as casually as she could.

'I want that list back.'

'OK,' said Rosie.

'What?' Ben looked at her in amazement.

'I said OK.'

'But you've been refusing to give it back. Why the sudden change of heart?'

Because you called me, thought Rosie. Because you took me out to dinner, treated me nicely for a change; and now it's sunk into my thick skull that you've only done this as a last-ditch attempt to get your damned client list back, after which you're going to drop me like a hot potato.

Aloud, she said, 'Does it matter? You'll get it back, if that's what you want.'

'What I *want*?' Ben looked at her as if she'd gone crazy. 'I've been chasing that list for weeks. And you've been refusing to hand it over. And now, without any warning, you're prepared to give it up just like that. So I'd like to know why.'

'Well, tough,' Rosie said sharply, biting into a chocolate with unnecessary violence.

'You're such a bitch,' said Ben, sitting back in his chair and staring at her as if she were an incomprehensible alien species.

'Yep,' said Rosie, demolishing another chocolate.

'You're not even going to apologise for stealing it, are you?'

'You started this, not me.'

'Jesus, she's off again,' said Ben to the ceiling.

'Don't talk to me like that.'

'Like what?'

'Like I'm a moron!'

'Oh, I don't think you're a moron,' Ben said nastily. 'Actually I think you're a very smart operator.'

'You mean, a scheming little cow.'

'If you like.'

'No, I *don't* like,' spat Rosie, glaring at him.

'Did you enjoy your meal?' said a tall and elegant honey-blonde woman who had arrived silently beside their table. She looked in concern from one to the other. 'I'm Venny Quinn, the co-owner. If there's anything wrong . . .?'

'There's nothing wrong,' Ben assured her charmingly.

'It was a wonderful meal,' said Rosie. 'Please give our compliments to the chef.'

'Micky will be pleased you enjoyed it,' said Venny, and glided off to fetch their bill.

Ben watched her go. 'What a gorgeous woman,' he said imprudently.

'Yes, isn't she,' agreed Rosie with a tight smile.

Ben turned his attention back to his companion. 'And sweet-tempered.'

'Bound to be.'

'And elegant.'

'Hey, *I* can do elegant.'

'Did I say you couldn't?' Ben shot her a half-smile.

'This dress isn't easy to wear, you know,' Rosie fumed. 'And this underwear *itches.*'

'I didn't think you wore underwear,' said Ben in surprise.

'I'm making an effort here.'

'Right.' Ben looked amused.

'Don't smirk at me,' warned Rosie.

'I was smiling at you.'

'Why?'

'Because you make me smile. When you're not making me want to break your neck.'

'Your bill,' said Venny, drifting back to their table.

'Thank you,' said Ben, giving her an even more dazzling smile.

'You don't smile at me like that,' said Rosie when Venny had gone.

'Like what?' Ben fished out his credit card.

'Like I was in full possession of my faculties.'

Ben let out a laugh. 'I like your faculties,' he said, giving her a meaningful look. 'What few of them there are.'

'You're such a bastard,' said Rosie, but she was unable to hide a grin.

'All part of my charm.'

'I like your charm,' returned Rosie. She kicked off her shoe and lifted her leg so that her foot rested on his crotch under the cover of the tablecloth. 'What little you've got.'

'I don't think it's my charm you're interested in,' Ben said thoughtfully.

'You catch on fast.' Rosie kneaded the growing outline of his cock with her toes.

'Don't start anything you don't intend to finish,' Ben warned.

'Don't be so jumpy,' said Rosie, kneading harder.

Venny came back and took the bill and Ben's credit card. Ben's smile this time was rather strained. Rosie's toes were making inroads into his restraint. The feel of him and the obvious effect she was having on him were eating into Rosie's decorum too. She was feeling distinctly hot by the time they left the restaurant. By the time they had got into the Mercedes, she felt ready to rock and roll. And Ben didn't seem inclined to hold back, either. Under the cover of darkness and in the leather-scented comfort of the big expensive car, he leaned over and kissed Rosie until her head spun. And while he kissed her, his hand delved around her back, loosening the zip of the dress. He pulled it off her shoulders and down her arms, then sat back.

'Good God, black underwear,' he murmured, and kissed her again.

'I told you I was wearing underwear,' said Rosie between heated kisses.

'Black lace,' observed Ben, running one hand over the flimsy fabric. 'And it scratches?'

'Something awful,' admitted Rosie.

'Take it off then.' He bit her lower lip gently. 'Take your pants off too.'

'I'll take the bra off,' said Rosie. 'But not the pants.'

'Why, are you worried I'll jump you the minute your cunt's uncovered?'

'I'm not worried you will, I *know* you will.' Rosie fiddled behind her with the clasp. 'Why do women wear these things anyway? They're excruciating.' She yanked the clasp open and shrugged the bra off down her arms. 'Oh Jesus, the relief,' she moaned, rubbing at her abused skin.

'Let me help you with that,' said Ben, and grabbed a handful of tit.

'What if someone comes by?' asked Rosie anxiously. They were parked in a road, one car among many other parked cars, but occasional pedestrians walked past. There was just enough light cast by a distant street lamp for them – and others – to see what they were doing, and she was sitting here stripped to the waist, her naked breasts being fondled and her nipples sticking out like crazy.

'They'll think I'm a very lucky man,' said Ben, and got back to the serious business of kissing her senseless while his hands moved over her breasts, pushing them up, clasping them warmly, squeezing them, pinching her nipples.

'Oh, I love it when you do that,' groaned Rosie, leaning back against the upholstery as his mouth took over from his probing fingers. As he tongued her breast, causing arrows of pleasure to shoot down from nipple to clit, his fingers pushed up under her dress. Rosie was glad she hadn't worn tights; but she was wearing some black lacy hold-up stockings, and when his fingers hit that strip of bare silky skin above them she nearly went into orbit.

Rosie clutched at his neck as he licked and bit at her aroused nipples, and she felt his hand move up quite roughly, until he could grasp the thin triangle of material that covered her bush and pull it down.

'I said I wasn't going to take my pants off,' said Rosie breathlessly, feeling a flood of wetness down there as he yanked them down to her knees.

'That's OK.' Ben grinned, his teeth a flash of white

in the half-darkness. 'I've done it for you.'

And he pulled the pants down to her ankles, and off. Instantly his hand returned to her crotch, smoothing down over her bush and into her well-lubricated crack to tweak her clitoris into a frenzy.

'Oh God,' Rosie wailed hopelessly.

'Come on,' said Ben urgently, and pulled her up and across him, so that she straddled his lap. It wasn't exactly comfortable – she was almost crushed against the steering-wheel, but there was room enough for her to unzip him, and to take out his towering penis.

Ben grasped her breasts as she speared herself upon his cock. Their panting breaths seemed to fill the car's warm interior as Rosie pushed down eagerly. Realising that Ben couldn't move in this position, she took the initiative, pumping her hips madly up and down on his engorged organ, enjoying the feel of its heat and size slipping and sliding in and out of her as she moved.

Ben squeezed her breasts and licked her nipples as she continued to ride him, grasping his shoulders to steady herself. Ben's fingers snaked back between her wide-spread legs. She felt his fingers at the point where they were joined, curiously touching his own sex-slippery pole as she moved up and down on it, then touching her opening and pushing an experimental finger in beside his cock to feel her, so open, so excited. And then his thumb settled over her clit and rubbed at her with unexpected briskness. Rosie let out a cry and pumped at him harder.

Desperately aroused now, Ben leaned back and

watched in the very subdued light as she rode him to orgasm, her breasts bouncing madly, her head thrown back, gasping and groaning, completely self-absorbed. God, she really loved sex with him. And he loved having her. He felt his orgasm hovering now, threatening to overtake him; his cock was too sensitised to stand much more of this; his balls felt as if they were bursting, pushing up so that every time she slapped down onto his cock, they connected with her ass. The sensation was acutely arousing. His wetness was mingling with hers. They were both breathless, both clinging and clutching at each other. He kept his thumb firmly on her clit, pushing and rubbing and pinching at her little magic button as she bounced up and down on his cock. She felt so delicious. So tight and yet so accommodating; so wet and yet she was grasping him firmly, taking him in, in, in, with a kind of relentless rhythm until there was only one possible outcome.

He felt his climax erupt then, his balls contracting – oh God, such a feeling – and then the pleasure spilling over like bubbling champagne, the pressure so intense in his cock and then releasing, releasing. The contractions made him moan and writhe and clutch at her hips to keep her there, open, willing, waiting to receive him, and the mad hot spurt of his seed into her, again and again, in endless spasms of excruciating pleasure so that his thumb on her clitoris was suddenly rough, almost hurtful. Rosie screamed and came so that he felt her contractions too, felt her pleasure, felt her soft acceptance of all he had to give.

*

They drove back to Rosie's place not long after that, in silence. The earlier awkwardness of the atmosphere between them had descended again. She had half expected that he would take her back to Janina's flat, but no, he took her back to Richmond. He did come and see her to the door, but said he wouldn't stop for coffee. He seemed thoughtful, reflective.

'I suppose you want your list back now,' said Rosie, when he was about to turn and go.

'Oh.' Ben paused. 'Yeah, OK.'

Rosie went through to the office, unlocked the desk drawer and took out the list. She went back into the hall. Ben was still standing just inside the open door. This is it, she thought. This is where the fun stops.

She gave him the list.

Ben looked at it, and then at her. 'This is it, then,' he said, echoing her thoughts.

'I guess so.'

'No reason for us to bother each other any more.'

'None at all.'

'Well, thanks. Goodnight.'

And he went, just like that. Rosie closed the door behind him. Well, that was the end of it. And she told herself that she was glad. She went through to the kitchen and looked at the roses in the sink. She got a vase out from the cupboard and grabbed the scissors from the drawer. She filled the vase with water from the tap and unwrapped the ginger ribbons and peeled off the lime-coloured tissue paper. She started snipping the rose stems off on the diagonal to make them keep better, humming a cheesy old song under her breath as she did so. It was 'Everything's Coming Up Roses', and it cheered her up. A bit.

Chapter Seventeen

So Rosie awoke next morning to the grim knowledge that she was right back where she had started. Money was going to be tight again without her work at Lulu's and without Ben's client list to tap into. And on top of that, Ben was out of her life. She wasn't quite sure how she felt about that yet.

She showered and put on clean jeans and a mauve T-shirt and trainers, and ate toast and drank coffee. Then she wondered why Lulu was late, and checked the appointment books, and discovered that it was Sunday, so Lulu was not due in until tomorrow, and of course there was no work to do.

The Sunday papers came through the door shortly after she had made a fresh pot of coffee, wondering what the hell she was going to do with herself all day, so she took them to the couch and sprawled there and read them all – the supplements, the financial pages, even the football coverage. Then she went out and tidied up her miniscule little garden, and washed her beloved Beetle, and washed her crappy old van too, to show willing.

By then it was time for lunch, so she rummaged in the fridge and found mouldy cheese, overripe tomatoes and wilted lettuce. She jammed two slices of bread from the freezer into the toaster to defrost it, then made herself a sandwich, washing it down with tap water because she didn't have juice.

On her way to the kitchen to wash the dishes, she passed the roses. They were in their vase on an occasional table beside the window. She paused and looked at them. Wondered if she should just bin them. Decided not.

She sighed, and went to do the washing-up.

Monday was better. Monday morning was taken up with one of her old and much-valued clients, Virginia McCabe, who was a former Justice of the Peace, and intensely interested in her garden. Rosie was digging out another border for her; Virginia was fed up with all that bare lawn.

'What are you going to want planted in here?' Rosie asked as she sectioned the turf off into neat squares, lifting each one with a shovel and laying it aside to make loam.

'A beautiful golden conifer, with a cotinus in front for contrasting colour.'

Rosie considered the suggestion. The gold of the conifer would look superb against the burgundy-red of the cotinus. 'If you put some orange crocosmia to the side there, that would be a terrific combination.'

'You're right,' said Virginia, pleased. Leaning on her walking stick, she watched Rosie carry on sectioning turf. 'So what's been happening in your life, Rosie? Anything exciting?'

'Nothing special,' lied Rosie. 'You?'

'I don't get out much,' said Virginia with a smile. 'Is business good?'

'Oh, OK.' Rosie shrugged, shovelling turf.

'Competition must be fierce these days.'

'Yeah, it is.'

'Another firm put a flyer through the door just a couple of weeks ago, saying they were looking for more work and that their rates were reasonable.'

Rosie straightened. 'Did they? Do you still have it?'

'Sussing out the competition?' Virginia asked archly.

'Something like that.'

'It's indoors with all my other bits and pieces,' said Virginia. 'I'll fetch it out.'

When the old lady emerged from the house again, Rosie had cleared the new bed of turf and was busy wheelbarrowing them down to the composting area at the bottom of the garden, where she stacked them back to back.

'Here you are,' said Virginia, brandishing the flyer. 'Keep it if you want. I'm not interested in another gardener – I'm very happy with you.'

Rosie looked at the flyer. Countryman Gardens was in bold green script, and the blurb suggested knowledge and effort and diligence and, yes, reasonable rates. In the centre of the flyer, just above the contact numbers, was a head-and-shoulders picture of Ben Hunter. Handsome bastard, she thought.

'He's a very handsome man, isn't he,' commented Virginia.

'Very,' agreed Rosie.

'I think if I were twenty years younger I'd be very interested in procuring his services.'

Rosie looked up at Virginia, who winked.

'Virginia!'

'Well, don't tell me you'd kick him out of bed.' The old lady laughed.

Rosie said nothing. If this was Virginia's reaction to the flyer, then wasn't it reasonable to assume that Mrs Squires and her other female customers had reacted to the sight of Ben in the same way? He hadn't deliberately pinched her business; he'd offered a service, and her female clients had taken one look at him and decided the offer was too good to pass on. Only the older ladies, like Virginia, had stuck with her. And the men. Well, the straight ones anyway.

'He's good-looking,' said Rosie, handing the flyer back.

'Keep it. It's of no use to me, and it's a bit of free research for you.'

'Thanks.' Rosie stuffed it into her jeans pocket, feeling uncomfortably aware that she had misjudged Ben. But what the hell, that was all water under the bridge now; it was all history. 'So what about some crown fritillaries at the front here? Orange ones against that gold – that would look amazing.'

'Yes, that would be fine.'

'I'll get some ordered.'

Of course life wasn't at all flat now she'd seen the last of Ben Hunter. She still had her own work to do, and she still had some friends. She had even made some new ones, in particular Joanne from Lulu's place, with whom she seemed to get on very well. They had lunch together mid-week at a local Italian restaurant.

Rosie, knowing Joanne always looked drop-dead gorgeous and was into designer gear, did her best to arrive at the restaurant looking a bit more presentable than normal. She put on her one and only gooseberry-green skirt suit (she'd bought it for a distant cousin's wedding two years ago, and it had been languishing at the back of the wardrobe ever since) and her tan mules, and carried her straw bag which had cost two pounds fifty down the market, but looked as if it had cost a lot more.

'Hey, you look hot,' said Joanne admiringly when Rosie joined her at the table in the bustling restaurant.

Rosie was glad she had made an effort. Joanne was wearing a pale pink suit in some glaringly expensive fabric, studded with gold buttons and edged with black braid. Rosie *suspected* it was Chanel. Teamed with a black bag and black shoes, and with her sleek dark hair neatly slicked back and flicked up on her shoulders, Joanne looked a real eyeful, a million dollars. No wonder Ben gets the hots for her, thought Rosie dismally.

'You look wonderful,' she said truthfully, sitting down.

'Well, it all takes time and effort,' said Joanne with a laugh.

'Yeah, don't you get sick of that?' queried Rosie. 'And all that expensive underwear. Why does no one warn a person how uncomfortable it all is?'

Joanne laughed softly and poured Rosie some Chablis. 'You're a bit of hick, aren't you, Rosie?'

'I'm a *lot* of a hick,' Rosie admitted.

'A country girl?'

'I come from a little village near Winchester. Went to the local agricultural and horticultural college. Thought of gamekeeping for a bit. Then considered woodland management. Thought I might even be a river-keeper, but river-keepers tend to keep the jobs in their own families, there are no openings. So I settled for plain old gardening.'

'Did that cover garden design?' asked Joanne, interested.

'Of course.'

'And you came up to London why?'

'To make money.'

'Like it?'

'It's OK.'

'Ben hates it.'

'Does he?' Rosie gave her drink a lot of attention.

'He won't stick it for much longer.'

'How long, would you say?' asked Rosie, sounding casual.

'About a year, I'd guess. Maybe less, if you give him his client list back.'

'I already have.'

Joanne's black brows rose in surprise. 'You have? Well, good for you.'

Rosie shrugged. 'It seemed the fairest thing to do. I mean, I didn't want to put him out or anything. I didn't want the poor sap having to sleep with me all the time, just to get that list back.'

'Is that why he slept with you?'

'Sure it is.'

'You really think that?'

'Of course.'

'You think Ben's that calculating?'

Rosie was saved from having to reply by the arrival of a beautiful young Italian waiter at their table. He looked from Rosie to Joanne with glowing dark eyes, and took their order with lots of smiles and flirtation.

'Don't you just love Italian men?' drooled Joanne as he departed. She watched his backside twitching perkily as he made his way back to the kitchen, and sipped at her Chablis.

'Mm, yes,' said Rosie, uninterested.

'Ben's from the country too,' said Joanne, looking acutely at Rosie.

'I know. He took me down to see his place.'

'Did you like it?'

'It's lovely.' Rosie sighed, and sipped the wine.

'Rosie, you're getting me down,' chided Joanne.

'Sorry.' Rosie straightened with an effort.

'Come back to my place this afternoon,' said Joanne. 'I'll cheer you up.'

It was not an empty promise. Snagging two of the most delectable Italian waiters when the restaurant closed, Joanne took them all back out to her place on the river in Marlow. This time, Rosie saw more than the gardens, the river and the house's beautiful exterior. This time, Joanne showed her and the two waiters the big indoor pool house.

Rosie wondered what it must be like to live like this, in the lap of luxury, supported by a rich and mostly absent husband. Bloody marvellous, probably, but she suspected that it wouldn't really suit her – although Joanne seemed to thrive on it.

She could only gawp in amazement at the pool house's plush interior. It was like a huge conservatory, with the pool, a huge azure oblong made up of contrasting green and white tiles, slap bang in the middle of it. Large softly cushioned sun loungers were dotted here and there all around it. At the far end there was a grotto, with an aviary of rare birds squawking and fluttering in comparative freedom. Set into the base of the grotto was a tinkling fountain, and to the side of that there was a comprehensively stocked bar. At the end of the pool house where it joined the main building, there were changing cubicles.

'There are spare bathing trunks in there,' said Joanne

casually to the two dumbfounded Italians, Gianni and Luco. 'Just help yourselves.'

'What about me?' asked Rosie.

'There are women's spares in there too.' Joanne grinned. 'Don't worry, I'm not going to lend you my discards. I know there'd be a lot of slack up top.'

'Well, I'd manage if you threw in a couple of pineapples.' Rosie grinned.

'We have pool parties all the time,' said Joanne. 'So I keep a selection of sizes at the ready.'

Joanne was as good as her word. Inside her own little private cubicle, Rosie sorted through a rack of swim-wear. She found a lime-green bikini in her size, and put it on, emerging hesitantly to find that the two Italians were already splashing about in the deep end, and Joanne was fixing them all cocktails at the far end, while wearing a modest fuchsia pink one-piece swimsuit.

'Who wants a Long Slow Screw Up Against A Wall?' she flung over her shoulder.

The Italians thought this was extremely funny, but agreed that they would try the drink and see if they liked it. Rosie sat on one of the sun loungers and watched the two men slithering through the water like otters at play, racing each other from one end of the pool to the other.

'There's a lot to be said for youth,' said Joanne a touch wistfully, casting a glance at the two men as she brought the tray of drinks round to Rosie's sun lounger.

'What does that mean?' asked Rosie, taking a cocktail and sipping it as Joanne settled on to the other lounger.

'My husband's fifty-five,' said Joanne. 'Twenty years older than me.'

'Ah.'

'When he gets home from work, he mostly wants to slump in front of the television. And halfway through the evening, he's generally asleep.'

'I see.'

'So if you are wondering why I go for thrills – well, I guess that's your answer.'

'I'm sorry.'

'Oh don't be sorry.' Joanne took a hearty slug of her drink. 'Oh, that's delicious. Look, I'm making the best of things. I know what his limitations are, and I accept them in exchange for all this. And to keep myself sane, I play around a bit. Well, a lot.'

So much for Joanne and her enviable lifestyle, thought Rosie. She sipped at her drink. God, it was strong. It seemed to go straight to her legs, via her crotch, then it zoomed back up and settled in her stomach with a pleasurable glowing effect. She felt like the kid on the porridge adverts, warmly insulated from the outside world. She felt great.

'They're very energetic,' said Rosie, watching the young men in the pool.

'But not exactly Cambridge material,' admitted Joanne.

'Energy and brains is a lot to ask.'

'Ben Hunter's got both,' remarked Joanne.

'True.'

'I think – you know what I think, Rosie?'

Rosie suddenly realised that Joanne was slightly drunk. They'd downed a lot of Chablis at lunch. She realised that she was a bit squiffy, too. 'No, what?'

Joanne wagged a finger at her. 'I think you should snap him up.'

Rosie laughed. 'I don't think he wants to be snapped.'

'I think you're wrong.'

'I think *you're* wrong.'

'No, you are.'

'No, you.'

'What is this?' asked one of the Italians – Rosie thought it was Gianni – hauling himself out of the pool and padding over to where they sat. 'Are you arguing?'

'Having a lively debate,' said Joanne, patting her sun lounger. Gianni sat down and took a drink.

Rosie noticed with amusement that Joanne was eyeing him up like a shark eyeing a guppy. And he was very good-looking. Dark-skinned and dark-haired, and beautifully toned, and the trunks he wore, just plain and very brief black ones, did nothing to disguise the healthy bulge at his crotch.

Luco pulled himself out of the pool and came over to Rosie's sun lounger. She handed him his drink with a smile. Another perfect Italian stallion, she thought, and had to admit to herself that Joanne had exceedingly good taste.

'So what is this debate?' asked Gianni.

'Whether or not Rosie here should take up an offer.'

'He hasn't offered,' objected Rosie.

'What do you want, to have it written in blood? Ben's not the sort to beg.'

'This Ben is handsome, yes?' asked Luco, draining his drink.

'Very,' said both women together.

Luco pouted. 'More handsome than me? I don't think so.'

And he stood up and struck an impressive body-builder's pose. Gosh, he was really good-looking, thought Rosie. But lately she was finding that only blond hair and piercing blue eyes really turned her on. Whereas Luco was very dark. But she supposed she really ought to make an effort, if only for her own sake. Some fun would do her good. It had all been getting far too heavy with Ben Hunter, and she was, she told herself bracingly, well out of it.

'Yes, but we can't really tell, can we?' she said purringly. 'Not while you're wearing *those*.' Rosie indicated the black trunks he was wearing.

'No problem, *cara*,' shrugged Luco. He put his empty glass down on a small cane table, and quickly bent and pulled the trunks down. He stepped out of them, then straightened and put his hands on his hips, proudly displaying his naked cock to Joanne and Rosie. They gazed admiringly. Luco had an exceptionally nice body.

'Now tell me, is this Ben Hunter as handsome as me?' he demanded.

What an arrogant git, thought Rosie. And of course Luco wasn't as attractive as Ben. Ben had *presence*. Ben had charisma. Ben had more than the average number of brain cells. But still, Luco did have his charms. About six inches of them, from where she was sitting. His penis had risen up like a cobra to a snake charmer's flute, and was standing erect against his dark-haired lower belly.

'Honey, no one's as handsome as you,' Joanne told him reassuringly. 'Except possibly Gianni, unless he's too shy to compete?'

'No, I will compete,' Gianni grinned with confidence. He stood up and dropped his trunks to his ankles, then straightened with them still draped there. He held out his hands, palm up. 'Now what about this, uh? You like this fine Italian cock? Better than Luco's?'

It certainly was a very fine cock – longer than Luco's, but slightly thinner. Chunky was the word that came into Rosie's mind as she stared at Luco's nude penis. Then she looked at Gianni's, and thought that this was a veritable surfeit of riches. Two gorgeous men flashing their naked cocks at her – and truthfully, she suddenly felt so hot that she felt she could handle them both, without Joanne. Her bikini bottom was growing damp from her juices. Her nipples were sticking out. She'd never had a swarthy Italian before, not even one. And now she wanted two!

'Now we see you, uh?' said Luco, indicating Rosie's and Joanne's swimwear. 'You take the clothes off?'

'Rosie?' asked Joanne, as she lay back on her sun lounger. 'Come on, get them off. After all, I brought these two back here to cheer you up, remember?'

Rosie looked at Joanne in wonder. Did Joanne actually mean that she was going to let Rosie have both men?

'I want to see you getting it on with these two,' said Joanne, to clarify matters.

'But what about you?' asked Rosie, not wishing to be selfish.

'Oh, I'll get mine later,' Joanne said casually. 'Sometimes I just like to watch.'

'Come on, *cara*,' pleaded Luco. 'At least the bikini top, yes? I want to kiss your nipples.'

I hope you're intending to do rather more than that, thought Rosie, *much* more than that. She felt incredibly hot now, aware that the attention of both men was focused lustfully upon only her. She reached behind her and undid the bikini top. Carefully, keeping an arm over her naked breasts as they spilled free, she slipped the little scrap of material off and dropped it on the tiles.

Gianni chuckled at this. He kicked his trunks aside, his cock waving about as he moved. God, you could hang a flag off that, thought Rosie.

'Come, show us your breasts,' he said encouragingly.

Rosie dropped her arm, placing both hands flat on the lounger. Their eyes seemed to devour her as they stared. She felt her freshly bared nipples almost returning their stares. Her teats prickled with lustful sensations, and passion stabbed at her groin, making her clit twitch and grow.

'Do you like them?' she asked unnecessarily. If the two men had been erect before, they were as stiff as flag poles now.

Proud of her assets, Rosie stood up and lifted her

arms behind her head, pulling her heavy mass of red hair up and away from her neck. By so doing, she raised her breasts in the most provocative way.

'That's so sexy,' Luco moaned admiringly.

'I want to see her bush,' Gianni said hungrily. He looked into Rosie's eyes. 'Is it red, like your hair on your head? Do you have a hot red bush? That means you are a passionate woman.'

'Yes, it's red,' said Rosie, wondering if she was really stripping off in front of two naked men, while Joanne watched from the sidelines.

'Prove it, then,' said Gianni.

'Maybe it's not red,' said Luco. 'Maybe she dyes her hair red. Maybe she's a brunette like Joanne.'

'Nope,' said Rosie. 'I'm a true redhead, and I'll prove it right now.'

Rosie undid the ties at the bikini bottom's sides, and tossed the thing to one side. She performed the same sleight of hand over her bush that she had employed over her breasts. They didn't catch a glimpse between the material being whisked away and her hand closing over it.

'Ah, such a tease,' moaned Gianni, almost in pain with longing. He touched a desperate hand to his cock as he gazed at her naked breasts, her belly, her nude and vulnerable hips. But her bush, the greatest prize of all, was still hidden from his eyes. 'Show us, *cara*,' he begged.

Rosie took pity on them and took her hand away. Both men stared ravenously at her fiery red bush, their eyes searching eagerly beneath the furry triangle for the outline of her sex lips, for that secret little slipway that led to heaven.

'A true redhead,' marvelled Luco, giving his straining penis a salutary tug.

'Let's go in for a swim,' suggested Rosie, and she dived sideways into the water.

Caught by surprise, the two men stared for one dumb moment before they too hit the water and raced after her.

'That's cheating, Rosie!' shouted Joanne, laughing. 'You know damned well I wanted to see it all.'

Gianni caught her first. Laughing madly, Rosie turned in his arms, her breasts bobbing enticingly up under his chin as she linked her arms around his neck. She wrapped her legs around his waist, felt him wrestle his cock down into position and then push up madly, slipping inside her. Oh, that was wonderful! Rosie let out a scream of delight as Gianni, steadying himself with one arm on the pool's edge, pumped at her with desperation.

But then Luco caught up with them, and wanted a piece of the action too. Coming around behind Rosie, he trod water. Rosie felt his hands, hard and caressing, on her naked buttocks, pushing them wide. She felt his fingers delving into her crack, touching Gianni's furiously thrusting cock as it worked in and out of her, then sliding back up, holding her fleshy globes wider apart, and then she felt the tip of his penis pushing against her sensitised anus, pushing firmly but gently, and she was opening to him, letting him come into her back there – oh, Jesus, so good. She was a man sandwich, trapped between two hard-muscled bodies while under the water they both pumped lustily at her.

The frantic pressing of Luco's chest and belly against her back was driving her ever tighter in against Gianni, so that her clit was coming into brisk contact with his pubic bone every time he thrust. Rosie reeled, drowning in delicious feelings as the two men pounded at her. She grabbed at the side of the pool, groaning and shrieking at the wonder of it, her head thrown back, her breasts gleaming above the water. Luco clamped his hands over them, rubbing her tits, abrading her nipples and that, coupled with Gianni's bumping against her clit, tipped her finally, swiftly, right over the edge.

She came crazily, screaming again, pushing down on to the two cocks that so busily serviced her – and looked up, panting, and saw Ben standing grimly looking down at her from the edge of the pool.

Chapter Eighteen

'She set me up,' Rosie said dazedly to herself as she sat in Ben's – or rather Janina's – Mercedes and was driven back into town by a tight-lipped Ben. 'I cannot believe it. Joanne set me up.'

'What?' asked Ben in obvious exasperation, his hands clenched on the steering-wheel as if it was her neck.

'Joanne set me up. She invited you over this afternoon, didn't she.'

'Yes.'

'Yes! There! You see? She invited you over so that you would catch me with Bungle and Zippy back there, and fly into a jealous rage or some such nonsense.'

'Really.'

'Don't look at me like that!'

'Like what?'

'Like you don't believe a word I'm saying. I'm telling you, she set me up with those two, and I think she must have spiked my drink with an aphrodisiac at lunchtime.'

'Such as?'

'Well how the hell should I know?' It was Rosie's turn to looked exasperated. 'Some exotic herbal concoction, *I* don't know. Hey, I've jut been date-raped.'

Ben shot her a cold look. 'Rosie. It didn't look like any sort of rape from where I was standing. You were *enjoying* it. Two of them. At the same time.'

'Is there a law against that?' demanded Rosie, annoyed by his censorious tone. What had gotten into him all of a sudden? He was the last person to preach a strict moral code to anyone. He was ready for sex anywhere, at any time, and with whoever he fancied at that moment. And he was having a go at *her* about shagging two men at once? For God's sake!

'Not that I know of,' said Ben, but he still looked mad enough to kick her ass.

'Then why the histrionics? And will you slow down? Why do you always have to drive so fast?'

And why do I have to keep watching your hands on the steering-wheel, and those strong hairy forearms, and thinking impure thoughts? wondered Rosie privately. She hated the fact that she was sitting here fancying him like crazy, when he was trying to make her feel like seven kinds of shit. Maybe the exotic herbs hadn't worn off yet. Or perhaps she was just a hopeless case where he was concerned. Yeah, that was more likely, she thought grimly.

Ben didn't slow down until they hit heavy traffic and the big car had to crawl along with the rest of them. He admitted to himself that he had been driving too fast.

He had been driving too fast because he was angry. And he was angry because, much to his own amazement, Rosie had succeeded in shocking him.

Two men, he thought.

Two men going at her at once – and she had loved it!

And now she was trying to say she'd been set up by Joanne. Which was a possibility, he had to allow that much. Joanne was a bit of a schemer. And it did seem suspicious that Joanne had been leaving all the fun and games to Rosie. That was most unlike Joanne. And what had she phoned him for, really?

To say the coast was clear, and why not come on over. She had not mentioned the two Italians, and she certainly had not mentioned Rosie. No, she had let him stumble across Rosie being serviced by those two in the pool house, and there had been a glint of satisfaction in Joanne's dark eyes when she saw that her ruse had worked.

Because he was jealous. He could admit it to himself, but to no one else. When he had seen those two pawing at Rosie and worse, he had felt a most peculiar feeling. He had felt – for the first time in his life – that he wanted to smash someone beyond recognition. To wreak havoc. In fact, it had shaken him. It was an aspect of his normally easygoing personality that had never surfaced before, and it had unnerved him, and when he was unnerved, he got angry. He recognised now how very possessive he was of this red-haired, lippy little hoyden, and recognised too that this was a clear danger signal. This had to stop. And it had to stop *right now*.

Whatever his feelings were for her, they had to be more firmly controlled. It was lucky that he hadn't completely lost it back at Joanne's house; and he was holding on to his temper by the thinnest of threads even now. What Rosie needed was some stern discipline. And what *he* needed, angry and rattled as he was, was to see her punished.

Rosie couldn't believe it. He'd done it to her again. Brought her back to Janina's flat, stripped her with quite unnecessary roughness, and tied her to the bed. The bastard. And now she knew, she just *knew*, that the whole humiliating but desperately arousing scenario was going to be played out again. He was going to usher in Luke and Daniel, and he was going to watch while they jumped her, and he was going to make her piss in that damned pot again, and if she ever got loose she would break the thing over his stupid head.

But it wasn't Luke and Daniel Ben brought into the bedroom this time. It was Janina.

'Have a good business trip?' quipped Rosie mulishly, wanting them to see that there was no way they could frighten her.

'OK,' said Janina, smiling down at her as she lay there staked out like a pioneer after an Indian attack.

And what the hell was the woman wearing? pondered Rosie, glancing down Janina's statuesque body. A lot of shiny black PVC. Well, not a lot. Various bits of PVC. A black PVC choker that highlighted the paleness of her skin and the rumpled blondeness of her long tumbling mane of hair. A bra with holes cut in it, allowing her nipples – nice nipples, very nice indeed – to jut out. A tight belt, cinched in to accentuate the smallness of her waist. And a PVC thong that just about covered her bush. And boots! Leather spike-heeled boots that came up to mid-thigh. God, that was sexy. And she had in her hand – what was that she had in her hand? It looked like a whip. Like one of those cat-o'-nine tail whips they had in the Navy in the eighteenth century.

Oh no.

'Look, I'm not a Conservative MP you know,' said Rosie, straining frantically against her bonds. 'I don't get off on corporal punishment.'

'The object of the exercise is not to "get you off",' Janina said patiently, pacing around the bed. Ben was standing just inside the door leaning against the wall, hands in pockets and a thoughtful expression on his face, watching the two women.

'Oh? Then what is it then?' demanded Rosie.

'It's to punish you,' Janina said silkily. She trailed the whip's tails down over Rosie's belly and between her open thighs. Rosie shuddered.

'I've got a very low pain threshold,' Rosie lied.

'Oh dear. That is unfortunate.'

'I'll scream very loudly.'

'Scream away. There's no one in the entire block at this time of day.'

Janina trailed the whip on to Rosie's legs, and down to her feet. She dangled the tails against Rosie's soles. Rosie let out a yelp.

'Don't do that! I'm ticklish.'

'Are you really,' said Janina with a catlike smile. And she shimmied the tails against Rosie's feet while Rosie squirmed and cursed at her.

'Ben says you've been a naughty girl.' Rosie's eyes spurted tears as she twitched like a marionette beneath Janina's cruel ministrations. 'And naughty girls have to be punished. Ben, do you want to whip her?'

Ben's eyes met Rosie's. 'No, you go ahead,' he said, and left the room.

Bastard! How could he do this to her? How could *Janina* do this to her? She'd stopped tickling the soles of Rosie's feet, and was now taking aim with the whip, and Rosie could not believe it, but she was really going to do it, and Rosie felt shamefully, horribly aroused.

'Ow!' she screeched as the tails of the whip whacked the soles of her feet. God, that Janina had a powerful swing on her. Janina swung again, swiping even harder at Rosie's feet. More tears spurted down Rosie's face, but she was horrified to find that wetness was seeping from elsewhere, too. She was turned on. Either Joanne really *had* slipped her something at lunch, or she was turning into a nymphomaniac.

'Oh!' she squealed, as the whip struck again – across her ankles this time, stinging her skin like mad. And her nipples stood up as if beginning to take an interest in the proceedings.

'Dirty little bitch,' muttered Janina, seeing the evidence of Rosie's desire. She swung the cat-o'-nine tails and hit Rosie's inner thighs this time. One of the tails even stung her crotch.

'Oh you cow,' gasped Rosie in pain and ecstasy.

'Ha! Did the dirty little bitch like that then?' crowed Janina, and whipped her again, harder, and this time the thing hit her clit. 'Is it turning you on? Let's see.'

Janina, with clinical detachment not entirely borne out by the state of her own nipples, thrust a finger between Rosie's thighs. She rummaged busily in Rosie's crack and Rosie felt Janina's digit push up inside her. Quite easily, too.

'Goodness! So wet,' Janina said admiringly. 'Wet enough to take a man now, I think. Ben!'

Ben came back into the bedroom. He had a glass of brandy in his hand and a grim expression on his face. He stared at Rosie as she lay there, panting, almost mindless with passion and pain.

'She's ready for you,' said Janina, like a receptionist apprising a doctor of the patient's receptivity.

And she was, she was. That was the awful part. Rosie watched in a daze as Ben drained the glass and put it down on a side table. She watched in growing alarm as Janina moved back to allow Ben access to the bed. She pulled against the restraining scarves as he clambered between her legs and started to unzip his trousers. She swore at him as he pushed his trousers down on to his thighs, revealing his big erect cock.

'See, she's wet,' said Janina.

'God, what a pair of perverts you are!' yelled Rosie.

'Shut up,' advised Ben. He didn't even untie her

ankles. He just nudged up close against her crotch, pushed his naked dick down and suddenly it was surging up inside her.

'Ahh,' groaned Rosie. It was excruciating. It was exquisite. Because her ankles were tied, her legs were almost flat to the bed, which meant that his cock, oh God, his wonderful glorious cock, was pressing up against her G-spot, and his pubic bone was rubbing against her clit, and as his hips started to piston back and forth against her the sensations were so acute that she felt she might actually faint from the force of them.

Janina was standing right by the bed, taking a keen interest in the proceedings. Rosie wouldn't have cared right at this moment if an entire rugby club had been grouped around the bed passing bawdy comment. Ben was inside her, slipping and sliding and heating her beyond redemption and she had no shame, no care, no feeling beyond the desire for him just to go on with what he'd started.

And Ben wasn't about to stop. His head was thrown back, his eyes closed – he could have been fucking *anybody*, Rosie thought in dim outrage – and his hands were digging cruelly into her wide-open thighs as he chugged in and out of her. Her whole being seemed focused upon his penis, its movements, its size, its heat, its power. She loved it.

Janina leaned over and casually tweaked Rosie's nipple as Ben rode her. Then she drew back and let fly with the whip again, right across Rosie's breasts, and it was torture, but it was wonderful. It was pain and pleasure and it was altogether too much. Stimulated beyond endurance, Rosie came, screaming and crying, but Ben seemed unaware of her except as an inert sex object, a pair of quivering breasts, a set of spread legs and a hole in which to rut. He pushed on, even when Rosie had collapsed back, spent, on to the bed. He pushed and pushed and shoved and dug at her, until his own release came, and he spilled hotly into her, his contractions almost violent, almost painful judging by the way he screwed his face up. Then he slumped, relaxing, tension draining away from him. Without once looking at Rosie, he pulled back, tucked his cock back into his trousers, zipped up, climbed off the bed, and left the room.

'He's really angry with you,' said Janina in explanation.

'He's not among my top one hundred guys to spend a fun day with, either,' said Rosie with an attempt at lightness. The old post-fuck blues were sinking in now. And she didn't like Ben being at odds with her. She was surprised how much she disliked that.

'You two seem to fit together,' said Janina, tossing the whip on to the floor and starting to loosen Rosie's bonds.

'He's a bastard,' said Rosie, rubbing at her wrists when Janina had freed them. 'I hate him.'

'What a liar,' chuckled Janina, untying Rosie's ankles. 'You adore it when he's inside you.'

'That's just sex.'

'Don't knock it,' advised Janina.

Freed at last, Rosie sat up. Her feet stung a bit. So

did her crotch, and her inner thighs, and her breasts. She was just grateful that it was Janina who'd used the whip, and not a stronger person like Ben. If he wanted her punished so much, why hadn't *he* whipped her? He could have. She shivered at the thought. More pain, but she would have loved it too, taken pleasure from it. God, was she sick, or what?

'Go and shower off,' Janina said kindly.

So she did, in the big luxurious shower room that could easily accommodate half a dozen people. She had a long, sensuous and relaxing shower, taking her time over it. Taking more time than she strictly needed or wanted, because she kept hoping that Ben would walk in, naked, and shower with her, and perhaps even resume what had begun in the bedroom against the cool tiles of the shower-room walls. Melt a little and kiss her breasts, and smile at her, and sponge her body down, and get aroused and make love to her again.

But he didn't, and she dried alone and, dressed alone, and because when she emerged from the bedroom the flat seemed to be empty again, she left the flat and went and hailed herself a taxi to take her back to Richmond.

Chapter Nineteen

After a couple of weeks had passed, Rosie felt that she was getting the whole thing back in proportion again. Basically, all her friends were traitors and all men were bastards, but none more so than Ben Hunter. So she was glad to be kept fairly busy with gardening work to take her mind off it all. And she showed up bright and early for the new-client consultation in Hackney, keen to get what looked like becoming a major job.

The builders were working in the otherwise empty detached Edwardian house, and Rosie was flirted with outrageously when she arrived. The foreman took her through to the back garden, and Rosie stood there, waiting patiently for her prospective client to show up. While she did so, she surveyed the garden.

It couldn't be called a garden. It was a corporation tip in miniature – yes, that was a better way to describe it. There was an old cast-iron bath in one corner. A chicken coop and a tattered run in the other. A pile of builders' debris blocked the centre of an extremely unlovely and unimaginative concrete path that ran like a tramline from the top of the garden to the bottom. There were straggly, unhealthy looking trees down at the far end and, as Rosie stepped down to take a closer look, see if there was anything salvageable down there, she twisted her ankle pretty painfully on the uneven and frost-damaged steps.

She rubbed at her ankle and sighed. Behind her, hammering and drilling and Radio 1 made a cacophony of sound. Out here, there was just this sad mess of a place. She walked – more carefully now – to the bottom of the garden. There was a lilac – she could rescue that. But the rest of the stuff would have to go. A pity about access being only through the house, because this would be a big, messy job. But at least the carpets weren't down yet and the residents weren't *in* residence, so that would make life easier.

She hummed to herself as she strolled around the perimeter. At least the fences appeared to be in good order and, apart from the trees at the bottom, there was no disastrous planting to sort out. There *was* no planting. Just this tatty horrible old lawn and a bit of soil at the edge. She took a tiny container out of her jeans pocket and bent and scraped up a soil sample to work out whether it was acid, alkaline or somewhere in between. Recapping the container, she slipped it back into her jeans and then straightened as if shot when someone behind her said; 'What the *fuck*?'

She whirled around. 'Oh damn and blast,' she said in deep irritation.

'What are you doing here?' Ben asked furiously.

'I'm meeting a prospective client to discuss the renovation of the garden,' Rosie said flatly. 'What the hell else would I be doing here?'

'So am I,' said Ben, looking at her nastily. 'You're not up to your old tricks again, I suppose? Poaching other people's work?'

'Look, this client phoned me and asked me to meet his representative here for a consultation and to work out a quote. So far as I know, he's no one's client and so he's up for grabs, OK?'

She looked at him. Wow, he looked good. He always looked good. But now his tan was darkening as summer got under way, and it made his eyes bluer than ever.

'This is a very big job,' said Rosie, wrenching her eyes off Ben and looking back towards the house. 'Total renovation.'

'Yep,' said Ben, and Rosie knew that he was thinking exactly the same as her. A total renovation would pay handsomely. It would make a big difference to her finances, which were limping along a bit. But it was worrying that they'd invited Ben over too. The Polish chap she'd spoken to on the phone, Mr Patenski, hadn't indicated in any way that he was going to go down this route. It was the route for beating the price down, for getting two experts on the spot and letting them fight for the contract. And the lowest quote would secure it.

Oh well. That was business, she supposed. And then she saw Joanne come out on to what passed for the terrace, throwing a flirtatious comment back over her well-clothed shoulder at one of the builders. Joanne picked her way cautiously down the rickety steps, and approached the two speechless gardeners with a broad smile.

'Ben! Rosie! Thanks so much for coming, both of you,' she gushed, throwing her arms wide in a welcoming gesture. She air-kissed Rosie on both cheeks and then gave Ben a smacker on the lips. 'Goodness, you two look so well. How are you?'

'Fine. We're just wondering what you're playing at,' said Ben, refusing to be charmed.

'Yeah, right,' agreed Rosie. 'Last time I saw you, you set me up for a fall. Is that what you're doing this time?'

'How can you think that?' asked Joanne, looking hurt. 'You spoke to my brother-in-law on the phone, I believe.'

'Is he Mr. Patenski?' asked Rosie.

'That's him. Leo Patenski. He's bought this place as an investment, and I'm overseeing the interior work, and of course the garden. Gardens are just so important now to the feel of a home, don't you think? And I thought to myself, who do I know who could do a wonderful job and really bring this garden to life? Well, it was obvious. You two. Ben and Rosie.'

'Forget it,' Ben said brusquely. 'I've got my own team I work with.'

'Me too,' said Rosie, whose only team was Lulu and who usually hired subcontractors when she needed help with heavy stuff.

'Now are you sure about this?' sighed Joanne,

looking put out. 'Because that's the deal, you see. You share the contract – or you don't get a sniff at it, either of you.'

There was a silence during which both Ben and Rosie did rapid calculations. They both thought that the project would be worth around fifteen to twenty thousand pounds, and that was seven and a half each, hopefully more, and it would come in very handy.

I suppose a big job like this would almost take you up to the amount you need to buy that field by your place in Sussex, Ben?' oiled Joanne.

'How did you know about that?'

'Lulu told me.'

'And how did *she* know?' He eyed Rosie beadily. 'As if I couldn't guess.'

'All right, all right. I told her. I probably shouldn't have.'

'No you shouldn't.'

'But I did.' Rosie blushed guiltily. 'Listen, don't flatter yourself. I don't want to work with you. I'd rather have my arse rubbed with a brick. But we can't turn down a job this size, it'd be madness.'

'Can't we? Just watch me.'

'Well, that's a shame. Because the deal's non-negotiable,' said Joanne. 'Either you do it together, or it goes to another firm altogether. All or nothing. And listen.' She looked at them both acutely. 'Is bad feeling between you really worth losing a job this size for? Only I don't think it is.'

'You're scheming again, Joanne,' warned Ben.

'Scheming?' Joanne opened her beautiful dark eyes wide in innocence. 'On the contrary. I'm trying to help out my friends and, to be fair to both of them, to give them equal shares. Now if they can't be amicable and adult about it, is that my fault?'

Silence fell again. Ben looked at Rosie. Rosie shrugged.

'We'll have to work out the quote together,' Ben said bluntly.

'Seems logical,' said Rosie.

'I don't like this,' said Ben.

'Don't think you're alone in that, pal,' snapped Rosie.

'But you'll do it?' asked Joanne hopefully.

Ben let out a breath. 'Yeah, I'll do it. Providing she keeps out from under my feet, OK?'

'I do have a name, you know,' Rosie objected.

'Yeah, "Trouble",' said Ben.

'Well, if that's how you feel, let's not bother.'

'Suits me.'

'Wait!' Joanne intervened hurriedly. 'Ben's willing to undertake the commission. Rosie, are you?'

'So long as he understands that I expect equal input in the design,' Rosie said sniffily. 'I've got a very advanced garden-design computer program.'

'Ben?'

He shrugged. 'I've already said. We'll work it out together. But I always work out the initial design freehand.'

'That's archaic,' tutted Rosie.

'I don't give a shit. It's the way I like to work.'

'Well, why don't you both work out a plan separately, then get together and blend the two? That would work, surely.'

'It might,' Ben said grudgingly.

'It'll be slower than it need be, but yes, OK, it'll work out.'

'So it's a deal,' Joanne said firmly.

Ben and Rosie glared at each other.

'It's a deal,' they said in unison.

'Ha!' Joanne looked at them both and shook her head. 'Well, I hope you prove me wrong, but I give you a fortnight before you kill each other.'

'This is ridiculous,' said Ben four days later as, for the third time, they failed to agree on the plan.

'You can say that again,' snarled Rosie.

Ben had come up with a very structured layout – a typically male design, Rosie thought scathingly – incorporating lots of structural bits and pieces as a dominant backdrop to the planting. But Rosie's was completely different. In hers, the plants were to the fore, and the hard landscaping was only there to support them.

'Ludicrous,' said Ben, feeling uncomfortably crowded by having to work in tandem with someone else. That that someone was Rosie only made it worse. Her very presence seemed to abrade his senses like sandpaper. 'That just looks horrible. So girly.'

'Well, I am a girl,' said Rosie.

'It's too soft. There's no backbone to it.'

They were in Rosie's sitting room, staring at the computer screen. It was getting late in the evening and Rosie's eyes felt gritty and her temper felt strained. She hated working with anyone else. She was used to being her own woman, her own boss. She wasn't used to having her work criticised, and she found that she didn't like the sensation. But she kept remembering how Joanne had mocked them, saying they wouldn't last two weeks without mayhem occurring.

'Look, can we combine that rusted-metal monstrosity of yours with the ornamental cabbages? Or what if we put the glass dome *behind* the fountain instead of in front of it?'

'It's not glass, it's PVC. What if we forget the whole damned thing?' snapped Ben.

'Not an option,' Rosie said crisply. 'We want that cash, remember.'

'Oh God,' moaned Ben, standing up and stretching. Rosie heard his shoulders snapping as tension was released. 'This is a nightmare. Why did I ever agree to this?'

'Because, as I said, we want that cash.'

Ben turned back and looked again at the screen. 'So what do we do?'

'We halve the planting on my design, halve the hard landscaping on yours, then blend the two seamlessly together,' said Rosie, attempting a smile. 'How's that?'

'Probably awful, but let's try it.'

'I'll restructure it on screen, you make us some coffee, OK?'

*

Five days later, they had the plan. Then they showed it to Joanne, who showed it to Leo Patenski, and the thing was approved. Ben ordered in the necessary supplies for the landscaping, leaving Rosie to order the plants.

'How's it going with you two?' asked Lulu one day in the office.

Rosie shrugged. Ben was at the builders' merchants sorting out supplies, and she was thumbing through catalogues and compiling a list of plants. She had a huge list of plants, because it was quite a large garden. She had yuccas and lavender, rosemary and Jerusalem sage for the hot spot near the deck. Fatsia Japonica, dicentra and persicaria for the far end under the lilac tree. Ornamental rhubarb, cornus and hostas for the boggy area she was going to create. And she wanted to put a few baskets up on the house wall to pretty it up a bit, so there were surfinias, lobelia and trailing fuschias to be ordered for those. She always ordered in threes, or fives, or sevens – odd numbers looked more natural when the plants matured. And she *never* ordered a single plant to put in, unless it was a big specimen like gunnera, or a tree fern.

'So-so,' she said cautiously.

'No tantrums? No fights to the death?' teased Lulu.

'Plenty of tantrums, but we're both still breathing.'

A red flatbed truck pulled up outside. Both Lulu and Rosie peered silently through the window as Ben jumped out, shut the door, and approached the flat.

'That's one very good-looking man,' Lulu sighed admiringly.

'You ought to try working with him,' said Rosie, and went to let him in.

'Hi Lulu,' said Ben as he came into the room, bringing with him a gust of fresh air and another of healthy clean male. 'You got those plants ordered yet?' he asked Rosie. 'Because the rest of the stuff'll be there on Monday.'

Rosie nodded, fighting a stab of irritation.

'The plants will be there by Friday, which will give you and your crew the whole of the week to get the landscaping done.'

'You can give us a hand on that,' said Ben. 'Rake out the topsoil and get the water feature set up.'

'I'm not working with Luke and Daniel,' said Rosie, feeling her face start to burn as Lulu looked from one to the other of them. She doubted she would ever forget them in the bedroom at Janina's flat, with her tied to the bed and them enjoying every minute of it.

'Why? They don't bite.'

'You know why,' said Rosie through gritted teeth.

'Listen, I thought we agreed we needed this contract?'

'We did.'

'So toughen up. And are you sure Friday's a definite? Because I want the whole thing completed by the weekend, or Leo's going to get difficult and start chiselling bits off the bill.'

'I said so, didn't I?' Rosie barked.

'Would anyone like a cup of tea?' Lulu offered sweetly.

'No!' they snapped in unison.

'This is what I like to see,' said Lulu with a grin, going off to the kitchen to get a cuppa for herself. 'Good working relations.'

'I'll see you on Monday,' said Ben, and left.

On Monday Rosie was round at the house, as agreed. So was Ben, and so were Luke and Daniel. Daniel, ever the charmer, just sneered at her, but Luke blushed crimson as he caught sight of her, and thereafter kept sneaking furtive looks at her breasts and her ass whenever he thought she wasn't looking. Ben announced that the skip was there, so what were they all standing around for – were they waiting for it to fill itself?

They got to work. They cleared away the cast-iron bath and the builders' rubble and the chicken run, excavated half-dead trees, got the pneumatic drill and the ear-protectors out and broke up the ghastly concrete path, lugging the shattered bits through the house and into the skip, which was soon full to the brim. Then they cleared the surface of the old lawn. The topsoil arrived in perfect time so they spent the remainder of the day carting it through the house and spreading it around the garden.

Rosie felt dirty and exhausted by the time five o'clock arrived.

'See you tomorrow,' said Ben, and he and his two workmates piled into the red flatbed truck and vanished into the distance.

Probably gone to the pub, thought Rosie. Rotten bastard! Who said the age of chivalry was dead? After all the work I've got through today, would it really have hurt him to invite me along? she thought, feeling ridiculously hurt.

But truthfully, a couple of hours in the pub with Daniel and Luke eyeballing her wasn't exactly her idea of fun. A hot bath and a TV dinner and then an evening of couch potatodom suited her much better. She trudged through the house.

'Going home, gorgeous?' asked one of the Aussie builders, a dark-haired charmer with twinkling eyes.

'Yep. Worn out.'

'That's a shame. We could have had a drink together. There's a pub just round the corner.'

Yeah, I suspected there might be, thought Rosie, feeling even more put out by this confirmation of her suspicions. And she was even more put out to find that she wasn't even faintly interested in the beautiful tanned Australian plasterer. She was just tired. And sad. And she was going home to be tired and sad in private.

Monday set the pattern for the rest of the week. She was there raking and fixing and filling and carrying alongside the men; and she was pleased to find that, although severely exhausted by the end of each day, she could match the curmudgeonly woman-hating Daniel and his sly young sidekick Luke pace for pace. Matching Ben's pace was quite another matter.

No wonder he looks so fit, she thought, as she watched him peel his shirt off in the noonday heat and keep right on working on the deck. He *was* fit. He was a regular bloody Hercules, in fact, and she couldn't keep up with him for even half a day. Although she tried. God knows she tried. And it was by trying so hard that she managed to drill a slice of skin off her index finger, inflicting a small wound which hurt like hell and produced an astonishing amount of blood.

'Damn!' she said in pain and shock.

'What's up?' Ben looked up and saw the blood dripping, and came over. 'Hurt yourself?'

Oh, she was so pleased that Daniel and Luke were off getting some bits from the builders' merchants. She could just imagine how Daniel would jeer, and how the spineless Luke would titter in collusion, and their inference would be clear: useless, stupid woman. Nothing but trouble. This was bound to happen. She's only good for one thing, after all.

'The drill slipped,' said Rosie, fumbling for a tissue to stem the flow. Goodness, there was a lot of blood. It dripped on to the deck. Ben snatched up his shirt and wrapped it quickly around her finger. He grabbed her elbow and held her forearm aloft.

'That'll stop it,' he said calmly. 'Give it a few minutes, then I'll get a plaster from the truck. You OK?'

She wasn't OK. She felt her head getting swimmy. It was the heat, and she was getting dehydrated, and now she was bleeding copiously.

'Sit down here.' Ben put an arm around her waist and guided her down onto the finished part of the deck, where there was shade cast by the house wall.

'I'm sorry,' Rosie said woozily. 'I feel so silly.'

'Here, drink some of this.' Ben uncapped a half-full bottle of mineral water and brought it to her lips. 'Maybe you've been overdoing it.'

'No, I'm fine,' Rosie lied.

'You're not fine. Rest here in the shade. Had enough to drink?' Rosie nodded. God, he was being really *nice*. 'Just keep your arm up. Let's have a look.'

Ben unpeeled the shirt-tail from around her finger. It oozed blood more sluggishly now. Ben rewrapped it.

'It's ruining your shirt,' Rosie said weakly.

'It's just a shirt,' Ben shrugged. He got a cloth out of his jeans pocket and tipped some of the water out on to it, then applied the cool damp cloth to the back of Rosie's neck.

Oh, no. Now he was being too nice altogether. Now he was being so nice that she felt her eyes starting to fill with tears.

'I'll be OK,' she said, trying to push him away.

'Hush up, Rosie,' Ben said, gently dabbing at her brow with the cooling cloth and then returning it to the back of her neck. He smiled at her from dangerously close quarters. 'Even when you're about to pass out cold you're still obstinate.'

'Ha! Look who's talking.'

'Is it stopping now?' he asked, taking another look at his blood-sodden shirt-tail. 'Yeah, that looks all right. Just as well. We couldn't afford to spend four hours waiting about in A & E, could we.'

'You're all heart,' said Rosie, wriggling away from him in earnest now. The bastard! That's all he was worried about – whether or not the work would be done on schedule.

'Hey, what did I say? It was a *joke*, Rosie. Cool down.'

'Oh pardon me,' sniffed Rosie. 'It's just my finger's throbbing like mad and I feel dizzy. Excuse me if I didn't realise you were exercising what passes for dazzling wit around here.'

'Stay there,' said Ben, standing up. 'I'll fetch the antiseptic spray and the plasters.'

He was back in moments. And he sprayed her throbbing finger with a local anaesthetic and disinfectant, then carefully wrapped it in a large plaster.

'Feeling better now? Not dizzy?' he asked, moving the water back towards her lips.

'Fine,' Rosie said grumpily. Then she looked at him and softened a little. 'Thanks.'

'It's no problem.' He leaned closer and kissed her. Then he kissed her again. Then Rosie's arm went around his neck and the kiss deepened and lengthened until there was a sudden eruption of catcalls from the window above them. They looked up – and four builders grinned back down at them.

'Nice work if you can get it, pal!' called one.

Ben smiled and stood up, giving Rosie a hand to get back to her feet.

'Listen, you want to go on home now?' he offered. 'We can manage here for the rest of the day. Everything's running fine.'

'No, I'll be OK,' Rosie assured him. She felt a bit shaky, and that dynamite kiss hadn't helped in the least, but she was damned if she was going to creep off home like the weak little woman when there was work to be done here.

The afternoon wore on. Daniel and Luke returned and some more work got done. The fountain and the ornamental PVC dome was in place, the rills were in operation, the deck was down, and a mixer was chugging away out at the front of the house, making the cement to lay the York stone paving. When they packed in at five, Rosie was nearly dropping with tiredness, but since Ben had been so nice to her she felt able to extend at least a tentative hand of friendship.

'Gonna invite me round the pub?' she asked him chirpily as they gathered up the tools.

'What?' Ben looked at her blankly.

'Round the pub. Where all three of you go after work.'

Ben shook his head. 'Rosie, we don't go round the pub after work. I drop Luke and Daniel off home, and then *I* go home, and take a shower and fall asleep in front of the telly. Janina's off on business again. Dublin this time.'

'Oh. Right.'

Rosie almost smiled at her own stupidity. And she had been picturing them quaffing beer and having a laugh at her expense. While all the time he had been going home alone, cleaning up and eating alone, watching TV alone, until he fell asleep. In fact, he had been doing exactly the same as her.

Really, she ought to stop jumping to conclusions.

Like the one where he'd been pinching her female clients. Like the one where he was a money-grabbing bastard. Like the one where he led a rampageous social life, totally unlike her own. Much to her own disgust, she found that she was beginning to see Ben Hunter as others had probably seen him all along. As a nice, decent and extremely sexy man who had a single ambition that she had unwittingly thwarted.

She watched him get into the flatbed truck and fire up the engine, then climbed tiredly into her own little van and pointed it towards Richmond. This work schedule of his was punishing. She was knackered. But there was only this week to get through, and then they would part company – and this time, it would be for good.

Chapter Twenty

Friday came around quickly. Most of the day was a series of minor panics, but the thing was more or less done and dusted. Finishing touches were put in, and Rosie's lavish planting was thoroughly watered. At a quarter past four, Rosie switched on the fountain. The soft tinkling filled the garden. The rills flowed smoothly, and the bog irises in the pool that they flowed into at the far end of the garden seemed to glow like sunshine, lighting up that formerly dark and gloomy corner.

With Daniel and Luke out front supervising the removal of the skip, Rosie and Ben were free to sit down on the living-willow bench and watch the water catch the sun.

'Of course, it'll take a couple of years to really grow into itself,' said Ben.

'I always tell the clients three. Three years,' said Rosie, aching and weary but, looking around at the finished result, deeply satisfied. 'It wasn't so painful, working together, was it?' she jibed.

'Nope, it was OK,' said Ben, watching the water. 'Bearable, anyway.'

'What time did Joanne say she was coming?'

'Five.'

'Right.'

They had finally settled with Joanne on eighteen thousand five hundred pounds. That was – Rosie had worked all this out well before now – nine thousand, two hundred and fifty pounds each. Ben had funded the hard landscaping materials from Countryman Gardens; Rosie had paid for the planting through Coming Up Roses. The two bills were similar, within a couple of hundred pounds.

She looked around the garden, and admitted to herself that Ben's landscaping did look good, and the planting was bold enough to stand up to it. The whole design was harmonious and pleasing to the eye. Which was surprising, considering the way things had been between the two of them. She was pleased with herself. She had behaved in an adult fashion, and so had Ben, and they had worked the whole thing out between them, with some success. With *considerable* success. She hadn't enjoyed working with Daniel and Luke, but she had kept her head down and tolerated them, and she had got through it.

Yes, she was pleased with herself. Tired, granted. Filthy and sweaty, certainly. But pleased. Not least because she had come to an important decision, and felt at peace for the first time in weeks.

'Better put the tools away,' she said, hauling herself to her feet.

'Yeah,' said Ben, and they worked together in silence, packing up, until five o'clock came around and Joanne, punctual as ever, came sweeping out on to the palm-dotted deck and looked upon the garden and found it good.

'You clever old things,' she marvelled, mincing down to join them by the fountain in very unsuitable high-heeled mules. She was immaculate in a white catsuit and lots of gold jewellery. She made Rosie feel – as always – like a walking sartorial disaster zone. Joanne was about to kiss Ben, and air-kiss Rosie, when she took in the grubby state of the pair of them and decided against it.

'This is absolutely wonderful,' she said, looking around instead.

'Thanks,' Ben said dryly.

'Shouldn't we have a bottle of champagne to celebrate?' Joanne demanded.

'Curiously enough, I don't have any to hand,' said Ben. 'This isn't a TV show, Joanne, this is reality. You can have bottled water, if you want it.'

Joanne screwed up her nose. 'No thanks.' She fished in her dainty little shoulder bag and pulled out her chequebook and a very costly-looking gold pen. 'I'm so pleased, I can't tell you,' she said, scribbling quickly. 'It was nineteen thousand, yes?'

'Eighteen thousand five hundred,' said Ben.

Joanne wrote the cheque and held it out to them both with a teasing smile. 'Now, who should I give this to?'

'Give it to Ben,' said Rosie. 'It's his.'

Both Ben and Joanne looked at Rosie blankly.

'Well yes, darling – his and yours,' said Joanne.

'No, just his.'

'What are you talking about, Rosie?' asked Ben.

'I'm giving you my share,' said Rosie breezily. 'Call it a gift, call it an apology for all the hassle, I don't care. But it's enough to buy you that field in Sussex, isn't it, and I want you to have it.'

'You can't do that,' said Ben, shocked.

'I just did,' Rosie said positively. She shook Joanne's hand, then realised that her own hand was very dirty and smiled sheepishly. 'Sorry about the dirt, Jo. And it's been very nice knowing you, and I hope we'll meet again?'

'Of course we will,' said Joanne, completely wrong-footed.

'Good. Goodbye then. Bye, Ben.' And with only the briefest of smiles at him, she left.

It was so nice just to get home, to take a long hot bath with wine and candles, the whole works, and then to put on her very unglamorous terry-towelling white robe, yank a brush through her dusty hair and collapse on to the couch.

She looked over at the Whisky Mac roses. They were almost over now, and the baby's breath had deteriorated to the point where she had discarded all those stems yesterday. She had been trimming a little more off the roses every day, and changing the water, and they had kept really well, considering, but maybe now it was time just to consign them to the bin.

Well, maybe she would. In a minute.

For now it was nice just to sit here with the sun spilling in the window and the silence all around her, and to feel the aches and pains of the day slipping away. After a bit she levered herself upright and popped a frozen meal into the microwave. Then she switched on the television and collapsed back on to the couch.

And then the doorbell rang, and she swore.

It would be politicians canvassing for votes.

Or it would be her crotchety upstairs neighbour complaining about the noise of the television.

Or a double-glazing salesman.

Or Jehovah's Witnesses keen to foist their views upon her.

I'm not going to answer it, she thought. When it rang again, she ignored it. The microwave pinged and she went through to the kitchen. When she came back someone was holding up the flap of the letterbox and peering in.

'For God's sake open the door,' Ben said irritably.

Rosie dumped her tray on the coffee table and went and opened it. He was cleaned up and wearing fresh jeans and a white shirt. He was carrying another two-dozen bunch of Whisky Mac roses.

'Splashing all that cash around?' she quipped, taking them from him.

'Hardly. I just thought the others must be nearly over by now.'

'They are, nearly.'

'Well, there you go.'

'I suppose you'd better come in,' said Rosie, shooting off into the kitchen to plunge the roses into water. When she came back into the sitting room, Ben was standing at the window staring out. She looked wistfully at her TV dinner, then flicked the remote at the TV to turn it off, and carried the tray back into the kitchen.

When she came back into the sitting room again, Ben was sitting on the couch.

'So, what can I do for you?' Rosie asked formally, wishing she had some clothes on and not this threadbare and exceedingly unsexy robe.

Ben grinned. 'I thought you'd never ask. You can come here and kiss me for a start. If anything else occurs to me, I'll let you know.'

Rosie shook her head and put her hands on her hips.

'Look, I don't have to kiss you, Ben. I don't even have to see your ugly mug anymore. All bets are off. The job's done, you've got your money for your nursery business, it's finished.'

'So let's go out like two civilised people and celebrate,' said Ben.

'I'm tired,' Rosie said truthfully, irritated that he looked so fresh and spruced up and not tired at all after such a long, hard day at work.

'Am I asking you to do anything? Let's take a drive.'

'Do I have to dress up for this?' Rosie asked wearily.

Ben shook his head. 'Nope. Wear anything you like. Only –' he grinned beguilingly '– not that damned robe. You know those jumble sales, and the stuff that's left, that's too downright awful even to *give* away and gets chucked in a skip round the back? Well, I think that robe belongs in that skip.'

'Listen, you aren't exactly anyone's idea of Savile Row tailoring on show,' retorted Rosie, although he was absolutely right. She really, really ought to dump the thing. But it was sort of comforting. She'd had it for ages and was attached to it like a child to a particularly gross comfort blanket.

'Can you get changed and save the lip for later?' Ben asked nicely.

'Oh, all right then.'

Rosie went into the bedroom and peered unenthusiastically into her wardrobe. She pulled out clean jeans and T-shirt, and shrugged both on. Just to be fancy, she brushed her hair too, and scowled at herself in the dressing-table mirror. Her heart was thumping a wild tattoo in her chest, and that made her even grumpier. What was it about that man? Why could she never, ever resist him like she should?

'Look,' she said when she came back into the sitting room, 'I just want to say that I am not going to be tied up tonight. Have we got that clear?'

'Did I say you would be?' Ben asked innocently, but there was nothing innocent about the expression in his eyes as they swept up over her.

'You never say,' Rosie pointed out. 'You just do it.'

'Good point.'

'So not tonight.'

'It's a deal.'

*

And somehow she just knew where he was taking her. As Ben guided Janina's Mercedes through the traffic and out of London, heading south, Rosie just knew. She said nothing. She was too bushed to protest. If this was a kidnapping, if he was, despite his assurances, going to lash her to the bed and have his evil way with her, then so be it. It was so soothing, being driven, and it was sort of sexy too. She sank back into the soft leather seat and watched Ben's hands on the wheel, and listened dreamily to Schubert or some such damned thing and, before she knew it, Ben was nudging her awake.

'I wasn't asleep,' Rosie said defensively.

'Sure,' said Ben.

Rosie looked around. The car was stopped in the little lane outside his cottage. Ben was unbuckling his seat-belt. Rosie fumbled for hers and scrambled out. Ben came around to her side of the car and put a casual arm about her shoulders. She winced. They ached from all the work she'd done, and her spine felt stiff from the journey.

'Oh, we're here,' she said stupidly, stifling a yawn as she peered at the garden. It was a truly lovely garden, she thought, just coming into its own now as early summer started to take hold. There were a few rhododendrons out in bloom that had been in bud last time they came here. Shocking tones of orange, lemon, scarlet and bubblegum pink rioted all down one side of the plot, and the weigelas were loaded with blossom too. 'Oh, you've got a Florida,' said Rosie, yawning and indicating a shrub with a variegated leaf and a shock of frothy pink blooms. 'And a hawthorn. That's lovely,' she said, spotting a tree loaded with white blossom. She sighed and wished that this were her garden, instead of that sorry little excuse for a plot she rented in Richmond.

'How tired did you say you were?' asked Ben, pulling her in against him.

'Exhausted,' said Rosie, through another yawn.

'Feel weak?'

'Mm.'

'Too weak to fight me off?'

'Am I going to *have* to fight you off?' Rosie asked suspiciously.

'Only if you want to,' said Ben, starting up the path.

Rosie followed, stretching elaborately as she went. 'Just no tying up, OK?' she pleaded.

'OK.' Ben opened the front door and picked her up and carried her, much to her surprise, indoors.

'Whoa!' she protested as he kicked the door closed behind them and went straight up the stairs with her. He kicked open the bedroom door, went over to the four-poster, and tossed her on to the mattress.

Rosie bounced like a frog on a lily pad in a churned-up lake. She clutched at the coverlet for support.

'Listen, haven't you heard of observing the niceties?' she complained. 'Making a girl something to eat first, fixing her a drink, putting on some smoochy music and *then* throwing her on the bed?'

'I think niceties are overrated,' said Ben, shucking off his jacket and unbuttoning his shirt. 'Why not cut straight to the chase?'

'Chase!' Rosie let out a hollow laugh. 'This isn't a chase, pal, this is a *fait accompli.*'

'Is that a complaint?' asked Ben. He'd stripped off his shirt now – oh, that body! – and was kicking off his shoes and socks. Without hesitation he then got to work on his jeans.

'Not a complaint as such, no,' allowed Rosie, watching him avidly as he pulled his jeans down and off. No underwear, she noticed blissfully. Maybe they don't make underwear strong enough to contain that thing, she thought, watching his cock rise up as if searching her out.

'I thought you were too tired,' said Ben, straightening and observing her interested gaze.

'Not that tired,' she said with a happy sigh. 'I mean, I'm still *breathing.*'

'You can just lie back and think of England,' suggested Ben, kneeling on the bed and starting to tug her T-shirt up over her head.

'Mfph,' said Rosie from under the T-shirt.

'What?' Ben gave a final tug and the T-shirt and Rosie parted company.

'I said, I probably will.' Ben's lips fastened on to her nipple. His hands were at work on the waistband of her jeans. She heard the zipper go down. Then she felt him unlacing her trainers and wrenching them off. Then her jeans, down over her thighs, over her knees and ankles, and off, landing somewhere in a far corner of the room as he flung them aside. His hand slipped between her legs.

'God, you're a fast worker,' moaned Rosie, throwing her arms around him.

'Still tired?' murmured Ben against her breast.

'I may not be able to manage this,' teased Rosie.

Ben bit her nipple, pulling it out with his teeth.

'Ow! Bastard,' she complained huskily, shivering with sudden need.

'You love it.'

'Ha! Says who?'

'Your body. Your body never lies.'

'Maybe I *am* too tired,' Rosie said waspishly. 'What have you hijacked me down here for anyway? Just for this?'

'I object to the "just",' said Ben. 'But there was another reason, too.'

'Oh?' She was running her fingers through his hair and sniffing its fresh grassy scent. She didn't much care why he'd hijacked her at all. To hell with it.

'Yeah, I wanted to ask you if you want a partnership in a country-based nursery business, that's all.'

Rosie nearly fell off the bed. 'You *what*?'

'I'm coming back to Sussex. Selling the business in London to Daniel and Luke, and buying that field I showed you next door, and living in the country. And I just wondered, you know, if you might like to come and, well, sort of live with me, and be a partner in the new business.'

'You're such a bastard,' Rosie said accusingly.

'*What?*' asked Ben.

'Springing this on me now, when I'm tired out and

aching, with my hair all dirty and my manicure shot to hell.'

'So that's a no then?' Ben grabbed a handful of red hair when she went to jump off the bed. He started reeling her in like a fish on a line.

'It's probably a no, yes.'

'No? Yes? Which?'

He'd reeled her in and she was kneeling between his legs now. Ben's hand slid around her waist and settled on her buttock. He squeezed it fondly.

'Well, I suppose it's a sort of tentative yes,' said Rosie, feeling that the room was growing unaccountably hot for some reason. Should her heart really be beating this fast? Maybe she ought to get her blood pressure checked.

'Tentative?' Ben was back to teasing out her nipple again. It made concentration just a little difficult.

'Sort of.'

'Yes?' Ben pulled her closer. 'Yes?' he mumbled against her naked belly.

'Oh, all right then,' said Rosie, smiling and grabbing his thick wheaty hair in both hands and casting her fate to the winds. 'Yes.'

Two weeks later Lulu was helping her pack up her stuff at the Richmond flat, and moaning profusely while she did so.

'I knew you were headed for trouble with that man,' said Lulu, as she lobbed cutlery into a box. 'That man is just too damned sexy for any woman's safety, if you ask me.'

Rosie dumped another overflowing box by the front door and dusted off her hands.

'Well, I didn't ask you,' she said sweetly.

'I liked this job,' complained Lulu.

'You'll get another one. Probably Daniel and Luke could make use of your services.'

'Is that so? Well they can just go and whistle, because my services don't come cheap.'

'Yes they do,' retorted Rosie.

'You're right, they do.' Lulu grinned and started on the desk. She opened the top drawer, beheld the sex-toys catalogues and chocolate bars within. She sighed wistfully, unwrapped some chocolate, took a bite and closed her eyes in bliss.

'Give me a bit of that,' wheedled Rosie, coming over to the desk.

'You only eat chocolate when you're under stress,' said Lulu, breaking off a piece reluctantly. 'So what's the stress this time?'

Rosie shrugged and gobbled down the chocolate.

'I don't know, Lulu. Am I doing the right thing? Is it going to be a complete disaster?' She picked up the sex-toys catalogue, opened it and looked suitably scandalised by the contents.

'Look at it this way,' Lulu said encouragingly. 'Even if it's the worst match since Charles and Di, you'll have fun along the way.' She patted Rosie's shoulder kindly and indicated the catalogue. 'Keep that if you want. You're probably going to need it.'

Rosie tossed it into the nearest box.

'So you think I'm worrying over nothing?' she asked anxiously.

'Girlfriend . . .' Lulu chomped down the last piece of chocolate with obvious relish. 'Be cool. After all, everything's coming up roses.'